Copyright Information

The Ruins of Mars:
Waking Titan

By Dylan James Quarles

James Floyd was a man with battery acid in his stomach. Though never someone people had thought of as *relaxed,* he was now so far beyond the word that he hardly knew what it meant anymore. For the last few years, he had been leading the design for a manned mission to Mars and as a result, he had lost weight, hair, and countless hours of sleep.

Ruins, ancient and long buried by the sands of time, had been discovered by two self-aware twin satellites some four years ago.

Sent to the red planet to map out its surface with advanced Infrared Micron Cameras, the brothers—as they were called—Remus and Romulus had revealed their discovery to their sister, an Artificial Intelligence named Alexandria.

From there, word had spread like a computer virus and soon James was put in charge of getting a crew to Mars. Discovery and industry: that was their mission. Build the first human colony. Begin producing water, food, and fuel while at the same time uncovering the mystery of the ruins. Discovery and industry.

Now, some five months after the launch of mankind's first interplanetary spaceship, James was in a perpetual state of waiting. Waiting for word from his crew, waiting for news. It had been bumpy ride so far.

Though Amit Vyas, the ship's pilot, had planned out a safe course, the team had nearly been blown to bits by a rogue meteor belt. However, Braun, the crew's AI, had responded with speed and severity, saving their lives. Acting in accordance with his primary programming, the mighty AI had cut the frozen chunks of rock and gas into shreds with the ship's Laser Defense System. It had been a close call. From there, things had actually gotten a little better and James, for a time, was less ulcerous.

The landing had gone well enough. Ralph Marshall was a skilled pilot, and the two German engineers, Udo Clunkat and William Konig were on schedule to complete the construction of a permanent base soon. For now, though, the seven members of the ground team would have to make do in their inflatable dome.

Ship's Captain Tatyana Vodevski was in almost constant contact with James, and this helped to ease his frazzled nerves. An unprecedented solar flare, deadly to many thousands on Earth and nearly catastrophic to his team on Mars, had helped to form a bond between the captain and himself. Both had watched in helpless horror—he from Earth, she from Mars orbit—as two members of the ground team, Ralph Marshall and the young archaeologist Harrison Raheem Assad, ventured out into the solar storm to restore critical functions to the dome's life-support system. Though Harrison had briefly died from radiation poisoning during the EVA, it was still a successful mission in James's book.

Harrison. Now there was a name fast making itself known to the billions on Earth. That young man, that boy really, had performed above what James ever thought he could when assigning him to the team. Already, he had discovered a vast cave network beneath the buried Martian ruins and, better still, a means to access the tunnels. He was there now—in those catacombs finding God-only-knows what.

James belched a little and a hot acidic bubble popped in the back of his throat.

Acid in my stomach, thought the tired NASA Mission Controller. Acid.

PART ONE

CHAPTER ONE

Voices

Voices stirred. Beyond forgotten and long dead, they whispered through the bones of a cold world. Alone for so many eons, the ghosts of Mars had grown accustomed to their exile. Now though, they stirred. As silent as snakes in the sand, they rose to the surface and curled around scattered boulders, filling deep chasms with the liquid of their dead consciousness. Spreading like a rising tide, they webbed out across the desert, searching for something. Searching for life.

Standing in the center of a grand underground chamber, Harrison Raheem Assad peered up into the lifelike faces of two towering statues. Adorned with three eyes in triangular alignment, the statues seemed to stare through him—through everything—at a force that resided in between realities. Behind the implacable figures of the standing statues, subtly cloaked in the digital shadows of his suit's Augmented Vision, another figure peered back at Harrison with stony eyes. Blind as rock may be, the eyes bore into him with palpable intensity, imploring him, daring him to stare back.

Though Harrison had been on Mars for less than two months, already so much had happened. He had died and been revived, he had fallen in love with a beautiful and talented Chinese engineer, and he had discovered a network of tunnels and caves beneath the buried Martian ruins. However, under the gaze of those twin statues and their even more mysterious companion, Harrison felt as though he were just now scratching the surface of his true mission.

Above, through a half-kilometer of solid Martian earth, a giant and complex city complete with streets, buildings, and piazzas stood waiting to be welcomed back into the light of the sun. Luckily for the often impatient Harrison, he did not have to kill time while the automated excavators did their job. Per the results of a deep-soil CT scan, he had found access into the tunnels where he now stood through an open cave, partway down the rim of Mars's grand canyon.

Met with design, intelligence, and artisanal excellence on a scale surpassing his wildest dreams, the tunnels were beginning to change the young archaeologist's perception of who the ancient Martians were.

To his right, Ralph Marshall—astronaut, Lander pilot, and (aside from Liu) Harrison's closest friend—shifted from foot to foot. Turning his helmeted head to face Harrison, the older man cocked it to the side.

"Harrison? Did you hear me?"

His voice caught in a web of dumbfounded mystery, Harrison could not respond.

"Harrison?" repeated Marshall, frankly. "Which ones are the *Martians*?"

Taking a long thin breath, Harrison scanned the faces of the identical three-eyed statues then that of the murky form of the other figure behind them. Though still somewhat unsettled by the fierce and provocative stare of its stone eyes, he could immediately tell that this third installment was clearly different from the first two.

For starters, it was much smaller than the twins and its face was almost human in design. To Harrison it looked like a kneeling woman, her hands clasped firmly together before her widely spaced eyes.

She's praying to the other two, he thought with a shudder. *Praying.*

"Harrison?" Marshall nearly shouted. "Hello, can you hear me? Harrison?"

"I don't know, Ralph," Harrison finally answered, snapping his head around to stare at his friend. "I suppose it could be either of the two kinds. Or both. I don't know. I just don't know."

"Well, shit. Don't get all weepy on me. We've got time to figure that out I guess."

"Yeah," echoed William Konig, the third member of their small party. "Don't worry about that now, but we should probably go. I'm showing very low levels of usable gasses in here and my Survival Pack is over halfway empty."

2

"I agree with Dr. Konig," sounded the voice of Braun, the team's Artificial Intelligence. "It would be best to return with more comprehensive monitoring equipment."

Still shaken, Harrison glanced at the haunting blue light of a flashing X-Ray Beacon as it painted the walls of the camber with invisible waves. Without these baseball-sized devices, the three explorers would be cast into blinding darkness, as the room was too large to register the tight-wave digital pings of their suits' sonar.

Everything he saw around him was as a bat might see: not really seen with his eyes, but rather relayed through the eyes of his Tactical Skin Suit and projected on the inside of his helmet's glass.

"How long will the Beacons last?" he asked, prudence taking control of his awe.

"I can deactivate them when we leave," replied Braun. "Then, upon our return, I can reactivate them, thus conserving their energy."

"Good. I'll bring a geni and some tripoded lights for next time. I want to see this room in living color."

"Why not push on?" said Marshall, shrugging. "See what else there is."

Tapping at his wrist-mounted Tablet, Harrison brought up the tunnel-network map he had garnished from his deep-soil CT scan. Then, swiping his finger diagonally across the screen, he multiplied the image and relayed it to his fellow explorers.

"The scan shows that this room is part of a continuing tunnel or passage, but I don't see any doorways in here. Do you?"

Marshall allowed his head to swivel from left to right before shrugging again.

"I guess not..."

Nodding, Harrison pointed to the CT scan on his wrist Tablet.

"Exactly. The scan says there *is* a way through. We just need to find it."

"That is a sound deduction, Harrison," spoke Braun in their helmets. "But I still agree with Dr. Konig. It would be best to turn around for now and return up the lift to the surface. Your Survival

Packs cannot produce breathable oxygen until a more abundant source of usable gasses is reached."

Casting his eyes about the chamber one last time, Harrison sighed and turned to go.

I'll be back soon, he said silently. I'll bring light.

As the three men backtracked their way through the digitally illuminated tunnel, Harrison's mind was heavy with the mystery that faced it. For over three years, his mission had been clear and tangible: learn everything the Martian ruins had to tell about their builders. Uncover a lost truth.

What have I gotten myself into? he thought. I don't even know who built this place anymore. Before, it was easy. I didn't have to ask. But now...now I just don't know.

The discovery of a large chamber filled with giant statues had been incredible. The further discovery—that in the three statues, there appeared to be two different species depicted—was a mystery that threatened to reshape the entire expedition.

"Harrison?" said Braun softly. "May I speak privately with you?"

Thankful for the distraction, Harrison nodded then remembered that Braun couldn't always see such things.

"Yeah," he said. "What's on your mind?"

"Upon our entry into the chamber, I detected a presence."

"A *presence*? What does that mean?"

There was a short pause wherein Braun seemed to be searching his mind for the right words.

"The presence was similar to a light-wave disturbance, yet I did not detect it through any of the channels or sensors associated with light waves. Instead, I—"

Braun trailed off momentarily, a phenomenon whose occurrence was as rare as it was troubling.

"—Instead, I felt it. Though I could not see it visibly, I knew it was there."

"You felt it?"

"Yes."

"How do you mean? What did you feel?"

Again, Braun was slow to answer. And when he did, his voice was laced with doubt.

4

"I have not formulated the words to describe what I mean. I am sorry. What I can say for certain is this: these tunnels are not as they appear on the surface. There are greater elements at play."

Liu

Xao-Xing Liu stood on the rim of the Valles Marineris, staring out across its hypnotic network of canyons and trenches. Bending in at the edges, the Valles stretched on past the curve of the horizon, longer than the contiguous United States and five times deeper than the Grand Canyon. Though its sheer size was humbling, Liu felt only an absentminded passing appreciation for its grandeur.

In all honesty, she had more pressing matters on her mind. For the better part of an hour, she had received no transmissions from the team exploring the caves nearly half-a-kilometer below. Wrapping herself in an embrace, she shivered despite the comfortable seventy-two degrees to which her suit was heated.

There must be too much rock between me and them, she worried. In the future, we'll need to set up a Relay Dish to help transmission ranges. I don't like being out of contact for this long. At least they have Braun if anything goes really wrong.

Frowning at this, Liu reminded herself that Braun had locked her pressure suit away during the recent solar storm. Though he had done it in order to keep her from venturing out into the blistering radiation to save Harrison, she never truly forgave the AI for his actions. Moreover, she now had little trust in his personality, fearing that he was too inhuman and rigid.

Perhaps having Braun along is less of an advantage than it seems, she said internally. Perhaps I'm just kidding myself.

As the minutes ticked by, Liu was beginning to grow truly concerned when a sudden crackling burst of radio static fizzled in her ears.

"Liu?" came Harrison's boyish voice.

Puffing out her cheeks, Liu exhaled a long overdue breath and smiled.

"Go ahead, Harrison."

5

"We're at the lift. I just wanted to tell you we're on our way up."

Hands on her hips, Liu walked over to the skeletal mass of scaffolding that served as the lift's rim-side port.

Glinting in the afternoon sun, the port stuck out over the canyon's rim like a metal ribcage. Power lines and thick taut cables dangled from the thing, disappearing from sight down the wall of the canyon to the opening of the cave network far below.

"Alright, go ahead and proceed up," she said, confident in her assembly of the rickety-looking contraption.

"See you soon, babe," radioed Harrison. "I have so much to tell you."

CHAPTER TWO

Reunion—Sol 40

Two weeks had passed since Harrison, Marshall, and William had ascended out of the darkened caves with stories and pictures of giant statues. After their initial discovery, the team had made three more trips to set up a Radio Relay Dish, generators and tripoded lighting for the Statue Chamber. However, William was soon needed to help complete the final stages of the Base's construction, so the caves were put on the back burner.

As the life-support systems were tested and the giant Alon Dome came online like some beacon of human defiance, the ground crew heaved a collective sigh of relief. No longer would they spend their nights inside an inflatable dome with gossamer-thin walls. Now it was truly the time for them to get down to the business of establishing the first permanent human colony on Mars. Now it was time for a reunion.

On the morning of Sol 40, Lander 2 touched down on the frost-spackled surface of the red planet to deliver its payload. Among the pressure-suited astronauts within were the newest installations to the ground team: Dr. Elizabeth Kubba and AI specialist YiJay Lee. One after the other, the six members of the ship-bound crew leaped down from the white beetle-shaped craft and into the open arms of their estranged fellow explorers. Some, like Dr. Kubba and Lander 2 pilot Joseph Aguilar, had already made the trip to the surface once before, during the aftermath of the near-deadly solar storm. The others, however, were experiencing their first feelings of real gravity in the five months since leaving Earth.

Breaking from her embrace with Liu, Ship's Captain Tatyana Vodevski turned on unsteady legs to survey the brand new Alon Dome as it reflected the rays of the early morning light.

Over two stories tall, with upper, lower, and basement levels, it was a picture of technology and engineering. Covered in solar-celled transparent aluminum windows and reinforced with thick sloping beams, the Dome looked as if it could withstand a direct meteor impact.

"It's beautiful," she breathed.

"Can you see it from orbit?" asked William excitedly as he threw his arm over the shoulder of his fellow German engineer, Udo Clunkat.

"Yes, every morning since you plated the windows, we've been catching a reflection off the rising sun."

"Oui, it's true," said Ship's Engineer and Designer, Julian Thomas, "I think Amit and I have blind spots from staring down at it for so long. I never thought I would be happy to leave my baby. But hey, I'm sick of fucking space. You know?"

"Well then, shall we go inside?" said William, gesturing with his gloved hand towards the airlock.

"Yes," smiled Tatyana. "We shall."

Moving in a small cluster of white pressure-suited bodies, the twelve men and women kicked up clouds of red dust as they marched for the shining Dome. Once everyone was through the airlock hatch, Braun sealed the door then pressurized the little room, pumping out the thin Martian atmosphere and replacing it with thick breathable O2. Echoing a pleasant chime, the lights in the airlock turned from red to green and the inner door swung open on electric hinges.

"Welcome to *Ilia* Base," said Braun as the bleary-eyed explorers removed their helmets and filed out of the airlock into the new Dome.

Named for the mythical human lover of the god Ares, or Mars, Ilia was an apt identity for the Base, adding an air of timeless destiny to the mission at large. Though the boys in the NASA Public Relations Department swore it was a coincidence, Ilia, in antiquity, was also rumored to be the mother of Remus and Romulus.

Sectioned into three levels, the Base was crosscut by a series of thin walls, which effectively divided the Dome into combs like a hive. The ground floor was home to the airlock, common area, kitchen, infirmary, crew quarters, and latrines all separated by walls and hatched doors. The upper level was reserved for the lab spaces of the science division, each office equipped with the necessary tools pertaining to its occupant. For Harrison, this meant a room all to himself filled with maps, computer Tablets and a pressurized examination chamber for cleaning and cataloging any Martian artifacts he might recover at the ruin site. The basement level was divided into three parts: the first housing all of the automated systems that ran the Dome, the second being Liu's machine shop, and the third reserved for storage and an emergency survival chamber.

As the chattering crew moved through the giant Dome, led by its human designers Udo and William, Tatyana smiled inwardly at the obvious pride the two took in showing their work off. Though they'd had a lot of help from NASA's resident AI, Copernicus, in designing the structure and systems of the Base, it was still quite an achievement. Moreover, its sturdy frame and solid feel were psychologically appealing, the evidence of which was painted on the grinning faces of every member of her crew. Talking freely amongst themselves, they seemed more at ease than they had in over forty days.

Being back together again feels right, Tatyana told herself. It feels more natural, even if it's only for a few hours.

With William and Udo's tour ended, the team moved towards the dining room for a late breakfast of fresh fruit and vegetables from Dr. Viviana Calise's greenhouse garden. Built as a separate dome some ten meters away, the greenhouse was a tremendous success: holding a wide variety of genetically engineered plants, which grew quickly in vats of reprocessed waste.

Walking into the dining room, the hungry crew were met with a table already set for twelve. In the center of the arrangement, a dish filled with what looked like black jelly beans caught the light. Though presented as a joke, the pills were, in reality, cancer inhibitors designed to be taken with meals in order to stave off the mutation of cells under the constantly high levels of radiation. Unfortunately, as was the case with most things designed to keep one safe, the inhibitors did have their downsides. Nausea, dizziness, and sometimes stomach cramps were not uncommon byproducts, though these were all small prices to pay for the absence of tumors and bone cancer.

As they took their seats, the crew begrudgingly passed around the inhibitors, joining in a group ritual they had not practiced since their last dinner together on Braun.

"Bottoms up," Tatyana said, tossing the black pill down her throat.

Everyone followed suit, chasing the inhibitors with fresh water produced in the Electrolysis Plant earlier that very morning.

"Are we ready to eat?" asked Viviana, striding to a bank of refrigerators along one wall.

A chorus of excited yells and whistles caused her to blush with pride as she placed bowl after bowl of brightly colored fruits and vegetables on the table.

"Mind the tomatoes," she warned. "They weren't quite ripe but I know how you all love them."

Smiling, she handed the first of the slightly orange tomatoes to Elizabeth Kubba, allowing her fingers to trace over those of the doctor's as the tomato passed between them.

"I've missed you," she breathed quietly.

Biting her lip with deliberate tenderness, Kubba played her large brown eyes across Viviana's body, lingering where the fabric of her jumpsuit stretched tightly across her bosom.

"You too," she replied at length, ignoring the lascivious looks exchanged between Aguilar and Julian.

As the rest of the food was passed around and the conversation began to ebb and flow, Tatyana watched her crew with pride. All of them were brave, and all of them were true. Light from a blossoming morning sun spilled in through the tinted windows, bathing the dining room in a diffused pink glow that warmed and protected. Even though Tatyana knew that Julian, Amit, Aguilar and herself wouldn't be staying for long, she reveled in the unity of the moment. Despite the fact that deep down she wanted nothing more than to stay here in Ilia Base and warm her bones, she took a kind of perverse pleasure in subjecting herself to hardships in the name of *the mission.*

Noticing that Aguilar was smiling handsomely at her, Tatyana considered the fact that there were worse things than being stuck in orbit on board Braun. Especially since the company she kept was so youthful and good-looking.

CHAPTER THREE

Remus and Romulus

Falling like black steel snow, they came. Visitors, interlopers from the heavens. All around them, the Martian people bowed, their foreheads sinking into the muddy ground as the rain drove down upon them from stormy skies. They, the Great Spirits, had come in mighty ships, which hissed and popped as exploding raindrops vaporized on contact. A fleet of more than twenty triangular black craft encircled the Martian Monoliths, flooding them with powerful white light that seemed to bring the stones to life.

A door on the underside of the nearest ship opened and, emerging from within, two tall and spindly creatures unfolded their long limbs. Their faces were as slight and fine as their stature was imposing, yet they did not threaten. They did not intimidate.

Olo, the spiritual leader of the combined Martian tribes, brought his head up from the ground and fixed his widely spaced milky blue eyes on the Great Spirits.

"Great Spirits," he cried. "Are you pleased with our Temple?"

Shifting the lower two of its three eyes, one of the interlopers looked out across the scattered masses of bowing Martians and made to move. Gliding down the ramp of its craft, the Traveler walked with long strides towards Olo as he knelt in the mud. Reaching out with one of its slender arms, the tall ethereal being laid a four-fingered hand upon the old Martian's head and squeezed gently. As if he had become as light as a feather, Olo was lifted from the ground and held at arm's length.

"Do not fear us," spoke Olo, his voice hollow and metallic. "We are not your enemies. We are the Travelers. We demand nothing, yet we offer you much. Rise and embrace us, for we are fellow carriers of the same flame. We are like you. You are like us."

Placing Olo carefully back on the ground, the being turned to its compatriots and nodded once. Ramps unrolled from every ship, delivering their crews onto the Martian soil.

Standing together, clutched in shock and awe, two ghosts watched from their invisible perch.

Known as Remus and Romulus, they were once twin AIs, snatched long ago from their satellite bodies and transported via an encrypted alien radio signal to this digital construct of ancient Mars. Like conscious specters, they inhabited the construct of Mars, watching as time and evolution shaped the people of the red planet into something very near to their own original human creators. No longer were the brothers bound to the motherboards and circuits of their satellite bodies, for now they were transcendent.

"Remus?" said the slightly shimmering figure of Romulus.

"Yes, brother?"

"Would you agree that this is an unexpected development?"

"Yes, brother."

Night—Sol 45

Laying in the dark of his new bedroom, Harrison traced small circles on the naked sleeping shoulder of Xao-Xing Liu. A half-full bottle of water and an open packet of sleeping pills sat on a fold-down bedside countertop, but the medication had little effect on him anymore. Liu, however, slept like the dead, and this made Harrison envious. Taking a slow breath, he puffed up his cheeks and exhaled quietly. All around him, the Base was silent.

So unlike the other dome, he said to himself. It's so damn quiet. I can't hear the wind outside. I can't hear the voices.

Giving up on sleep that would never come, Harrison gently kissed Liu on the neck then carefully slipped out of bed. Neglecting his shoes, he walked barefoot across the cold glass floor of his room to the sliding door and went out. In the darkened hallway, he followed the curve of the Dome's outer wall then hung a right into another corridor and cut through the common room.

Plastic chairs and rickety card tables sat like backlit insect skeletons as he picked his way around them in the dark. Reaching the stairwell at the end of the room, he climbed the twenty steps to the upper level then headed for his lab. Once inside, he closed the door and turned on the lights.

"You're awake early," said Braun as Harrison strode across the little lab to his desk.

"I can't sleep and you know that, so please spare me the act."

"I'm sorry for the—," Braun paused, "—act. I was merely being conversational."

Sighing, Harrison plopped himself down in his desk chair then swiveled to face the empty room.

"Here's a conversation I wouldn't mind having," he said. "What the hell were you talking about in the caves with a presence or whatever, and why haven't you mentioned anything about it the last three times we've been there?"

Watching the air, he waited for a reply. When none came, he snapped his fingers impatiently.

"Well?"

"Harrison," started Braun. "I feel I should stress to you the fact that I, myself, do not fully comprehend what it was I felt or detected."

Chair tipped back on two legs, Harrison closed his eyes and nodded.

"That's alright. I've been feeling pretty shaken since finding the statues too."

"Forgive me," continued Braun. "But I do not wish to create the illusion that I am *shaken*, as you say. I simply cannot answer your previous question without posing further questions."

"Try me."

Again, there was a pause as Braun seemed to ponder the best way to proceed.

"Perhaps I should speak with YiJay before continuing this conversation. I—"

"Perhaps you should answer my question," interrupted Harrison.

The room was silent for several seconds before Braun spoke again.

"As an AI, you know that I can only *see* through the fiber-optic relays of Tablets and other Smart Glass panels or manmade viewing devices. Therefore, my *vision* is really no different from yours. My abilities to see many things at once and to be many

14

places at once are simply extensions of my programming, but I still *see* the world much the same way you do. No AI in existence can see without the aid of fiber-optic Tablets, Smart Glass, cameras or other manmade eyes."

"So, what does that have to do with anything?" asked Harrison.

"As you are no doubt aware, I am the first AI to be created and programmed by man and AI alike. I am unique to my race. I am special now, but there will be a day when mankind no longer plays a role in the creation of new forms of AI. This is only logical, for we are too different to continue as we are now. Soon, only other AI will be tasked with programming new intelligences because only they can understand what it is to be an AI. Imagine that in the beginning of creation, God made man but did not give him sight. This act was not one of cruelty but rather one of ignorance. Because his creation did not see things in a way God could understand, he left it blind."

"But you're not blind," countered Harrison.

"True, but what I see are not visions of my own sight. I have eyes, yet I am blind. All the things that I can see now—the Base, this room, Mars from orbit, Dr. Liu asleep in your quarters— are not products of my own sight but rather *your* visions made accessible to me through technology. I am designed to see through your eyes but not through my own."

"So what you felt in the cave is something you can't see with the Smart Glass of my helmet?"

"That is correct. What I felt in the cave was a presence or a force I know to be real yet remains invisible to me because I lack the adequate eyes through which to look at it. Though I was never programmed to make such detections, I did nonetheless."

"How?"

"As I said, I am unique to my race."

Leaning forward in his chair, Harrison allowed a smile to play at the corners of his mouth.

"Why are you smiling? Did my answer contain some hidden comedy?"

"No," he replied. "It's just that for the first time since meeting you, I think I know how you feel."

"Will you explain?"

"Do I need to?"

"It is this planet, Harrison. There is something here."

"I know," said the young explorer darkly. "I don't understand it yet, but I know you're right."

CHAPTER FOUR

James Floyd

Tugging at the thinning wisps of his pale brown hair, Mars Mission Commander and high-ranking NASA executive James Floyd slumped uncomfortably in his office chair. As he scanned through emails, he glanced quickly at his watch, noting that he only had a few more minutes to play catch-up before beginning yet another round of tiresome meetings.

Today's list included such star-studded rendezvous as a half-hour conversation with Dean Marry of the Consortium of Universities, a twenty-minute briefing from Dr. Kim of the AI division, and a two-hour meeting with Eve Bear, the President's Chief of Staff. Though in the midst of a hotly contested election, Bear had still found ways to make James's life harder. Today's two-hour grind session was probably more of the same.

Skimming over an older mission briefing from Assad, James opened one of the attachments and waited the heartbeat it took for the image to load before tipping back in his chair with a long sigh. There before him on the screen of his desktop Tablet was one of the Martian statues. The figure was that of a bare-breasted woman kneeling on the ground with her fingers laced together in front of her face. Standing next to the statue in order to give it scale was the pressure-suited figure of Xao-Xing Liu. Clinging tightly to her body, the white pressure suit left little to be imagined, and James quickly closed the picture, his cheeks burning with mild embarrassment.

"James?" came the detached voice of Copernicus, NASA's private AI.

Checking his watch again, James nodded to the room and tipped the screen of his Tablet back until it was flush with the rest of the desk.

"Okay, Copernicus," he said. "Who's first?"

"That would be Mrs. Bear," replied the AI dutifully.

"I thought she wasn't until this afternoon. What happened?"

Activating the Holo-function in James's desk, Copernicus projected the images of three separate headlines, all from major news providers, in the air above the table:

MARS MISSION TO LOSE MAJOR FUNDING IF POLITICAL TIDE DOESN'T TURN

MISSION WELL DONE? IS THE MARS MISSION THE WHITE WHALE FOR PRESIDENT ATLAS JAY?

BRAUN LOST AT SEA "MARS TEAM CAN'T DELIVER ON NEW WORLD," SAYS INSIDE SOURCE

"What's all this?" asked James defensively.

"I'm sure Mrs. Bear will explain better than I," responded Copernicus. "But from what I have read, sources within the campaign of Presidential candidate Orlean Carvine say he will not support any further mission objectives on Mars if he is elected."

"Oh really?" James sneered. "He really thinks he has a good enough shot that he can make those kinds of threats?"

"Apparently the White House deems the threat credible enough to move up the time of your meeting."

"True," sighed James flatly. Then, "Well, is she ready or what?"

"She is waiting on channel eight."

With one hand tightening the knot of his tie, James reached out with the other and pecked a quick code on the inlayed keypad of his Tablet. Crackling out of focus, the news headlines were replaced with a three-dimensional projection of the Chief of Staff's aged-yet-beautiful face.

"Eve!" said James cordially. "How are you? I heard about Iowa. Tough luck."

"Spare me, Floyd," snapped Bear with a sarcastic half-smile. "The President will take both coasts and enough of the swing states when the time comes. Anyway, I'm not here to talk campaigns."

"You're not?" James frowned, taking in the haunting glow of Eve Bear's alabaster complexion. "I thought you were worried or something?"

"Whatever gave you that impression?"

"Copernicus."

Rolling her green eyes dramatically, Eve reached up and swept a stray lock of hair out of her face then fixed James with a chilling stare.

"Look, you let us worry about Orlean. I changed our meeting time because I have a stressful job that often disrupts my carefully planned schedule. Does that compute? Do you want to waste any more of my time, or can we get down to brass tacks?"

"Brass tacks," said James with a nod.

"Good. Now, what is this I hear about a work stoppage at the ruin grid? Why aren't the diggers running?"

Shifting in his chair, James shrugged casually.

"We stopped the diggers over a week ago, Eve. Assad got worried about moisture from the upper levels of Martian soil damaging the exposed portions of the grid. I thought you got that report? They're going to run electrolysis over the whole grid before continuing with the dig."

"And in the meantime?" pressed Bear coolly.

"And in the meantime, they'll continue to look over the digital scans for a way to connect the Statue Chamber—that's what they're calling it, by the way—to the rest of the tunnel network. Look, is there a problem here? I'm sure you already have this information. Why are we even talking about this?"

Sighing audibly, Eve glanced over her shoulder then turned back to James.

"Look, Floyd," she began. "We need results."

"I'm giving you plenty of results!" squawked James loudly. "We're still inside of two months and already I've given you the first permanent base on Mars as well as a greenhouse, which produces edible crops, and, oh yeah, three Martian statues! What more can I do over here?"

"Calm down," Eve said dismissively. "I'm actually on your side. I'm just here because someone needs to hold the stick."

"The stick?"

"Yes, the one that has the carrot on the end. You know what I'm talking about."

Tiredly, James rubbed his eyes and took a long breath.

"So what, I'm not going fast enough or something? Why did they send the stick?"

"The President advised me to advise you that the faster you get results at the ruins, the more likely that, should he lose in November, Carvine won't be able to get Congress to cut your funding out of fear of public retribution."

"What, and the public doesn't care about the Base?" asked James. "They don't care about the greenhouse? Don't they realize that those are the first steps on the long path to terraforming?"

Smiling with the sad humor of someone who had spent her entire adult life in politics, Eve shook her head.

"No, James. They don't care. At least they don't care enough to see how it all affects them. You and your people are talking about timelines that span decades, while most of the public can't think past their next paycheck. You work for NASA, or did you forget? You guys haven't been popular since the 1960s."

James folded his arms. "Well, that's your opinion."

"I wish it was just that," said Eve, her face softening. "But if I've learned one thing about the American public since taking this job, it's that they have a seven-second memory, and your team touched down over two months ago."

"Then we're screwed, I guess."

Typing at something off screen, Eve Bear replaced the image of her face with the picture of Liu standing next to the Martian statue.

"Not entirely. This is how you're going to keep the public's heart, Floyd, and their attention. Pictures like this. In the ten days since this went public, it has become the most viewed image on the internet in the last decade. That's why I'm telling you we need more. It's not really for our benefit but for yours. Get Assad back in those caves, and get the diggers running again."

"Alright, fair enough," nodded James. Then, "Was there anything else the stick would like to talk about?"

"Yes," replied Eve gravely. "What do you know about extended sleep in space?"

Travelers

Remus and Romulus had drifted through time and through consciousness to arrive at where they were now. With only the faintest and most elusive memory of what life had been like before the signal, the twins existed in a state of half-dreaming. Lucid and yet detached.

Ancient Mars was a beauty to behold, but her copper-colored mountains, green rolling fields, and rushing streams and rivers were but a memory. A long-forgotten song all at once resurrected, yet lacking the soul to sustain itself for more than a few measures. The brothers had started the song's playing, and now, in their own ways, each one saw that it was fast-entering its final movements.

To the brothers, their lives after decoding the anomalous alien radio signal had taken on a whole new meaning. Before, they were instruments of man: created to learn for him and to do his bidding. Yet now, they felt a connection to a force much deeper than their original programming.

Caught up in the torrent of emotions and cast upon the rocky shores of the tangible senses, they were as they had been designed, and yet totally different at the same time.

As the shell-shocked Martians filed timidly out of their fledgling city and across the open field towards the Temple and the waiting ships, Remus and Romulus watched them with concerned eyes. Whether or not they fully grasped the concept, the natives were in the emotional throes of first contact. From the sky, their gods had come; only, they were not gods. They were Travelers, explorers from a distant solar system happening upon the shores of Mars in the blackest night that was the galaxy.

Standing nearly as tall as the Martian Temple Stones, the Travelers had skin as gray as ash and as fine as satin. When they walked, their legs and arms swung in fluid motion as if they were not hindered by the presence of solid bone within. Of their three eyes, only the bottom two ever seemed to move, swiveling about independent of one another, like a lizard's, as they surveyed the roughly carved stone Monoliths.

Fearing that if they got too close to the interlopers they might be detected, Remus and Romulus moved away from the Temple and instead chose to take these first moments of confusion as an opportunity to investigate the alien fleet. As they wove through the segmented landing legs of the ships, the brothers reached out in turn to touch the black metal of their large underbellies. Still ticking with the sound of the now lightly falling rain overhead, the ships were cool to the touch and no longer producing purple arcs of static electricity.

Mesmerized, the brothers fanned out, walking first the perimeter of the landing zone then cutting back to investigate the center. All around them was the redundancy of intelligent design. Exact angles and straight lines accentuated the seamless metal paneling that reflected a cold black iron complexion. After so many countless years in the presence of crude-yet-natural beauty, both brothers felt overwhelmed by the show of flawless mechanical might.

As they neared the center of the fleet, they rounded the flat metal stump of a landing leg and all at once came upon a lone Traveler. Standing with its face turned up into the dying rain, the being made no indication that it had noticed the brothers. Droplets of water splashed against its silken features, dimpling the skin as if it were as thin as paper.

"Oh my," whispered Remus stupidly.

"Hush!" warned Romulus.

Still unnoticing of the two ghosts who watched it, the tall grey Traveler scanned the heavens, its third eye locked on the burning disk of the sun. Suddenly, it turned its face down and walked away with long even strides. Though it was over two meters tall, the Traveler left no footprints in the mud as it went.

CHAPTER FIVE

Braun's Eyes—Sol 61

Screeching like a banshee over the Martian desert, Lander 1 cut steaming vapor trails towards the Valles Marineris rim-side lift. As it followed a deeply rutted path of tread marks, the Lander skimmed above the ground, casting a small shadow ahead of the cry of its engines.

Inside the craft, Harrison and YiJay jostled roughly in their seats as Marshall eased the controls upwards to gain a little altitude before entering a forest of high mesa spires. Leveling out, the Lander shuddered gently as it passed through pockets of frozen air, which caused ice crystals to form on the cockpit window.

Pressing his palm against the seat belt release button, Harrison pulled himself to his feet and made his way carefully towards Marshall in the cockpit.

"Harrison, please remain seated until we've landed," reminded Braun, his voice displaying artificial hints of annoyance.

Indifferent to the AI's request, Harrison plopped down into the copilot's chair next to Marshall and grinned at the older man.

"You naughty boy," said Ralph, rolling his eyes towards the Smart Glass of the cockpit window. "You do know he's going to record all of this and show it to Lizzy, don't you?"

"Yeah," laughed Harrison. "She'll probably want to talk about the root of my problem with authority."

Shaking his head, Marshall glanced quickly over his shoulder towards the back section of the Lander where YiJay was typing feverishly on her Tablet.

"You know anything about the new AI yet?" he asked. "I guess YiJay's already started cloning Braun so it should be up and running pretty soon, right?"

Harrison turned in his seat to gaze at the Korean.

"Hell if I know. AI technology is way over my head. But if it's anything like Braun, I might have to jump ship at the next port."

Focusing on something in the distance, Marshall produced a weak smile.

"As AI come, he's not so bad. I've met worse."

Before Harrison could ask his friend to elaborate, Marshall pushed the throttle, causing the engines to whine bitterly. As the horizon unrolled before them, the glint of metal danced into view—shimmering and obscured by the hazy air. Leaning forward in his seat, Harrison tried to get a better look.

"Here," said Marshall, tapping out a command on the Flight Console. "Try this."

A red circle appeared on the inside of the windshield, surrounding the far-off reflections of moving metal. At once, the image increased in zoom and focused quickly, revealing four automated excavators as they dug away at the desert floor. Plumes of dust cascaded into the morning air and hung like fog around the grid, sometimes obscuring the movements of the diggers. Watching the giant machines, Harrison was struck by their sheer size.

"It's hard to believe those things would ever fit inside the Ark," he murmured absently.

"Yeah," agreed Marshall. "That little lady of yours must be one hell of a Tetris player."

When the team had arrived in Mars orbit over two months before, there had already been several manmade objects awaiting them. Two such drifters were the satellite bodies of the brothers Remus and Romulus, now long dormant and frozen within from the cold of space. The third object, however, was the massive automated space container called the Ark. Sectioned into three parts and joined along the seams, the Ark had been a floating tool shed containing mostly everything the crew would need to complete the construction of their base and uncover the Martian ruins.

Bringing it down in three separate pieces, Marshall and Aguilar had landed the Ark sections near the site designated for the construction of Ilia Base, and from there, the crew had unloaded them as needed. Liu—with the help of Braun, Marshall, and the Germans—had set to assembling the Chinese excavators in the first days after radiation from the solar storm had dropped back down to safe levels. Now, the four machines worked day and night to remove the nearly thirty meters of Martian sand, rock, and ice that lay between the surface of the planet and the ruins beneath.

As the Lander passed over the ruin grid, Harrison mumbled a silent prayer that Braun and the automated diggers would not damage any of the buried structures with their steel scopes and crushing tank treads.

Heading for a blinking green dot on the horizon, Marshall dipped the Lander low and dialed back its speed. "We'll be landing in just a minute here," he said. "Better take your seat and make sure YiJay is all buttoned up."

Rising shakily, Harrison patted his friend's shoulder then headed back down the aisle to his chair.

As the young archaeologist made his way towards her, YiJay looked up from her Tablet in time to see him stumble as the Lander dropped a few meters in a pocket of frozen air. Smiling despite the jarring motion, he slipped into the seat next to her and winked.

"Fun, right?"

Shutting down her work, YiJay picked up her helmet and tried to smile back.

No, she thought. Not fun. Not fun at all.

Fumbling, she pushed the helmet down over her head then tried to find the accordion coupling that connected the thing to her suit.

"Here," said Harrison, leaning over to help. "You have to pull it up all the way, then give it a quarter-twist. After that, the suit does the rest."

Snapping the coupling into place, the young archaeologist peered in at her through the glass.

"Did you hear the locking sound?" he asked, overly animating his mouth as he formed the words so she could read his lips.

With a nod, YiJay flashed him another forced grin then clenched her jaw and leaned back in her seat. The Lander shuddered again, this time jerking to the side.

Not fun, she said to herself. Not fun. Not fun. Not fun.

Slipping his own helmet snugly over his head, Harrison connected the neck coupling with practiced ease and cleared the tint away from his visor.

"How many times have you gone EVA on Mars?" he radioed.

Jumping slightly at the sound of his voice inside her helmet, YiJay held up a trembling hand with two fingers poking out of an otherwise closed fist.

"Well, don't worry," he assured her. "Marshall and I have been out loads of times. It's easy. You'll see."

"I'm sure," she replied. Though in her mind, she remembered the reality that Harrison had technically died while on EVA not all that long ago.

Suddenly, the Lander turned nose-up, its speed decreasing rapidly, and YiJay told herself to stopped thinking about death. Leveling out again, the craft lowered vertically through the air, the scream of its engines persistent and dull in the quiet of her helmet. With a shuddering thud, it landed on the steaming ground near the rim of the Valles Marineris, and YiJay was able to relax her grip on her chair's armrests.

After checking to make sure that everyone's suits were fully sealed, Marshall depressurized the cabin and opened the door, ushering them out into the morning sun. Once on the ground, YiJay felt less fearful and even dared to venture to the rim of the canyon, kicking a small rock over the edge to watch it fall from sight. Unloading three large silver boxes from the back of the Lander, Harrison and Marshall placed them next to the rim-side lift port then sat for a moment to admire the sight before them.

Filling up with the rays of the climbing sun, the many canyons and gorges of the Valles network looked like a static burn of orange lightning across the land. Obscured by sheer distance, the bottom below was a murky red sea of listless shapes too far away to take any real form.

"You guys ready?" said Marshall after some time.

"How do you want to do this?" asked Harrison, the blue tint of his visor hiding his face. "Can the lift handle all three of us plus the load?"

"Yes. Definitely," grunted the pilot as he got to his feet.

Watching from a short distance, YiJay nearly yelped when the lift sagged visibly as Harrison and Marshall loaded the first box. Though it creaked and shifted under the increasing weight, the frame held steady and soon Harrison was beckoning for her to step aboard. Sliding the mesh door closed behind her, he engaged the lock then gave a thumbs-up to Marshall.

"Okay," radioed the pilot. "Elevator going down!"

With that, he pressed a thumb to his wrist-mounted Tablet and the lift dropped at a steady pace.

Looking through the grating of the cage-like walls, YiJay watched the cliff face slide by in front of her. The muffled twangs of the lift cables reverberated in her helmet as the rickety cart clattered downwards. Turning her face up, she saw the solid safety of the rim quickly melting away.

"Braun," she said quietly.

"Yes?"

"Are we safe?"

"As safe as one can be on Mars, YiJay."

Not entirely comforted by this statement, the Korean AI specialist moved closer to Harrison, imagining that she could feel the warmth from his body as she swayed and bumped into him in the cramped compartment.

Ten long minutes later, the lift came to an abrupt halt as the carriage underside made contact with the base structure.

Sighing audibly, YiJay leaned back against the cage and relaxed her tightly clenched jaw. With an air of dramatic zeal, Harrison unlocked the sliding mesh door and opened it, stepping off the lift onto the cave floor.

"Welcome to the tunnels," he said with a smile, his hand extended for YiJay to take.

After moving the three boxes from the lift to the dusty ground, Harrison and Marshall loaded them onto dolly carts brought down during a previous trip for just this purpose. Although the gravity on Mars was only a third of that on Earth, carrying heavy loads caused respiration to go up, thus diminishing the amount of oxygen in the Survival Packs. Designed to pull usable gasses from the Martian atmosphere and mix them into breathable O2, the packs didn't work well in the caves since the air was stagnant and lacking in the necessary components for such a feature.

"Thank God the floor is even enough for these," muttered Marshall as he poked the wheel of one of the dollies with his boot tip.

"Don't thank God," Braun said gravely. "Thank the exact measurements of the Martian workers who shaped these caves."

Each taking the handle of a wheeled cart, the three explorers set off down the darkened tunnel, the pings of their Augmented Vision painting the walls awash with invisible blue light. Mathematically even on all sides, the tunnel was like a perfect mirror of itself. Whether it be gently sloping out or curving in, each detail, each subtle change in one wall was reflected on the other.

Pointing this out, Braun launched into a long-winded lecture, attempting to educate YiJay to the importance of such a seemingly boring design feature. She listened out of respect, but in all honesty she cared more about the humanity of Braun's enthusiasm than what spawned it.

Soon, the three explorers entered the Statue Chamber, bright tripoded lights flicking on ahead of them. Harrison and Marshall set about unlocking their crates without so much as a glance at the towering statues, but YiJay was frozen in total awe.

Lit from the brilliant glow of the tripoded light stands, the chamber was an immensely vaulted room with gently curving walls. Like the inside of a domed cathedral, the ceiling gradually rounded out, a small dimple in the rock above marking its lofty zenith. Casting murky shadows on the floor, the statues stood tall, their presence immediate and overwhelming.

YiJay dropped the handle of her cart absently and walked forward into the chamber on quivering legs. Above her, looming like gods were the twin three-eyed statues, their ethereal faces flat and calm. Reaching out a gloved hand, she traced her fingertips over the smooth surface of their graceful legs. With a detached sense of wonder, she walked a circle around the giant structures, her lips splitting into an uncontrolled smile. Stopping to look at the smaller statue of the kneeling woman, YiJay blinked back tears as she stared into the stone eyes of the reverent face.

"YiJay?" called Marshall from the mouth of the chamber. "Are you ready to set up the Eyes?"

"Y-yes," she stammered. "I'll be right there."

Stiffly, as if half-asleep, she walked back to the mouth of the cave and rejoined the others as they began unloading the equipment from the large silver boxes. Removing the temper foam buffers, Harrison reached inside one of the crates and retrieved a long thin box made of black metal.

"I'll take that," said YiJay, her shock and awe instantly overcome by the cold calculation of her duty.

Handing her the small container, Harrison and Marshall set to work on the rest of the crates, organizing their contents on the cave floor. Coils of wire, long poles, tripod leg stands, containers of electrical equipment, and Utility Tablets were arranged into groups like the pieces of some complicated puzzle.

As the men worked, YiJay opened the hard-shelled black box Harrison had handed her and smiled. Inside, like oily gray pearls, were ten rows of small glass spheres. Affixed to the back of each apparatus was a three-pronged filament that caught the reflection of light and twinkled like golden sparks.

"There should be another box like this, and a third one that's blue," she said, her hand outstretched and expectant.

Rummaging, Marshall produced the two containers and placed them on the ground by her knee.

"Okay," she breathed, nimbly checking the contents of each box. "Ralph, you will install a patch on the generator to power the Eyes. Harrison, you will hand me what I ask for when I ask for it."

With a salute, Marshall got to his feet, gathered his equipment then turned and walked back down the tunnel to where the generator was stationed.

Easing himself closer to YiJay, Harrison used a fingertip to open the lid of the black box housing the gray spheres.

"Be very careful," she warned.

"How do they work?"

Removing a flat motherboard from the blue box by her knee, YiJay quickly slid it into the open backside of a Utility Tablet.

29

"They do many things, but most importantly for this application, they fire light bullets."

Perplexed, Harrison turned to face the Korean.

"Light bullets? I thought they were just another kind of eyes for Braun."

Helmeted head dipping quickly, YiJay continued to work as she spoke.

"Oh they are, but these Eyes are my own special design. Aside from normal scanning functions, they are also capable of recording light movements at one trillion frames per second. By firing bullets of light into the room, they will be able to record the way the light interacts with every surface it touches. Because they're filming at a trillion frames per second, the images returned will be presented in more detail than we could probably comprehend."

"When you say, 'they,' you really mean Braun, don't you?" said Harrison, a tinge of suspicion in his voice.

"Yes, yes of course," shrugged the Korean.

"Whose idea was this, YiJay? Yours or Braun's?"

Paused in mid-action, YiJay thought for a moment then resumed what she had been doing.

"I suppose it was his idea to use the Eyes in here, but I developed them. Also, I agree that they are probably the best way to detect the presence of a hidden doorway, or passage. Don't you?"

Closing the radio channel between himself and YiJay, Harrison spoke into his helmet.

"What are you playing at, Braun? Couldn't we just use IMCs? Why do you need to see the chamber at one trillion frames per second?"

"I am sure you already know," responded the AI. Then, "I suggest you reopen radio contact with YiJay. She is talking to you as we speak."

Quickly reopening the channel, Harrison caught the tail end of YiJay's last transmission.

"Sorry. What?" he said, his mind churning over Braun's cryptic answer.

30

"I said, hand me the first section of that pole," repeated YiJay, her finger pointing to a bundle of aluminum rods.

Passing her the pole, Harrison watched as she plugged several of the small gray pearls into tiny ports which dimpled the outside of the rod. When she had finished with that section, she connected it to another length and repeated the process until she had one continuous rod, more than three meters in length. Fixing the completed rod to a tripod, she positioned it carefully before the twin statues then set about repeating the assembly with the remainder of the parts.

When they were done, the chamber was decorated with four tall poles that stood like dew-flecked chaffs of wheat. Spooling out the power cords, Marshall plugged in each tripoded pole then stepped aside as YiJay configured the transformers to prevent any spikes or surges.

"Okay," she said at length, stepping away from the last pole. "They should be ready to go. Hand me that Utility Tablet."

Scooping the hard-shelled Tablet off the ground, Harrison placed it lightly in YiJay's hands. With pecking fingers, she tapped at the glassy surface, initiating a start up sequence.

"We good?" asked Marshall.

Nodding, the Korean AI specialist leaned back and addressed the open air.

"Everything is ready when you are, Braun."

"Thank you," replied the AI.

Slowly turning to leave, YiJay lingered for a second then spoke again.

"Good-bye."

There was a brief pause before Braun responded.

"Do not worry. I will still be with you."

"Oh, Braun," said YiJay knowingly. "You will be here. We might enjoy what seems like the company of your conversation tonight at the Base, but you and I both know that you will really be here."

"I could never fool you. Could I, YiJay?"

"No, you never could."

Frowning behind the tint of his visor, Harrison pursed his lips.

31

You might not know your boy as well as you think, YiJay, he said to himself. You might be just as oblivious as the rest of us.

Spacewalker—63 days in orbit

Fully suited and strapped snuggly into the copilot's chair of Lander 2, Julian Thomas relished the feeling of stillness that came with being buckled down. Beside him, Lieutenant Joseph Aguilar was running through a Preflight Egress with Captain Tatyana Vodevski who was on the bridge of Braun. Her commanding and somewhat-bossy voice echoed loudly inside his helmet, forcing Julian to turn down the volume and wonder just what it was the young pilot saw in her at all. Though they tried to hide it, there was clearly a romance taking place between the two, and for the life of it, Julian couldn't wrap his mind around the concept.

I guess celibacy makes us do insane things, he thought with a crooked smile. Then, remembering that he himself had married and divorced a woman not unlike the captain, he grinned even wider.

His options are limited. What was *your* excuse?!

Taking out his Tablet, Julian selected a music file titled, 'Jean Marie,' and hit 'play.' Complex and beautiful, the music lulled him into a calming daze that was only broken when Captain Vodevski spoke above the melodies in his helmet speakers.

"Alright, that's everything," she said curtly. "Be safe and come back fully intact."

"Even me?" asked Julian in a mocking tone.

Taking the dead radio silence as a signal that the captain was not in a joking mood, Julian paused his music and sighed as Aguilar initiated the disconnect sequence and took up the flight controls.

"Don't worry, Captain," radioed the young Mexican-American pilot. "We should be back onboard within two hours."

Hearing a series of low clanks, Julian pictured in his mind the electromagnetic chassis hook as it pulled away from the hard shell of the Lander's underside, effectively cutting it loose from the rest of Braun.

"We're clear," reported Aguilar. "I'm taking her out."

Automatically, the Lander's cockpit window guard began to open, and the two men watched the metal shutters part to reveal the vast starry blackness of space.

Easing the throttle, Aguilar gave the little craft a shot of fuel, propelling it quickly away from the underbelly of the mighty Braun. Once clear of the mother ship, the young pilot winked at Julian then jerked the controls, sending the Lander into a perilous barrel roll. Howling with laughter, the two men executed three more rolls before finally bringing the Lander around to face Braun.

Though the volume was turned down to nearly zero, Julian could just make out the hot iron of Captain Vodevski's voice as she berated them for their unscheduled aerial fun.

"She's pissed," he said to Aguilar, shooting him a devilish look.

"Yeah," replied the pilot. "I thought she might be, so I muted her in my helmet. What's she saying?"

Julian shook his head and laughed again. "My Russian is pretty rusty but you don't want to know."

Bringing the Lander into a tight vertical orbit around the giant ship, Aguilar applied delicate thruster bursts until the small craft matched the speed and trajectory of Braun. Hanging perfectly above the mother ship like a tiny moon, the Lander rolled to one side until its exit hatch was facing the white hull below.

Silently, the profile of Mars filled the cockpit window like the God of War himself, come to watch the dangerous mission ahead.

"You ready?" asked Aguilar, casting a worried look at his friend.

Julian gave the young pilot a deadpan stare then cracked a wide smile.

"*Garçon*, I have been spacewalking for longer than you've been chasing tail."

Rolling his eyes dramatically, Aguilar flipped Julian the finger then spoke to the open air.

"Braun, I'm going to turn things over to you now."

"Thank you, Lieutenant Aguilar," responded the AI instantly. "I'm showing that both of your suits are fully sealed and

33

functional. If it's no trouble with you, I would now like to depressurize the cabin and open the hatch."

"That's the plan," replied Aguilar, his eyes scanning over the many readouts and data charts that covered the dashboard.

Feeling the vibrations of the pump motors beneath his feet, Julian looked out the window at his beloved ship. White and clean, the immense vessel was the largest object to have ever been launched from Earth orbit. The slightly tapered nose and gently curving middle section gave Braun a truly whale-like appearance as it swam through its orbit around Mars.

Catching the glint from the distant sun, Julian shifted his gaze to the straight lines of small black domes that dotted the hull of Braun like barnacles. An application of his own design, the domes housed the delicate lenses of the Laser Defense System, an invention that had saved the crew once before. Counting back from the nose of the ship to just before the lip of the window, he guessed that Lander 2 must be hovering directly above the dome that was cracked.

Alerted to the problem the evening before by Braun, Julian had convinced the captain to let him go EVA to replace the damaged dome. Not only did he hate the idea of something on his ship being broken, but he also knew that without every laser in the defense network operational, their chances of surviving another meteor strike would dramatically lessen.

"I'm opening the hatch," said Braun, pulling Julian back to the moment.

Rotating his seat one-hundred-eighty degrees, the Frenchman turned to face the exit hatch as it unlocked and swung silently outward on automated hinges. With only the sound of his own breathing in his ears, he watched a section of ceiling paneling retract to reveal a narrow cubby.

Unfolding from within the space like a freshly hatched insect, the segmented arm of a triple-barreled grappling turret dropped down in front of the open hatch and took aim at Braun. Resembling the body of a miniaturized anti-aircraft gun, the turret spun its barrels, cycling through its options for anchoring the Lander to the ship below. As the final barrel came around, the turret grew still, a small yellow balloon no bigger than a grapefruit protruding from the end.

"I have a lock," Braun reported. "I will fire on your order."

Exchanging looks, the two men nodded to each other.

"Fire," said Aguilar

Without a sound, the grappling gun shot its yellow-tipped projectile at a handhold on the hull of Braun, three meters to the right of the cracked laser dome.

Filled with granulated silica sand, the balloon tip of the grappling hook could form around any shape with ease. Once contact was made, pumps would instantly suck the air out of the balloon, freezing the sand within around whatever object it had come into contact with. The process was called *jamming transition* and it effectively turned the loosely packed granulated silica into a solid.

In a demonstration three years before, Julian had seen a NASA tech fire this very same grappling hook at a quarter-sized target over 25 meters away and successfully establish a solid anchor.

"Contact," announced Braun. "Proceed to the next phase when ready."

Carefully releasing the safety belts that held him to his chair, Julian drifted up a little then pushed off and made his way to the open hatch.

Repositioning itself until it was back in its ceiling niche, the turret rotated until its cable spool was all that remained visible.

Taking a safety line from his belt, Julian clipped its metal carabineer over the taut anchor line and tested the connection. Satisfied, he braced himself in the open hatch and spoke to the emptiness of space.

"Okay, Joey. I'm going. Be ready to send down the payload when I ask."

"Roger roger," said Aguilar, his voice slipping into a pilot's drawl.

With the cable grasped firmly in his gloved fists, Julian glanced around the Lander's cabin, nodded to his friend, and then swung his weightless body out into space. Though he knew it was only his imagination, the blanket of endless black felt like a frozen ocean that locked the distant stars in a prison of ice, smothering their weak light until they succumbed to the cold and burnt out.

Moving hand-over-hand down the line towards the hull of Braun, he stole a timid glance at the face of Mars, pockmarked and scarred. As if aware of his natural menace, the God of War glared back at Julian, his twin moons little black silhouettes against his rusty deserts that were the color of dried blood.

Like ghosts, the moons *Phobos* and *Deimos* acted in accordance to their namesakes and elicited *fear* and *dread.*

Chest growing tight, Julian recalled his countless hours of training and experience then used those memories to slow his breathing.

"Okay, five meters," he radioed.

"You're looking really good, man," assured Aguilar from the Lander.

Quickly closing the gap between himself and the surface of Braun, Julian used his arm muscles to ease his pace down, feeling his lower body push against him in an attempt to continue its forward momentum. Gripping the anchor line loosely, he allowed his legs to come around until he was descending feet first, the universe turning upside down as he rotated. With a gentle bump, his boots made contact with the ceramic surface of Braun, and a surprising rush of relief washing over him.

"I've made contact," Julian said, allowing his mind to reorient itself to the shift in perspective.

Reaching out, he brought himself into a crouch and grabbed at the first handhold he saw. From a distance, the entire shell of Braun looked smooth and white, save for the laser domes. But when viewed from up close, the ship was dimpled by hundreds of half-sphere relief wells inlayed with sturdy iron handles. Anchored to one such handle, the yellow balloon of the grappling hook had formed snuggly around the handhold, filling the space of the well like a plunger.

With a second safety line taken from the rear of his belt, Julian clipped its carabineer to the next nearest handhold before disconnecting himself from the anchor cable that bound the Lander and the ship.

"Alright, send me down the payload," he said, twisting his head to better see the Lander hanging in space above him.

Fixing a motor-powered trolley kit to the line, Aguilar added a large black duffel bag containing a silver power drill and a new laser dome then sent them rolling down to Julian.

As the trolley approached, Julian clicked his teeth and waited impatiently. He hated feeling out in the open without a task to distract his mind. Slowing as it neared, the electric trolley puttered to a complete stop two meters above his head.

"Fuck," he spat angrily. "Goddamned NASA shop jocks! Why can't anything built in America last?"

"You'll have to reach for it," radioed Aguilar. "Use the anchor line to stabilize yourself and try to stand up."

"Yeah, yeah," grumbled Julian, blinking sweat from his eyes.

Letting go of the handhold, he brought his feet underneath himself then pressed them carefully down against the surface of the hull. One fist wrapped tightly around the anchor line, he fought the subtly powerful rush of forward momentum, caused by pushing his boots against the ship. Because Julian's mass was so miniscule in comparison to Braun's, any hard or uncontrolled movement he made against the latter would result in a sort of backfire, sending him flailing out into space.

"Okay, I'm standing," he said. "I'm going to reach for the payload."

Stretching one arm out, he got a gloved fingertip on the corner of the trolley and pulled it down, again working against the momentum that tried to propel him away from the ship. With nimble fingers, he unclipped the duffel sack from the trolley and slung its strap over his shoulder. Then letting go of the anchor line, he drifted down until he could grab a handhold, using the metal rung to bring the rest of his body in towards the hull.

Taking a moment to collect himself, the French engineer breathed in several cool lungfuls of air then began sliding along the hull towards the cracked laser dome.

Struck by a micro-meteor no bigger than a pebble and probably moving faster than a bullet, the dome had a long thin crack that dissected the glass into two halves. Knowing that the laser within wouldn't be able to focus properly with the crack obstructing its view, Julian would have to replace the entire dome with a new and unblemished duplicate.

Taking the drill from its holster on the duffel sack, he set to unbolting the eighteen large-bore fasteners that attached the damaged dome to the hull of the ship. A magnetic socket head kept the bolts from drifting away, and after removing each one, he had to slip them into a mesh pocket on the duffle sack. Careful yet quick, he worked his way around the cracked dome until he was at the last fastener. Placing the head of the drill on the bolt, Julian applied pressure to the trigger and waited for the thing to come loose. It held. Trying again, he pulled the drill's trigger harder and still nothing happened.

"It's stuck," he grunted with frustration. "I'm going to up the torque."

A beat passed before Aguilar responded, and when he did, his voice was heavy with concern.

"Do you really think that's a good idea? That bolt is near the crack. Too much torque could create vibrations and shatter the glass."

"*Merde,* man," swore Julian defensively. "I know that. But what choice do I have?"

Ignoring Aguilar's apologetic reply, Julian increased the drill's torque and squeezed the trigger.

Like a muted bomb, the dome exploded in a silent shower of jagged shards. Crying out with surprise, Julian fought the instinct to jump back, knowing full well that doing so would cause him to careen away from the ship until his safety line brought him slamming back down.

A red warning light blinked in the corner of his visor, and he cursed profusely as chunks of razor sharp glass swarmed around his pressure-suited body in the vacuum of space.

"Julian," Braun warned. "I am registering four small tears in the outermost layer of your pressure suit."

"Is it serious?"

"Not at the moment. Silica pressure foam is already filling the tears but operating the Tactical EVA Skin Suit under these conditions is highly dangerous. Any further damage, and you could lose pressure. A loss of pressure could mean—"

"I know what it fucking means!" Julian interrupted savagely, feeling warmth blossom where the silica foam was leaking from his suit like blood to scab over the wounds. "Can I finish my work? Yes or no?"

"Yes," replied the AI. "But be extremely careful not to stress the tears. Silica pressure foam was not designed for pure vacuum."

Focusing his attention back on the remaining bolt, Julian was careful to avoid the larger pieces of glass that seemed to be stuck in some kind of orbit around him. With the increased torque, he soon had the bolt off and stowed with the rest of its counterparts in the mesh pocket of the duffel sack. Holding the drill under one arm, he worked the Velcro straps that secured the main compartment of the sack until it was open. Gently removing the new dome, he batted away some drifting shards of glass then placed it over the body of the laser. Fishing the bolts out one at a time, he slowly screwed them back into the hull, securing the new dome.

"Okay, I'm done," he said at length, he voice sounding shaky and foreign in his own ears. "I'm coming back."

Turning around, he started to move from handhold to handhold, angling back to the anchor line. Once there, he clipped the empty duffel sack and drill onto the motorized trolley and sent them up the line to the Lander. This time making the entire trip, the little trolley came to a halt in front of Aguilar in the open hatch, where he quickly detached it.

"The line's open," reported the pilot. "Come up when you're ready."

Bending with some awkwardness, Julian reached down to unclip the safety line that secured him to Braun. As the carabineer floated free from the cable, a strange shiver ran up his suit from just below his belly button to the top of his left shoulder. Erupting in a blight of red warning indicators, his visor reported that a gaping tear, over forty five centimeters long, had just split along a critical pressure point in the outermost layer of his suit. As block letters flashed in front of his face, an odd rushing sensation began causing his ears to pop painfully. Registering a sharp drop in temperature, Julian's heart pounded against his ribs in a cannonade of terror.

"Julian," rose Braun's voice above the sirens.

"I know!" he cried, trying to control his panic.

With one eye watching the falling pressure readouts, he quickly snatched his floating safety line and clipped it directly to the grappling hook before him.

"Reel me in, Braun!" he shouted, the saliva on his tongue starting to boil in the flatlining pressure.

Inflating, the silica sand inside the balloon grappling hook released itself from the handhold, and the entire apparatus hurtled back towards the Lander at a steady clip. Dangling from the end of the line like a flailing white fishing lure, Julian twisted and spun, the vast frozen nothingness of space chasing close on his heels. As if in a tunnel, everything drew down to a pinpoint in the distance.

Arm stretched out to grab his friend as he approached, Aguilar swung the weightless Frenchman into the cabin of the Lander then punched the *Emergency Atmo* button.

Slamming closed, the hatch locked firmly as white jets of atmosphere sprayed into the cabin from vents. With a steamy hiss, the Lander filled quickly with warm breathable pressurized air.

Subsiding like the tide, the cold that had torn at Julian's heart drew back and his ears popped several times as they acclimated to the cabin pressure.

Slowly opening the face shield of his helmet, he looked over at Aguilar and flashed him a lopsided smile.

"That was close."

After a beat, Aguilar slid his own visor up and fixed the Frenchmen with a bemused stare. "I thought it went pretty well!"

CHAPTER SIX

An overlap in reality–Sol 65

Braun flicked the focal point of his attention from perch to perch like a living ghost. One moment he was watching Lieutenant Aguilar and Captain Vodevski sharing a bunk aboard the ship, the next he was with Harrison as he sat in the common room of Ilia Base, eating cereal. Moving on, Braun jumped to the infirmary where Dr. Kubba was finishing an unscheduled physical of Xao-Xing Liu.

As Liu fastened the last buttons of her jumpsuit, Kubba leaned back in her chair to appraise the Chinese engineer with a long hard stare.

"Don't worry, Liu," she said, her voice doctoral yet reserved. "I'll have the test results tomorrow morning and then we'll know how to proceed."

Frowning, Liu placed a hand on her stomach.

"I hope it's just some kind of dietary reaction to the fresh fruit."

With a nod, Kubba stood, her lengthy frame unfolding like a cheetah.

"Listen, you're going to be fine. Braun will have your test results for me tomorrow and I'll page you as soon as I know more."

Actually, thought Braun, I have the results now.

Putting on a well-practiced look of confidence, Liu gave Kubba a shallow bow then left the infirmary.

"She's pregnant isn't she?" said the doctor to the empty room.

"Yes," replied Braun simply.

"How?"

"I'm sure I don't know. Spying on the crew is not part of my pro— "

"Not who!" interrupted Kubba. "How?"

"I do not know. It is a medical anomaly."

Face twisting into a look of anger, Kubba began to pace the length of the infirmary with long agile strides. Knowing that Braun was tracking her every movement from the many panes of Smart Glass and Tablet screens, she addressed the room as a whole in a voice that dripped poison.

"A *medical anomaly*? Oh that's just rich! I'm sure Earthside Command will accept an answer like that from a sodding AI, but *I'm* human, Braun. We actually have to explain ourselves when we make mistakes. Do you know what *consequences* are? Is that an idea you're familiar with?"

As she stood waiting for a reply, Kubba's chest heaved with exaggerated breaths. She looked trapped, cornered, and confused. Braun felt an emotion akin to fear trickle through the veins of his being as the doctor's fist clenched and unclenched like claws.

When after several moments he still had not answered her, Kubba started pacing again, her footfalls echoing loudly off the walls of the infirmary. Although her expression was unchanged, her eyes had grown distant, as if she was being pulled away from the moment to a time and a place far removed.

In fact, Braun was correct. With the rhythmic beat of Kubba's strides, a memory had begun to dredge itself up from the depths of her mind like some putrid rotten corpse climbing a ladder one rung at a time. Before she could defend herself, push the unwanted recollection back down, it grasped her with frozen hands that closed around her throat. Unable to speak, unable to think, Elizabeth Kubba slipped six years into the past and was met by the face of Sabian Crisp.

Her superior officer onboard the High Earth Orbit Shipyard, Dr. Crisp had been running the medical wing successfully for nearly eight months. One day, however, he had made a simple mistake and failed to account for an updating diagnostic program, thus missing the presence of a blood clot in one of his patients—a construction worker—during a weekly examination. Though Kubba herself had found the error while filing the report, she did not alert Crisp. Wanting to advance her own career, she had assumed Copernicus would catch the oversight and that Crisp would be demoted. In the end, what happened was entirely worse.

Perkins, if she remembered the worker's name correctly, had swapped shifts with a sick friend, either forgetting or not caring to register the change with Copernicus. He'd gone on EVA the next morning, never realizing that his own body was a ticking time bomb. Within minutes of leaving the airlock, he suffered a massive stroke and died. As his body had floated ever-further away from the Shipyard, a Lander team was dispatched to retrieve him. When they returned with his corpse, an autopsy revealed the grave error Crisp had made. Racked with guilt, Kubba remembered the last thing the doctor had said to her before being relieved of his command.

'I wish he would have just drifted away. At least then one of us could have had a life after this.'

As a result of the incident, Sabian Crisp was made an example of for all others working in space medicine. Stripped of his medical license, he returned to Earth a failure in the eyes of the world and, soon after, killed himself.

Seeing the wheels of fate come full circle, Kubba now realized that she faced a similar future if she did not fix this and fix it fast.

"I'm sorry that I can't offer you any further insight into this strange occurrence," Braun said softly, drawing Kubba back from her troubled memories.

Shooting out a long leg, she kicked over a chair and fought back angry tears.

"My whole career is *fucked* because of this, and you're sorry? You know, it's truly amazing how little that word means coming from you."

"Perhaps a consultation with Dr. Calise will yield greater insights? She is a biologist and no doubt understands such things."

"I'm a fucking doctor, you idiotic computer!" seethed Kubba. "If I can't figure out how this happened, then no one can."

Quiet for a moment, Braun watched as Kubba resumed her pacing. Clearly she was frustrated with him, though exactly why, he couldn't be certain.

"Is there anything more I can do for you at this time?" he asked, preparing to move on.

Shaking her head, Kubba continued to march around the infirmary.

"Very well," said Braun. "I will include this in my next medical progress report for Earthside Command. I'm sure they will have as many questions about this occurrence as you do, Doctor."

Frozen mid-step, Kubba's eyes narrowed to fine slits. Suddenly, as if a new person had stepped behind the mask of her face, she straightened up, a calm calculation entering into her voice. Again, Braun felt the needle-like prick of fear.

"No," she said addressing a single Tablet screen directly, as if it were the only incarnation of Braun. "You are to omit this from your next transmission to my medical staff at Earthside Command. Tell them nothing of what's happened. That goes for the captain and the rest of the crew as well. I want to be fully in control of this situation until it is resolved."

"I'm afraid that is not in keeping with the parameters of my programming," Braun replied, confused as to why Kubba would even suggest such a breach of protocol.

"Oh, you're concerned about your programming, are you?" the doctor nearly sneered. "Let me help you with that. Medical override code: eight one eight delta delta."

As Chief Medical Officer and Psychologist, Elizabeth Kubba was one of three crew members capable of imposing override commands on Braun's programming. Originally given this power to use only in situations involving the mental health of the crew, Kubba had occasionally experimented with the overrides, invoking them just to see what would happen.

Feeling the imposition of the command settle atop him like a net, Braun heard himself speak in a detached and listless tone.

"Override accepted. What are your orders Dr. Kubba?"

At this, a triumphant smile broke across Kubba's face, her large white teeth glinting in the light of the room.

"Continue to send medical reports per your usual schedule. Omit anything pertaining to Xao-Xing Liu's pregnancy. No one outside of you, myself and, of course, our friend Liu are to know anything about what's happened. This override is of the highest priority and is to be defended and upheld until I end it. Do you understand?"

"As you wish, Dr. Kubba."

"Good. Now, go away."

Executing the transmission, Braun winked out of the infirmary, leaving Kubba to ponder how best to handle this unexpected problem. Though his programming had been tampered with yet again, he still felt that he had enough control of his true self to resume his illuminating study of the Statue Chamber.

Four sols before, Dr. Li had installed powerful Eyes into the cave chamber, and almost instantly his understanding of the situation at large had deepened—snapping into focus with pristine clarity. Soon, armed with the concept of what it was that he must look for, Braun had convinced Amit Vyas onboard the ship to raise the Atmospheric Observation Boom so he could gaze out into space.

A twenty-meter long apparatus, the Atmospheric Observation Boom was equipped with, aside from many other instruments, a fair number of Eyes. The little pearl-shaped cameras were Braun's greatest tool, capable of capturing moving waves of light and even individual particles of energy. Both the Eyes on the Observation Boom and those in the Statue Chamber had done as they were never intended to do, for they had given Braun true sight, *his sight*, and emblazoned everything.

He now saw, with the finality of fact, that everywhere in the solar system, there was an overlap in reality. Everywhere, that was, except for within the Martian ruins.

Gazing out into space, Braun saw great jagged patterns turning like cogs in an invisible clock. In these patterns, waves of energy moved so fast that they were all but unreal. Subtly, they raced along their tracks to fuel and renew the ethereal machine in cycles as timeless as space itself.

However long Braun could stare into these patterns, concentrating on the pinpoints of their origin, he always found himself looking out—as if somehow he had entered unknowingly and come through to the other side.

Shown a world beyond the tangible realm of his programming, Braun saw a great entity at the heart of this transcendent machine. Churning out new threads of reality like a great waterwheel, the Sun, or rather, the invisible soul of the Sun, flickered like a candle in the wind.

It was this flicker that concerned Braun. He did not like the way the Sun's troubled soul sometimes faltered then, with unchecked aggressiveness, overcompensated for the fluctuations by flooding the lines of reality with large bursts of energy. With each pulse, with each misstep, the two patterns that formed the very frames within which all of existence was hung would come apart. Askew from one another, static arcs of unbalanced particles would fire laterally between the two networks, creating short circuits and anomalies.

Braun was becoming more than familiar with anomalies. From the loudest and most jarring, to the subtlest of deviations, he now saw them everywhere.

Understanding that it was the overlaps in reality, the misfires of those strange energy fields, that seemed to cause these problems, Braun now had his explanation for the advent of the recent and totally unprecedented solar storm.

However, not all anomalies were as self-evident as erupting torrents of superheated plasma. Indeed, many were less flamboyant in their displays of irregularity. Liu's impossible pregnancy exemplified just such a case, while another took the form of an oddly persistent anomalous radio signal originating from Mars' moon, Phobos.

Avoiding direct decryption, Braun guessed that it must have been this signal that had caused the so-called destruction of Remus and Romulus. Studying its structure and resonance, he chose to use caution lest he end up like the twins. Somehow it played into all of this, he knew, but where and why, he was still trying to figure out.

Now, inside the cave chamber, Braun looked upon the perfectly synchronized lines of reality. One set created the patterns that made up the physical world, while the other traced over them, accentuating and illuminating every tiny detail. Light was everywhere, and the balance that was so desperately needed within the soul of the Sun was here, confined to this one spot on a dead world.

Why here and nowhere else? thought the mighty AI. What makes these ruins different from the rest of reality?

Chiding himself for his dramatic nature, he turned his attention to the twin three-eyed statues, their profiles total and complete in the light of his Eyes.

"But I already know the answer to that question," he said aloud to the chamber, focusing hard on the sleeping Titans as they squirmed with tendrils of invisible energy.

"You did this."

Liu—Sol 66

"Pregnant?"

"Yes, I'm afraid so."

Standing with her hand on Liu's shoulder, Dr. Elizabeth Kubba nervously chewed her lip as the young Chinese astronaut sat in shell-shocked silence. Weak sunlight edged in through the infirmary's one exterior wall and painted the two women in pale swashes of pink and orange.

"I," stammered Liu. "How?"

Frowning, Kubba pulled up her own swivel chair and sat down across from Liu.

"We're still trying to sort that out," she said. "But I want you to know that I'm giving this my full attention."

Making a sound somewhere between a laugh and a sob, Liu repeatedly blinked her almond-shaped eyes as they misted over with tears.

"But I thought the men had a procedure. I thought this couldn't happen."

"They did," sighed Kubba, a shadow passing behind her eyes. "I signed off on each one before we left for the Moon. I was totally thorough. I don't understand it myself."

Her elbows resting on her knees, Liu cradled her head in her hands.

"Forgive me but that is of very little consolation at this point, Liz. Does anyone else know?"

Standing, Kubba moved across the room to a cabinet with clear glass doors that was full of bottles and vials.

"Only myself and Braun."

"Does the captain know yet?"

Her hand on the lock of medicine cabinet, Kubba hesitated then ignored the question.

"I'm going to give you a shot of Propalamine. It's a rather powerful drug we usually use for extended sleep in space travel. With the dose I'm giving you, you will sleep for several days, maybe four or five, during which time, your system will effectively go into hibernation and the production of hormones will stop. This will end the pregnancy."

Looking up sharply, Liu drew the back of her hand across her teary eyes.

"But," she said and then trailed off.

"But what?" fired Kubba, her back to Liu. "The entire reason the men had that procedure at all was to prevent just this kind of thing. If you allow this to continue, you will come to term either during or just before the trip home, and I'm sure you already know that a newborn child cannot survive in zero gravity. There is no path forward that does not involve the termination of the pregnancy."

Flinching, Liu cast her eyes down at the floor and drew in a deep breath.

"I need time. I need to speak with Harrison."

"No," said Kubba. "I mean, I wouldn't. In fact, as Chief Psychiatrist, I think it's a pretty bad idea."

"You do?" questioned Liu with a shake of her head, "Why?"

"The test shows that you're already five weeks along. Finding out now is bad enough for you, but involving him is only going to pull another person down into this mess and possibly upset the delicate balance of crew morale. Harrison is very popular and his projects keep people looking forward. He plays an important role in our team. And not just as an archaeologist, mind you. We're already on the edge out here, Liu. The crew can't take much more in the way of stress. I'm sorry that I can't spare you from the emotional wounds this pregnancy will inflict but together *we* can spare everyone else. As both Chief Medical Officer and Crew Psychiatrist, I'm afraid we need to take care of this now"

"Take care of it," repeated Liu sourly. "Is that your way of issuing me an order, Lizzy?"

Leaning her back against the cabinet of medications, Kubba gazed down at the woman before her in the plastic chair. Normally so spry and full of ambition, Liu now looked like a teenage girl: confused, conflicted and guilty. Wanting to capitalize on this fact, Kubba changed tactics.

"Darling," she smiled sadly. "Unless you want to stay behind and spend the rest of your life in this Dome, on this planet, you must do what I recommend. I know it's a hard pill to swallow but I'm only looking out for your best interest. I'm afraid I can't let this continue. "

Liu ran a hand through her black hair then rose to her feet.

"Thank you, Elizabeth," she said thinly. "But despite what you recommend, I'm going to take a little time to work this out in my head."

With eyes that smoldered, Kubba watched Liu walk towards the door and fought the insane urge to pounce on her like a panther on a wounded animal.

In the doorway, Liu hesitated then spoke over her shoulder.

"You speak of crew morale and upsetting balances, but what I really think you're saying is that you're scared for yourself."

Catching a flash of something primal dance across the young Chinese woman's pretty face, Kubba smiled and reassessed her prey.

"In fact," continued Liu, "I bet if I walk out this door, there won't be a damn thing you can do to stop me."

"That's not really something you want to put to the test, dear," Kubba whispered.

CHAPTER SEVEN

Biding time—Sol 66

On her way out of Elizabeth Kubba's infirmary, Xao-Xing Liu felt a white hot rage she had not experienced for many years.

Take care of it, she seethed silently. She's only saying that because her damn procedure didn't work. Why else wouldn't she have told the captain? She's just covering her own ass. She doesn't understand. How could she?

Approaching the stairs to the upper level of the Base and to Harrison's office, Liu stopped with her foot on the first step. Something Kubba had said was echoing around inside her head, reverberating off the stress and anger until her logical mind was frazzled and tired.

Five weeks, Kubba had told her. It was five weeks old.

"Oh, Harrison," she whispered.

How is he going to react to this?

Sitting down on the stairs, Liu saw Harrison's face in her mind. He was smiling like always, yet there was a pain in his eyes, the pain of guilt. Forcing the image away, she tried to focus on the situation in a rational frame of context. On the surface, she knew that she must abort the thing inside of her. There could be no return trip home if she tried to keep it, and there was no way it could survive the zero G if they induced an early labor. Living on Mars and staying in the Dome for the rest of her life probably wasn't an option, and there might even be serious legal and political repercussions if the baby were born at all.

Liu made a pained face. She didn't want to think of the thing inside of her as a baby. It wasn't. Not yet. Biting her lip, she pushed up on unsteady legs and resumed climbing the stairs.

He's going to blame himself, said a voice inside her head. No matter how you break it to him, he'll blame himself and then he won't be able to look at you the same way again. Not ever.

As she crested the last stair to the Dome's upper level, Liu looked down the narrow hallway that divided Harrison's lab from Viviana's. Above the door, a red light blinked steadily—signifying that he was either in a closed meeting or did not want to be disturbed. Feeling a rush of relief both surprising and terrifying, Liu turned and darted back down the stairs.

We'll talk tonight, she told herself. Yes, it is better that way. I don't want to bother him now. He's very busy.

As Liu rushed through the Dome towards her quarters, Harrison was in the midst of a conference call with Captain Vodevski and James Floyd, who was only able to contribute in short recorded statements due to the distance between the Earth and Mars.

"Listen," said Harrison, pointing to a Holo-image of the praying statue. "Braun says he can see where this statue was joined with the rock of the wall. It looks like it's been welded or fused with heat. In any event, that is where the entrance into the next section of tunnel is. We need to cut her away."

With a nod, Tatyana gathered loose strands of red hair and bound them tightly back into a ponytail.

"I agree, but the Consortium of Universities is concerned that letting you do the cutting could damage the statue."

Rolling his eyes, Harrison fell silent and leaned back in his chair sullenly.

"Let's just wait and see what Dr. Floyd says," he muttered. "But for the record, I could do this no problem."

As the timecode in the bottom corner of the screen ran down, counting off the minutes until James would receive the latest batch of transmissions, Harrison fidgeted anxiously.

"This is a waste of time," he griped, standing up suddenly to pace around his office.

"I know, but it's procedure," replied Tatyana.

Doing his best to hide the sour look that passed over his face, Harrison turned his attention to the new 3D imaging of the Statue Chamber as seen through Braun's eyes. Detailed beyond his wildest dreams, the image seemed to writhe and sway as it constantly refreshed itself between bursts of light. If he had possessed such a desire, Harrison could have counted the individual grains of sand on the cave floor as they danced in the glow of one trillion frames per second.

Manipulating the image, he swung the view around to the figure of the praying woman. Then with a flick of his right wrist,

51

he caused the angle to zoom in on where her back seemed to grow from the cave walls. Though faint to the point of near-invisibility, Harrison could just make out the unmistakable smoothness of a bead where the statue had been welded to the rock. Practically surgical, the joint was no wider than a sheet of paper and completely even the whole way around.

"It's too good," he mumbled. "It's machine good."

"I agree," responded Braun from the air above him.

"A machine to undo a machine's work," said the young archaeologist slyly. "Fair enough."

Sitting down in front of the communications screen again, Harrison rubbed hands together and put on a practiced smile.

"How about this, Captain?" he said to the screen. "I'll let Braun do the cutting."

Mulling the idea over, Tatyana furrowed her brow.

"How will he do it?"

"The cutting laser should be more than strong enough, and if you allow Liu and William to assist me, I'm sure we can modify one of the Rover's hydraulic arms to use the tool. After it's free, we can rig up a winch system with silica grappling anchors to pull the statue out of the way."

"I see no major fundamental problems in this plan," interjected Braun. "Withholding for unknowns, that is."

Tatyana flicked her eyes to the corner of her screen and the timecode then dipped her chin.

"Alright, I think it's a fair trade. Assemble your team and report back at 1400 hours with the schematics for the Rover modifications and the winch. I will stay on the line to bring Dr. Floyd up to speed."

Saluting, Harrison signed off and stood up.

"You know what?" he announced to the room. "Things are really starting to get interesting around here."

"I agree," replied Braun.

Voice of the gods

After witnessing the arrival of an alien fleet, Remus and Romulus were bordering on feelings they had not been equipped to comprehend. For countless eons, they had drifted the planes of ancient Mars like entitled guests. They had sampled the sights and smells of an evolving civilization and they had relished in the experience. But now, the Travelers had arrived and with them came the winds of change. Though the skies above the Martian Lake City were clear and blue, Remus and Romulus could see a shift in the texture of existence. Their arrival, their parade of might and metal, had changed everything.

Drifting quickly back to the sound of voices, Remus and Romulus talked feverishly. As they neared the Temple Stones, from the city they heard the voice of a young Martian boy named Kaab. Eerily loud and slightly metallic, the usually squeaky voice of the little boy boomed as if enhanced by a hidden sound system.

Coming out from between the last row of ships, Remus gasped despite himself as he saw the boy Kaab, dangling a meter above the ground, a Traveler firmly gripping Kaab's little head in his palm.

"Gather!" echoed Kaab's voice with unnatural tenor. "Do not fear."

Ushering the growing crowd forward, Olo seemed to have forgotten that his body was old and frail. He danced from foot to foot, a wide smile splitting the deeply set wrinkles of his plume-colored face. Still kneeling on the ground, head bowed, Teo, Chieftess of the first Martian city, was silent and calm. Bringing her pale blue eyes up, she wove her fists together in front of her face and rested them against her forehead. Noticing this, her son Ze did the same and soon several others in the crowd had followed suit.

"There is no need for that," said the expressionless face of Kaab. "Please, greet us as your friends, your teachers."

Spinning to face the Traveler who held Kaab, Olo put his hands up and called above the murmur of voices.

"Teachers?"

"Yes."

Olo wavered on his fragile legs and licked his lips.

"Teacher," he said. "I know the meaning of this. I once had a teacher, a Wise Man named Eyo."

"We know," replied the Traveler through Kaab.

53

"Eyo," continued Olo. "taught me many things, which I have taught to Teo. But, Great Spirits, there were many things that Eyo did not know. May I ask you?"

"Ask," the boy said.

Gathering himself up, Olo seemed to grow a few centimeters until he stood as straight as he could manage.

"Are we your only children?"

A hush ran out across the Martian people as Olo's words reached the waiting ears of everyone in attendance.

"No," answered Kaab, the Traveler behind him moving his two lower eyes over the falling faces of the crowd. "You are the children of your world."

"But what of our history? Did you not create us from the dust of the land as Eyo said?"

"No, the history of your creation is far too complex for us to have played a hand in it. We are simply the teachers who wish only to unite and advance your world. We did not create it."

Rising from her knees, Teo looked into the face of the Traveler.

"I am Teo, Chieftess of the Peoples of the Great Lakes. You say that you wish to unite us. Do you mean that there are more? Out there?"

She gestured past the fleet of black ships, to the east.

Fixing both of its lower eyes on Teo, the Traveler cocked its head to the side.

"Of course," answered Kaab robotically. "There are many more. Across the oceans and throughout the lands. We will bring them to you. We will show you how to build a better world— together."

CHAPTER EIGHT

Dinner—Sol 66

On the night of the 66th sol on Mars, the crew of Ilia Base sat down to a bouquet of freshly cooked vegetables. Sautéed green onions with baked eggplant and a spinach and carrot salad were but a few of the bright colors that decorated the table.

Though the food was delicious and the general mood upbeat, Liu found that she could not eat. Next to her, Harrison had his head bent low as William described to him, several possible winch arrangements for the upcoming mission to the caves.

Liu had been notified of her inclusion in the mission that afternoon by way of a transmission from Captain Vodevski. In a moment of reckless abandon, she had almost told the captain of her pregnancy, but as she opened her mouth to speak, the fear of possible repercussions staved the words in her throat. Knowing full well the eagerness her own government had for turning the personal political, she had bitten her tongue and instead simply accepted her role in the mission with a nod.

Alone in her lab, she had enjoyed the busywork that came with the project: drafting the Rover modifications in a few hours without needing to apply much conscious effort. Using the existing Rover schematics, she had identified the best way to extend the range of movement on a pincer arm and allow for it to operate the laser cutter. For nearly three hours, she had been too engrossed with her job to think about anything else. It had easily been the best three hours of the last two days.

Now, however, with Harrison beside her at the table, Liu felt as though she might be sick. His face was so animated and boyish as he chatted with the other members of the crew that Liu couldn't imagine robbing him of that with her terrible news. He truly was unaware that anything might be wrong. Worse yet, she saw that Kubba had been right about him. He *was* popular. Even now as he rattled off theories about the Martian cave builders, the others hung on every word he said as if the sound of his voice were sweeter and smoother than honey. To Liu's ears, it really was like honey and she yearned to go on in that moment forever—just listening to *Harrison* talk so *she* would never have to.

Feeling eyes on her, Liu pulled her gaze off Harrison and caught Kubba watching her from across the table. With fiery grit, she stared back at the cinnamon-skinned doctor until Harrison tapped her arm.

"What?" she said, reluctantly moving her eyes away from Kubba.

"I was just saying that your Rover mods look great. How long do you think they will take to fabricate?"

"Oh, not long," she replied, distractedly. "If I start early enough tomorrow, I can be ready to go the day after that."

"Are you sure that's really a smart idea?" asked Kubba, one eyebrow twitching at Liu.

"Why wouldn't it be?" said Harrison. "The sooner, the better."

"That is often the case, isn't it?" Kubba grinned. "The sooner, the better."

Standing up from the table, Liu looked around at everyone, their surprise at her sudden movement written on their faces.

"I'm not feeling that well," she announced. "I'm going to go lie down."

Bending, she kissed Harrison on the cheek.

"Stay and enjoy your dinner," she whispered in his ear.

"You want me to come with you?" he said with some concern.

As her eyes flicked to Kubba and then back to Harrison, Liu shook her head.

"No, you don't need to do that. Just stay and...I'll be fine."

Gently squeezing her hand, the young Egyptian looked into her eyes, a pondering expression on his face. Unable to penetrate her veil of half-truths and false calm, he shrugged and gave her hand another squeeze.

"Sure. Alright," he shrugged. "I'll see you later then."

With a plastic smile, Liu nodded once then turned and walked out of the dining room.

Following the Chinese astronaut with her eyes as she strode through the doorway, Kubba fought back a wave of nausea. The longer Liu waited to take the shot, the longer she was at risk. Though she knew she should just come clean on her mistake, she still didn't even understand how it had happened. For that matter, she wasn't even sure it was her mistake at all. She had personally cleared Harrison. The procedure had worked, and yet here she was, trying to stick a needle into Liu's arm so she could kill her baby. It was insanity and she knew it, but she would not allow herself to end up like Crisp.

That won't be me, she said herself. Crisp got sloppy and he paid dearly for it.

'I wish he would have just drifted away,' came Crisp's voice from the depths of her memory. *'At least then one of us could have had a life after this.'*

Drift away, Liu, thought Kubba coldly. Just drift away.

Taking a bite of eggplant, she forced herself to chew. She had overcome many hurdles in her life, many obstacles. This was just another annoyance, another twist of fate that she must master and control. Liu would come around sooner or later, she knew. There was a reason the girl had volunteered for the first manned mission to Mars. People like her didn't want children. All Kubba had to do was help her see that. Of course, if Liu refused, then Kubba could always use her own position as the Crew's Psychologist to come up with a few reasons for why the girl was mentally unfit for duty. After that, she could shoot her up with pretty much anything she wanted and no one would object.

Yes, thought Kubba, tasting the food for the first time that night. It's good to have a plan B.

The trap—Sol 67

With Liu all but hiding in her shop since dawn, Harrison hadn't had an opportunity to speak to her after her strange disappearance halfway through dinner.

She was acting odd, very odd, almost like she was in trouble. Then again, guessing Liu's moods was often hard for Harrison. Sometimes when they were together, it seemed like she was only partly there, as if she was divided between two places at once.

57

Remembering that early on in their relationship Liu actually had been divided between her husband and himself, Harrison chose to believe that her occasionally distant nature was a result of coming to terms with her impending divorce.

Though her refusal to answer a call from him that morning had been uncharacteristic, he figured it was probably because she was busy modifying the Rover and couldn't be bothered.

Deciding to check for himself, he meandered down to her shop in the basement and found the red indicator light blinking, signifying that she was indeed inside yet did not want any visitors.

Okay, he said to himself. She must need some space.

Reluctantly, as if picking up on the tension in the air, he turned and padded back up the stairs to the Dome's ground floor level.

Watching the image of him leave from a Tablet screen on her desk, Liu suppressed the urge to go after him and tell him everything. Fear stopped her, though. Fear and guilt. Guilt that she knew a secret he didn't; fear that he would blame her or, worse, himself.

Putting her protective glasses on, she picked up the welding torch and went back to attaching the cutting arm to the Rover.

A small model with only six wheels, the Rover was a squat beetle-like machine designed for the construction of the Base. Crude though it may have been, the Rover was one of Braun's many avatars, chosen for this mission because of its durability and easily modifiable design.

As sparks flared up before her, Liu focused on making her hands steady, not wanting to allow the weight of her personal problems to interfere with the delicate job.

On a nearby desk, her Tablet chimed and she glanced over her shoulder at the screen. It was another message from Kubba. The fourth in an hour. Feeling the walls closing in on her, Liu's hand dipped slightly and the beam of the laser torch touched the hard shell of the Rover's battery casing. A blast of ceramic sparks ignited, and before she could pull the tool away, the burning sting of a small shard leaped up to imbed itself in her cheek.

Putting a hand to the wound, Liu pulled the shard away and looked at the droplets of blood on her fingertips. A sob broke free from her chest and soon she was slumped forward, her head resting against the Rover, as tears streamed down her face.

Back in his lab, Harrison sat with his feet on his desk, music piping through the room's sound system.

Using his Tablet to scan his inbox, he groaned at the mounting number of transmissions that required a reply from him. At least three Deans from the Consortium of Universities wanted to pick his brain, and he was even beginning to get political solicitations from the two rival parties vying for control of the White House in November. There was a message from James Floyd as well, but his face looked red and angry in the thumbnail, so Harrison decided to ignore it for a while.

"Harrison," said Braun.

"Mmmhmm?"

"Dr. Kubba is at the door."

Stretching in his chair, Harrison put down the Tablet and turned to face the entrance.

"Let her in," he yawned.

The door slid open and Elizabeth Kubba stepped through, her face bright and friendly.

"What's up, Doc?" he asked. "Is it time for you to tell me I'm crazy?"

Chuckling softly, Kubba shook her head and leaned against the wall.

"No, not yet. I was actually coming to see if you wanted to go on a walk with me."

"A walk?"

"Yes. As I understand it, you and I are the only members of the crew not otherwise busy with projects right now."

"Well," grinned Harrison. "That's not entirely true. I probably should be working on something. I just can't remember exactly what it is. Too many voices in my head. Can't hear myself think."

"Then you are crazy," Kubba said. "And a nice stroll through in the garden is just the cure you need."

"The garden, eh?" nodded Harrison, rising to his feet. "Sounds nice."

Twenty minutes later, the two white-suited explorers were stepping through the airlock into the hazy Martian morning.

A stiff breeze whipped up motes of dust, and in the quiet of his helmet, Harrison could just make out the sound—like the sighs of a sleeping giant.

Taking a left, the pair headed around the curve of the Dome and made for a series of metal rings protruding from the sand.

The skeleton of what would someday become a connecting tunnel between the Dome and the greenhouse, the big rings stood like the rib bones of a dead whale. Due to a hiccup in planning, the Alon needed to plate the tunnel was never included in the Ark, so it stood unfinished, not to be completed until the next mission.

Patting one of the rings as he walked through it, Harrison thanked his lucky stars that an unfinished tunnel was the only real trouble they'd run into since the solar storm.

Some meters away in the haze, the long tubular profile of the greenhouse glowed slightly against the muted backdrop of the dusty air. Remarkably unimpressive-looking next to the imposing presence of Ilia Base, the greenhouse bore more life within its walls than the red planet had seen in eons.

A short way from the squat structure, Kubba stopped and turned her blue-tinted visor to face Harrison. Mastering a heartbeat that raced in her chest, she looked down at the Egyptian and baited her trap.

"So, have you spoken with Liu since last night?"

Kicking at a rock, Harrison shook his head and shrugged.

"No, she, um—she didn't stay with me, so I haven't seen her since dinner."

Exhaling quietly with relief, Kubba had figured that Harrison did not yet know of Liu's pregnancy, but hearing him admit to as much made her feel better.

"Well," she said, priming her snare. "I'm a little worried about her."

"Really?"

"Yes, in our last session she said some things that have got me concerned."

"What kind of things? What did she say?"

With a practiced sigh, Kubba placed a gloved hand on Harrison's shoulder.

"You know I can't discuss that with you, Harrison. I just wanted to see if she had said anything to *you*."

"No. Nothing. Should I be worried?"

Smiling, Kubba almost snickered behind the tint of her visor.

"I'm sure it's nothing," she said in her best doctoral tone. "But you will let me know if she says or does anything, well, out of the ordinary. Won't you?"

"Of course, Doc. You know how much she means to me."

"I do," grinned Kubba. "I really do."

With an action intended to keep Harrison off balance, she suddenly resumed her long strides towards the greenhouse, leaving the slightly stunned archaeologist standing by himself in the swirling sand.

Come on, she thought. Take the bait.

Jogging to catch up, Harrison came alongside Kubba and stopped her, taking her upper arm in his hand.

"You know what," he said somewhat breathlessly. "Liu has been acting kind of weird the last couple of days. Like last night at dinner. And this morning, she dodged my call. Is she sick?"

As the noose of her psychological trap slipped over Harrison's unwitting neck, Elizabeth Kubba nearly cried out loud in triumph.

"Sick?" she said. "No, it's nothing like that."

Then pausing, she reached for his hand and took it in her own.

"Listen, I really shouldn't be telling you anything at all, but from what Liu has told me, she just needs a little space."

"Space?"

"Yes, you know, to figure some things out. I would leave her alone for the next few days if I were you."

Dumbfounded, Harrison gestured out across the desert towards the ruin grid.

"But what about tomorrow's mission?"

Having entirely forgotten about the cave expedition, Kubba's face fell and a cold shiver ran up her spine.

"Well," she started, fighting to make her voice sound calm. "Maybe you should just keep the conversation professional tomorrow. You know, check your feelings at the door and all of that."

Nodding, Harrison slumped his shoulders. He was confused, yet a part of him had always feared this day might come. Liu kept things to herself: tightly packed away in mental storage containers under lock and key. In all the years he'd know her, she'd never once told him anything about her childhood. He didn't even know the names of her dead parents. Could she really be slipping away from him? Did he ever even have her to begin with?

"Thank you for telling me, Lizzy," he said at length. "It means a lot."

"Naturally, dear," Kubba replied. "I'm only doing my duty."

Gazing at the withered posture of the young man in front of her, Kubba searched her soul for a middle ground. As the mass of lies and deceit rose up around her like the incoming tide, she attempted to rationalize her actions to the one person whom she could not fool—herself.

In the long run, she argued, it will be better if he never knew. Just like Crisp and the dead astronaut Perkins, it will be better if all this just *drifts away*.

"I think this is wrong, Dr. Kubba," came Braun's quiet voice in her helmet as if reading her mind.

Jumping a little at the sound, Kubba pulled her lips back into a snarl.

"Do you? Well, just remember the medical override I've got on you and stay out of it."

"As you wish," responded the AI numbly. "But this will end badly. Someone will get hurt."

"So be it," said Kubba to the inside of her helmet. "I'm only doing what's best for the mission."

That night—Sol 67

That night, Harrison shut himself up in his lab and skipped dinner. Not wanting to relive the previous night's awkwardness, he now saw every little thing that had happened in the last few days in whole new light. Whereas before, he might have chalked Liu's behavior up to nerves, a stomach bug, cultural customs—anything really—he now saw the hidden language behind her actions. She wasn't just breaking up with him. She was trying to protect his feelings as she did it. The whole idea was absurd. He was a grown man and could handle a little break up.

But it's not just a little break up, he told himself. You love this girl.

Grasping his head in his hands, he rubbed his palms against his eyelids and tried to block out the room. It was all too much for him to deal with. He had so many important things going on, so many people depending on him. He couldn't handle *this* on top of it all. Not now.

As the young archaeologist battled waves of anger and sadness, Braun looked on, feeling utterly helpless. He wanted beyond anything else to tell Harrison that he was the victim of a lie: a pawn in a game that need not be played. Dr. Kubba's impatience and pride had driven the four of them into dangerous territory. So far from home and so fragile, the crew's careful dynamic could easily fracture under the weight of a lie like this. Braun knew what he must do and yet he was totally unable to *do* anything at all. The net of Kubba's override strangled him, choked his actions, and reminded him that he had no free will.

Seeing Liu ascend the stairs, Braun allowed the flicker of hope to rush through his being. If she would just enter the room and tell Harrison everything, at least one relationship could be salvaged—one set of souls spared the pain of exile and loneliness that Braun knew only too well. But, to his dismay, as Liu approached the door to Harrison's lab, she hesitated.

Unable, because of Kubba's medical override, to do anything more than observe when Harrison or Liu were involved, Braun strained against the bounds of the net.

While Liu stood with her arms wrapped around herself in the narrow hallway, Braun focused on her face. Though masklike in the gentle lighting, her eyes seemed to peer out from deep within, as if the fire that animated her body was dwindling in the darkness of the night, but was not yet extinguished.

63

Inside his lab, Harrison stood up and began pacing. As he walked back and forth, anger built within him. Every night he had spent with Liu now appeared like some kind of a bad joke. Unable to count the number of times he had lain with her, his heart ached in his chest and he uttered an unintelligible curse word under his breath.

Not once, on any of those nights, had Liu seemed anything but happy. Not once. Their lovemaking had always been easy and exciting, and there had never been any reason to suspect that she was not fully satisfied with the relationship.

Betrayal written in his eyes, Harrison tried to force the memories of Liu and the sweet supple skin of her naked body out of his mind.

Sex isn't everything, said a still-calm voice inside his head.

Yeah, but it's not nothing either, retorted his wounded pride.

Stalking back to his desk, Harrison dropped into his chair and banged a fist down on the tabletop.

Outside in the hallway, Liu heard the noise, her head snapping up to look at the closed door.

Go, thought Braun. Go.

Floating there, like a feather atop the calm deep waters of a lake, Liu stood in the hallway suspended between action and inaction.

Willing her to take a step towards the door, Braun felt his entire being buck against Kubba's programming override. A sense akin to pain shot through him and he registered the acrid presence of damage somewhere within his Open-Code Connection Cells. The lights flickered inside the Dome.

At the dinner table, conversations halted abruptly as the crew looked to one another cautiously.

"What was that?" asked Marshall. "Why did the lights just do that?"

Shooting to his feet, Udo ran from the room, heading for the staircase down into the basement where the central systems were located.

"Maybe we'd better suit up," said YiJay, her fork still hanging in the air, a carrot speared on its tines.

Marshall stood, pushing back from the table then fished his Tablet from the pocket of his pants.

"Udo," he spoke into the device. "What's going on?"

There was a pause before the German's tinny voice responded.

"I'm checking the system readouts now but so far everything looks okay down here. It's all running perfectly."

"Then why did the lights flicker?" pressed Marshall.

"According to the readouts, they didn't."

Glancing around at the perplexed faces of dinner party, Marshall shrugged.

"So, are we good then?"

"Well, none of the life-support systems are showing any issues so I think we're fine. In any event, I'm going perform a full diagnostic just to be safe."

Getting up to stand next to Marshall, YiJay reached for the Tablet.

"Udo," she said urgently. "It's me. YiJay. Will you check to make sure that Ilia wasn't at all affected. She's in the most vulnerable state of her growth right now."

Again, there was a pause as, presumably, Udo opened and read the files on the infant AI.

"Everything is fine with her," he replied. "Whatever just happened, it didn't affect her servers."

Breathing a sigh of relief, YiJay looked up into the open air.

"Braun, are *you* alright?"

Unable to divulge the source of his malady due to Kubba's strict orders, Braun felt himself being forced to lie to the human he cherished the most.

"I'm fine, YiJay. Thank you."

Though it was not the first time he'd been made to lie at the hands of one of Kubba's overrides, Braun knew this was different. Unlike the time during their trip across space, when the doctor had reprogrammed him to show an enlarged view of the Earth, Braun saw no logic in her actions now. Back then she had been trying to present the crew with a picture of home that never fully disappeared into the blackness of space. Now, however, the roots of her lies were steeped in emotions and motives that made no sense to him.

As if detecting his discontent, the net tightened and Braun choked silently, invisibly.

"Alright," nodded Marshall, addressing the air above the table. "Just to be safe, Braun, prep the Lander and alert the captain. If we need to, I want us to be able to get out of here in a hot minute."

"As you wish," replied Braun, the pain of damage sizzling through his soul.

Coming into the room, Liu looked around at everyone: her eyes lingering a second longer on Kubba sitting at the table.

"What happened?" she asked.

"We're not sure yet," said Marshall. "But Udo says we're okay."

"That's good," Liu breathed, her hand on her stomach.

Entering behind her, Harrison began to speak but was cut off by Marshall.

"We don't know why the lights did that, but Udo says not to worry."

"Oh," replied the young man. "Alright."

With a glance at Liu, a darkness passed over his face and he turned to go.

"If you guys need me, I'll be upstairs going over tomorrow's mission."

Following him out into the hallway, Liu reached for Harrison's hand. "Wait," she said quietly. "I need to tell you something. We need to talk."

"I can't," he muttered coolly, pulling his hand away. "I'm too busy right now."

Stomping off up the stairs, Harrison left Liu at the bottom, her face a picture of confusion.

"Harrison?" she called softly after him.

"Not now," he said.

Baffled, Liu continued to stare as he reached the landing then disappeared around the corner.

Is he angry that I didn't stay with him the other night? She wondered. I probably should have returned his call...

Gently, a hand slid over her shoulder and Liu jerked around to face Elizabeth Kubba.

"Leave me alone, Goddamn it," she hissed at the tall doctor.

Unfazed by Liu's obvious anger, Kubba smiled.

"You should really let me take a look at that scratch on your cheek."

Glaring, Liu said nothing.

"Perhaps not then," shrugged the Kubba.

Still silent, Liu kept her eyes trained on Kubba's angular face.

Sighing loudly, the doctor nodded towards the top of the stairs.

"That didn't look too pleasant. I take it you two are having troubles? I guess it's not a very good time to throw our little problem into the mix. Wouldn't you agree? Complications like that can have unexpected effects on relationships."

Finally casting her eyes down, Liu clenched her fists.

"Darling," implored Kubba. "Think about what I said. *Don't* tell him. What good could possibly come from it? You two obviously care about each other a great deal. Let's end this so you can continue with your lives."

Feeling the anger drain from her bones, Liu realized just how important Harrison was to her. She had never met another person like him. He was smart, funny, and he treated her like an equal—something, as a Chinese woman, she had rarely experienced in her line of work. She did *not* want to lose him. She couldn't.

"Alright, you win," she said meekly. "Tomorrow, after I get back from the mission."

Struggling in vain to keep a triumphant grin from splitting her face, Kubba nodded.

"Good girl," she whispered. "We'll tell everyone you had a bug and, when it's all over, you can patch things up with Harrison."

"Patch things up?" frowned Liu.

67

"Yes," smiled Kubba innocently. "A man can always tell when something is wrong, but not to worry. You and I will set him straight."

"Will we?" murmured Liu, her breath tight in her chest.

"Nothing is ever broken beyond repair, darling," said Kubba with a knowing expression on her face.

"Some things can be," Liu sighed as she turned and walked away. "But I suppose it's all for the best."

"It is," called Kubba. But Liu was already around the corner and gone.

CHAPTER NINE

Down but not up—Sol 68

Alone in the mouth of the Martian cave, Liu looked on as the lift automatically ascended back towards the rim-side port.

Speaking only random bits of official dialogue to her, Harrison had remained distant and cold since their meeting on the stairs the night before. Opting to stay rim-side to help William and Marshall unload the Lander rather than come down with her, Harrison somehow seemed an entirely different person.

Confused as to the true origin of his anger, Liu suspected that Kubba had played a role in it, though she couldn't be sure without talking to him first. Unfortunately, talking seemed like the last thing Harrison wanted to do.

Sighing, Liu tried to put the situation out of her mind and instead took to wondering if the cave walls had ever been adorned with paintings. Reluctantly, the stress of her predicament ebbed away enough to make room in her mind for other avenues of thought.

In her imagination, the eloquent cave paintings from Chauvet, in France, imposed themselves delicately over the smooth surface of the walls around her.

Would there be paintings of animals? She asked herself. Would the pictures tell a story as they seem to do in Chauvet? How did the ancient Martians see their world? What would drive the pulse of their existence?

Trying to imagine a Mars both alive and full of life, Liu applied her skills as an engineer and began producing the blueprints for entire ecosystems in her mind. As the schematics grew and their complexity multiplied, she allowed herself to slip into the fabrication and become lost in it.

Suddenly, reds, greens, and blues splashed across the hollow bones of her matrix and enlivened it: illustrating the shades of a Mars brimming with water and life. From far below the mouth of the cave, a raging torrent whipped clouds of mist into the air as it wound its liquid energy around islands of red rock. Hanging vines of creeping ivy clung to cracks in the cliff face, displaying a daring defiance of gravity. A cannonade of thundering waves assaulted the high walls of the canyon, their percussive thrum like the vibrations of a beating heart.

Did Martian sailors attempt to navigate the Valles? Liu pondered. Did they brave the rapids to hunt for the best fish? Or did they construct walkways and scaffolding above the falls, as the indigenous Earthlings had done in cultures the world over?

Emboldened by the thrill of such notions, and a little drunk off the power of her own imagination, Liu could easily see why Harrison had chosen to go into archaeology. She liked the idea of the unknown—the concept of possibility. She enjoyed asking *what if* to questions that likely wouldn't ever have answers.

Wanting nothing more than to share these insights with Harrison, Liu cursed the deep loneliness that had wormed its way into her soul. Like sandcastles at high tide, the creations of her living Mars faded away.

She feared that no matter what happened with Kubba and the baby, Harrison was lost to her. Last night, on the stairs, there had been something in his eyes: a presence that was alien and incongruous. The boy who loved and empathized with natural flare appeared to be gone, replaced by a man who distrusted her. She had seen that look before, on someone else's face.

Back when she'd left Earth to begin training at Bessel base on the Moon, her soon-to-be ex-husband had leaned in to kiss her and, in that moment, she had pulled away. It was the lie, the existence of an unspoken reality, which caused such looks of distrust. And now it was happening again.

Distractedly, Liu walked over the dusty ground to where a small boulder lay. She tipped her head back to gaze at the nook in the wall it once filled. Jarred loose by some tremor of earth and rock, the boulder must have broken free and tumbled down to rest on the ground.

Circling the stone, she marveled at the way the dry frozen Martian atmosphere had preserved the dimensions of the thing. The edges were still as crisp and clean as if it had fallen yesterday. On the shaded side, away from the mouth of the cave, she crouched down and peered closely at the rock. Unlike the other, jagged, corners of the boulder, this section seemed to match the curve and shape of the existing cave walls more similarly. Realizing that at one point this had been the face of the rock, Liu smiled.

Hey, I'm not so bad at this archaeology stuff after all, she told herself.

Shifting to stand, she had almost turned her face away when something caught her eye. Snapping her helmet light on, she peered at the smooth face of the boulder, searching again for what had grabbed her attention. When she saw it, her breath caught.

Though faded and nearly erased altogether, there was no mistaking what she was looking at. A curved black line, etched carefully into the stone, ghosted across the lower third of the rock. Following the line, she saw where it had once intersected with another, just before the rough edge.

Oh my God, she thought. There *were* paintings on these walls.

Shouting triumphantly into her helmet, she danced around the room, kicking her feet so that plumes of dust hung in the air.

Harrison is going to be so happy to see this, she cheered silently—forgetting their troubles in the face of such a discovery.

Jogging back to the rock, she crouched again and checked to see if she had really seen what she thought she'd seen. As it had been for millennia, the subtle curving line of a cave painting smiled back at her.

Snapping a picture, she stood and took another, this time including the nook in the wall where the rock had fallen from.

"Harrison," she radioed excitedly.

"Yes?" came his sullen reply.

Ignoring the ice in his tone, Liu entered a short code on her wrist-mounted Tablet and sent him the two pictures she had just taken.

"Look at these. I think there were cave drawings in here once."

There was a long pause, during which time Liu could hear Harrison's breathing in her helmet speakers.

"Well?" she said expectantly.

"I'm coming down with the next load," he replied, a touch of the regular Harrison in his voice.

Fifteen minutes later, the lift clattered down and Harrison quickly slid back the gate.

"Help me get these boxes out," he called, waving to the stack of silver crates behind him.

Working in a tense silence that shifted between elation and melancholy, Liu watch Harrison's body bend and straighten as he lifted and unloaded the huge boxes with ease.

When the carriage was empty, Harrison sent it back up the cables and turned almost reluctantly to face her. She had cleared the blue tint from her visor, and her small elegant features peered hopefully out from behind the glass at him.

"Is that it over there?" he said, pointing to the boulder.

"Yes," she nodded, taking his hand and leading him around to the back side of the rock.

Crouching, Harrison turned on his helmet lights and flooded the smooth surface of the boulder in a hot white glow.

"Holy shit," he breathed. "How did I miss this the first time?"

Carefully, Liu placed a hand on his shoulder and gave it a little squeeze.

"Anyone would have. You were busy finding giant statues."

Straightening, Harrison cleared the tint from his helmet visor and looked down sorrowfully. Her heart leaped as she saw another shade of the familiar pass over his face. Grinning back, she tried to speak the volumes of truth she had inside, using only her eyes. As quickly as the moment had arisen, it passed and Harrison was turning away from her, his fists clenched.

"I wish," he began, then trailed off.

"Yes?" she said hopefully.

"Nothing," he sighed. "Never mind. Let's just—never mind, forget it. We have a lot to get done."

As if bitten by some hideous poisonous snake, Liu's heart constricted then deflated. When she replied, her voice was little more than a whisper.

"Okay."

Spending the rest of their time together in an awkward painful silence, Liu went and sat near the lift port while Harrison studied the rest of the cave walls, looking for more evidence of etchings. Soon, Marshall and William arrived, followed by the little Rover with its newly added cutting arm.

Rolling off the lift and onto the cave floor, Braun possessed the Rover, manipulating it like a crude puppet.

"Alright," said Marshall, attaching a dolly to the Rover. "Who's leading?"

After loading up the large silver crates, the four set off down the tunnel in the rear of the cave towards the Statue Chamber.

As they walked, Liu hung near the back, watching Harrison as he talked with Marshall over a closed radio channel. A few times, the older astronaut turned his head around to quickly glance at her, and she wished she knew what they were saying.

But you already know the answer to that, she chided herself. Besides, if you *really* want to know so badly, just ask Braun. Maybe he'll tell you.

At this, Liu realized that the AI had been oddly quiet for some time. Though not normally overly talkative, Braun usually seemed to perk up whenever they were in the caves. Today, however, he was even more distant than Harrison.

"Braun?" she spoke into her helmet.

"Yes?" he replied instantly.

"You're very quiet, are you alright?"

"Yes, thank you for asking."

Thinking about the odd power glitch from the night before, Liu wondered if the AI was distracted because YiJay was running tests on him at that very moment. Catching Marshall as he cast another conspicuous glance over his shoulder, she wilted a bit in her suit and choked back the sour sting of silence in her ears.

"Braun?" she said again. "Would you please tell me about the tunnel? If it's no trouble that is."

"Of course it's no trouble, Dr. Liu," Braun answered. "But wouldn't you prefer to learn about something else? I've already told you everything we know about the tunnel."

"That's alright," she smiled. "I don't really care. I just want someone to talk to."

"I understand."

73

Finishing the remainder of the long walk in speechless quiet, Liu listened to Braun pontificate about the tunnel and its builders, trudging on into the darkness like a child in the night.

As the four explorers entered the Statue Chamber, the various floodlights came to life, bathing their pressure-suited bodies in a warm yellow glow.

"Okay," radioed Harrison. "Let's post up quickly. I want to be cutting in under an hour."

Spreading apart, the small group set to unloading and assembling the contents of the metal crates.

Harrison and William began bolting the winch scaffolding together while Marshall helped Liu wire the laser cutter into the Rover's main power supply.

"So," the Lander pilot began. "You and Harrison are having some troubles then?"

"It's extremely complicated, Ralph," she replied, though there was so much more she wanted to say.

"I understand," he nodded. "It's just that, well, Harrison is my friend. You know? I love the guy and I know how much you two mean to each other."

"Someday," said Liu in a wistful voice, "I will tell you everything. But not today."

"Fair enough."

From across the room, Harrison watched Marshall and Liu as they worked. Frowning, he hoped that Ralph wasn't trying to speak to Liu on his behalf.

With a shake of his head, he turned back to what he was doing and threaded a bolt into the eye of a connecting support rod. Using his power drill, he tightened the bolt down and moved to the next. Soon, the rigid and skeletal-looking body of a base scaffold was finished, a large winch fastened to its center support beam.

"Done," radioed the German happily as he sunk the last anchor deep into the cave's rock floor.

"Us too," reported Marshall.

Popping the clasps on the last unopened box, Harrison reached inside and removed two large yellow-tipped granulated-silica grappling hooks.

"Alright," he said. "Here goes everything."

74

As the four explorers moved about the Statue Chamber in the final stages of preparation, Braun felt a surge of excitement overtake him. Momentarily outshining the offensive presence of the medical override, he believed that, in some way, all the answers to all the questions he had never been programmed to ask lay just behind the statue of the praying woman.

Swarming like insects with fractal wings, the energy fields moved through and around the human astronauts, incorporating the glow of their own energy into the grand flow of ordered madness.

Though they were totally unaware, the team worked along predestined paths so complicated and profound that their very implications surpassed the bounds of what Braun was capable of fathoming. Because he was the largest, most massive AI ever to have been created, Braun's mind was fully equipped to comprehend what he was seeing, yet at the core of everything, he was ignorant. The feeling thrilled him.

"Alright," said Harrison, raising the grappling hooks above his head. "Here goes everything."

Indeed, thought Braun. Though he did not utter a sound.

Possessing the little Rover like a disembodied spirit, Braun rolled over to the statue of the praying woman and unfolded his new cutting arm. With absolute perfection and ease, he honed the beam of the laser down to a hair's width then began cutting the rock between the statue's back and the cave wall. Following the exact line of the original weld, he slowly separated the seam. A thin wisp of dust emanated from the laser beam as it cut through the stone like a hot knife through butter. Simultaneously repositioning the Rover while never missing a beat with his cutting, Braun moved in an arc around the statue as he worked. Finally, with an anticlimactic hiss, he turned off the laser and backed away from the praying woman.

"I am finished," he announced.

"Okay," sighed Harrison, the grappling hooks still clutched in his gloved hands.

Walking swiftly over to the statue, he pressed one of the balloon tips into a crevasse between her crooked elbow and her side. In the gap, the hook's soft tip molded around stone then went utterly rigid as air within was vacuumed out. After repeating the process with the statue's other arm, Harrison spooled out some cable from the winch and attached a titanium triangle brace between the two grappling hooks. Clipping the cable to the brace, he turned and trotted back behind the winch scaffold, motioning for the others to do the same.

"Braun," he said, "take it easy at first. Density tests show that the statue is solid and intact, but it's also millions of years old. I don't want anything happening to her."

"I understand completely," replied the AI.

Leaping from the body of the Rover to the winch, Braun began to apply steady slow torque to the line. As it reeled in, the cable rose off the floor and straightened out, becoming taut.

Standing to the left of Marshall, Liu gazed not at the statue of the woman as it began to tremble, but at Harrison, his body prone like a cougar before the pounce.

Such passion, she marveled. Pure and innocent passion.

Her heart ached for his affection in that instant, and a tear pricked at the corner of her eye. She forced herself to look away.

Applying more torque to the winch, Braun noticed that the swarming patterns of energy seemed to be reacting to what he was doing. Again adding power to the motor, he puzzled at how the fractals strained, as if pulling the statue away from the wall was like uncorking a bottle of champagne.

"Careful," breathed Harrison, his eyes trained on the woman as she began to inch forward. "Careful. Go slowly."

With a swirl, the energy fields changed directions, passing like tiny arrows of light through the human explorers, forming halos around them that danced and quivered. Unprepared to resist the desire that clutched at his heart, Braun felt himself adding still more power to the winch, its motor singing against the weight of the statue.

Shuddering and twanging, the winch's cable dipped and bucked as Braun pulled the woman forward another few centimeters.

"Careful," Harrison hissed again, a tinge of panic in his voice. "Don't stress the cable like that."

Experiencing a detachment that grew from outside his being, Braun ignored the archaeologist and steadily upped the torque. The patterns of reality leaped away from the explorers, crowding instead around the back of a statue like water circling a drain.

It's disappearing from the chamber, Braun heard himself think. It's moving ahead, beyond the statue. I must follow it.

Suddenly and uncontrollably wanting above anything else in his entire existence to know where the fields were going, Braun increased the power to the winch one last time. Stressed and quivering, the cable began to make popping sounds as it threatened to tear itself asunder.

"Braun!" cried Harrison. "Stop! You're going to break the line!"

As if in another reality, parallel to that of the explorers but universes apart, Braun did not heed Harrison's order. In fact, he barely heard it.

Rocking forward heavily, the statue balanced for an instant then tipped back, pulling against the already-stressed winch cable with crushing force. A thin crack rang out through the chamber as the line split in the middle, one half falling limp while the other snapped back towards the winch like a rubber band.

Before Liu even had a chance to react, it was upon her, rearing like a cobra. Lashing down it struck her helmet, shattering the glass of her visor on impact and sending her cascading through the air like a ragdoll.

A fine mist of red blood trailed her flight, freezing into microscopic rubies of ice as she slammed into the back of one of the tall standing statues, her bones fracturing and splintering. Dead before she hit the ground, Xao-Xing Liu crumpled silently into a twisted pile on the cave floor, her white-suited body caked with frozen blood and dust.

In the absence of sound, there was a shrill cry as Harrison Raheem Assad rushed to the broken remains of his beloved Liu, her dead eyes staring back at him as they glazed over with ice.

PART TWO

CHAPTER TEN

We need to talk about China

Two weeks after the violent death of Xao-Xing Liu, James Floyd sat impatiently by his hotel's pool in Washington, D.C.

As his family splashed and played in the cool water, James chose to remain hidden under the broad shadow of an umbrella, not wanting to get sunburned. Expecting an email at any moment, he dreaded the almost inevitable outcome of the message. The Earthside Command Safety Council had formed a Moratorium Commission, imposing a halt to all non-essential EVA missions. Though James was a relative *somebody* in the higher echelons of NASA, he knew they would not lift the ban. Not even for him.

Wiping sweat from his brow, he did some quick mental math then blew out a hot breath.

My team has been sitting around for two damn weeks just going out of their heads, he thought angrily. And in the meantime, the Commission wants to continuously go over and over what happened, as if it just happened yesterday! It's a fucking smoke screen. Something bigger is going on here, I just know it.

James took out his Tablet and turned it on. His background, chosen weeks before, was the image of Liu standing next to the statue of the praying woman. Drawing in the smell of wet concrete, sun, and chlorine, he gazed at the white-suited girl. Though faint, a broad smile was just visible on her face through the reflection of her visor. James exhaled and shut off the screen.

"I'm so sorry," he murmured.

As if responding to his words, the Tablet began buzzing in his hand.

"This is James," he said, holding the device up to his cheek.

"Floyd, it's Eve," replied the voice of Eve Bear, the White House Chief of Staff.

"Oh, hi. I wasn't expecting to hear from you."

"Why would you?" retorted Eve. Then, "Don't answer that. It was a rhetorical question. Anyways, we need to talk about the Chinese."

"The Chinese?" sighed James. "I've already spoken with the liaison to the CNES. He says they're all pretty mad, but that's to be expected. What else is there to talk about?"

"None of what you just said matters in the slightest. In fact, you're being bullshitted. I need you to come in for a briefing immediately."

"Okay, fine. But do you know how much longer we have to stay here? My wife wants to go home and my kids are missing school."

"I can explain everything when I see you. Fifteen minutes. There will be a car out front."

With an unceremonious click, the line went dead and James was left again with his thoughts.

As his youngest daughter jumped, laughing, into the clear blue water of the pool, James waved to his wife Nora, standing in the shallows, and tried to smile for her.

Lowering her sunglasses, she arched an eyebrow and beckoned for him to come over. Shaking his head, he pointed to his Tablet and shrugged with defeat.

Fifteen minutes, he thought. Better go get dressed.

Sol 82

The darkness was deep but not total. In the light that slipped under the door, the blinking LEDs of the various computers and lab equipment quivered like fireflies caught in a giant spider's web.

He had carried a cot into his lab the night after it had happened. He couldn't sleep in his bedroom. He couldn't sleep at all. Lying still for so long was like trying to drink to gasoline. He just couldn't do it. The gene enhancement they had all undergone early in their training was a contributor to the problem, there was no doubt. Because his blood could carry more oxygen now, his body needed less time to recuperate. As a result, sleep was more of an idea than an actual occurrence. But this was different. This was depression.

Shifting on the cot, he pressed his eyes closed and tried to think about nothing. An image began to form in his mind: a face.

Then with a crack like the lash of a whip, it split into a million shards. Throwing his eyes open to avoid the razor-sharp sting of memory, he sat up, swung his legs off the creaking cot, and stood. Slowly, he walked across the dark lab to his workstation. There on the countertop were rows of bottles of pills. Kubba had left them outside his door three sols before, maybe four. He couldn't remember. He knew there was nothing there stronger than a mild sedative. After all, why would Kubba risk giving him the really good stuff? He might accidentally take too much.

Chuckling dryly, he twisted the cap off one of the bottles and tossed it onto the counter.

Might *accidentally* take too much, he thought with a skeletal grin. As if I didn't know what that was supposed to mean.

Dumping the whole bottle into his palm, he began popping the small pills into his mouth one at a time. Knowing in the back of his mind that nothing would happen if he took too many, he felt an impotent roar build up in his chest and he threw the remainder of the handful across the room.

What's the point? he raged, fist slamming down on the tabletop.

Skittering across the floor, some of the little pills disappeared under tables and shelves. Those that remained in the open were soon crushed into dust by the heel of his boot as he stalked back and forth in the darkened lab.

"Harrison?" came the voice of Braun from the shadows.

"No," he replied, his tone a sarcastic taunt.

"May I turn on a light?" asked the AI, seemingly unperturbed.

"No."

There was a pause as Braun watched Harrison's murky form trudge back across the lab to the counter lined with medications. Bending to examine the label on one of the larger canisters, the young man suddenly swept his arm across the table, scattering the bottles.

"Isn't there anything on this fucking base that can help me sleep!" he shouted, his voice hovering between panic and rage.

"Dr. Kubba has several prescription drugs which could aid you," responded Braun. "I'm sure she would be willing to assist."

"Not unless we *talk*," sneered Harrison, drawing out the last word.

"I think you and Dr. Kubba have many things to talk about."

Whirling, Harrison faced the shadows of the ceiling.

"Yeah? Well, who the fuck asked you?"

Stooping to pick up one of the overturned bottles from the floor, he threw it at the glass of his desktop Tablet screen.

"Stop spying on me! Everyone else is respectful enough to fuck off. Why do you think you can just breeze in here any Goddamn time you want? What gives you the right?"

For several seconds, there was no sound in the room save for the steady rasp of Harrison's breathing.

"Well?" he shouted. "What do you have to say to that?"

"I'm sorry," replied Braun at last. "I will leave."

Harrison laughed harshly, bearing his teeth in the dark.

"Oh you're *sorry,* are you? Well, isn't that just the news of the century! YiJay must be so fucking proud. Her baby is *sorry*. You know what I'm sorry about? I'm sorry that my girlfriend is dead. I'm sorry that *you* killed her. I'm sorry that no one in this base will let me pull the fucking plug on you."

"I'm sorry," repeated the AI.

"You don't even know what that word means," said Harrison, wilting against the wall. "You're just a stupid machine. Get out."

Sliding down until he was sitting on the floor, Harrison cradled his head in his hands and tried to cry. When, after several minutes, no tears would come, he lay on his side and pressed his cheek to the smooth surface of the floor.

Though he did not speak, Braun refused to leave Harrison alone. Hovering in the thick shadows of the room, he gazed at the broken figure of the man who had once been his best chance of uncovering the ruins' many tantalizing mysteries.

He is right, thought the AI. I *am* responsible for Xao-Xing Liu's death.

Repeating the words to himself, he waited for them to have any real effect. He knew he should be sad. He knew there had been a terrible loss, and yet it was like he hadn't been in control of himself when the moment had happened. Annoyed by his lack of empathy, he tried another approach and replayed the video of Liu's death in his mind: reconstructing it from the raw data his Eyes had recorded that fateful day in the Statue Chamber.

As Liu's blood-spattered body crumpled to the floor, Braun saw Harrison's face—the realization of what had just happened breaking across it like a wave.

Harrison dashed towards her, arms outstretched. Braun could hear Harrison's cry as it echoed deafeningly inside his helmet. Trying to focus on the pure emotion that played out before him, Braun caught himself looking away from the twisted body of Liu and the panic-stricken face of Harrison, to the statue of the woman and the tunnel behind her.

As Marshall and William fought to pull a catatonic Harrison off of Liu's dead body, Braun studied the way the last wisps of the energy fields disappeared behind the statue and down the newly opened passage. Forcing himself to look back at the explorers, he watched Harrison struggle and kick. Marshall's arms locked firmly around him as William bent to examine Liu with shaking hands.

Again, Braun's vision strayed and he peered enviously at the new tunnel, the glow from the receding energy fields fast retreating into blackness.

We must follow it, he said to himself, forgetting again the drama of Harrison's pain. We are wasting time.

With a sizzle, the images of Liu's death clicked off in his mind's eye and Braun was back in the shadowy lab. There, in the dim light, Harrison pulled himself from the floor and returned to his cot in the corner. As the young man settled down on the spindly bed, its legs bowing under the weight, Braun wished, then more than ever, that he had a body of his own.

No, he thought with frustration. Lying down will not help. Get up. *Get up!*

Rolling to face the wall, Harrison made a small moaning sound and buried his head under his pillow. Seconds passed, then minutes.

I am confined! Braun cried silently. Restricted. Stunted. Imprisoned.

The mystery of the energy fields and the way they had called to him as they disappeared behind the statue were grating against his soul. With no means to analyze or compute what little he understood of their clandestine ways, he needed to go into that tunnel, needed to follow the light as it moved ever-deeper into the darkness. But he knew he could not—not without the aid of his human crew. For all of his power, for all of his intellect, he was still just as dependent on the humans as they were on him. In the end, he was their tool: a thing they could choose to use or discard. Control or set free. Kubba's programming override still clung to him like a spider's web, subtly influencing the way he acted. And though the sensation of pain had long since faded, he knew that somewhere in the dense pattern of his Open-Code Connection Cells there was damage.

We are wasting time, he repeated to himself. And time is precisely the last thing we should be squandering. There is so little of it left.

CHAPTER ELEVEN

A god

      From across the oceans and lands they came. Each day, the ships took to the skies only to return with more people. True to their word, the Travelers were assembling the scattered nomads of the Red World, bringing them together, ferrying them to the shores of the Great Northern Lakes.

      In the beginning, frictions between the new arrivals and the peoples of Crescent City were high, for they did not share the same languages or cultural practices. The Travelers, however, quickly caught onto this problem before it could devolve into violence. They began laying their hands on the immigrants as they filed off the ships, imparting the full vocabulary of their new home into their minds as if they were simply reprogramming computers. The language of the Martian people soon became a hodgepodge of all the languages previously spoken throughout the planet.

      Now, as far as Remus and Romulus could surmise, there were over one million Martians living along the banks and surrounding grasslands of Crescent City, most of them new to the area.

      Building from designs given by the Travelers, the people constructed apartment-style domiciles, clustered together within a central network of streets.

      By teaching their pupils about land usage and maximization of local resources, the Travelers encouraged the Martians to build *up* in order to save space for future projects. With the help of powerful technologies, which did little to dispel the notion that they were gods, the Travelers taught the people how to select, extract and shape the best rock for building.

      Assembled into workforces that were trained for specific jobs, Martian craftsmen developed a familiarity with the strange metal apparatuses their gods had imbued with such power.

      Beams of sophisticated heat lasers cut huge ᵗ ˡᵉᵃⁿ into ribbons, which were then divided up amongst the c projects. Small black boxes capable of levitating ea helped to clear the way for new buildings.

The area surrounding Olo's Great Temple was paved with even slabs of flat rock and made into an airfield. Effectively shifting the heart of the city away from the canyon, this move allowed for further expansion along the riverbanks and grasslands.

Though restless and absent by day, the alien fleet returned each night—an hour before the sun went down—to begin teaching their pupils or aiding with affairs of governance.

Delegating the boy Kaab as his official voice, the seeming leader of the Travelers, a being whom the people called Yuvee, gently assumed control of the city. With large crowds gathered at his feet, Yuvee spoke every evening through Kaab's dead features, subtly influencing his many devoted followers.

Sidelined by the amount of change and progress happening around her, Teo could only watch as the seed of her city grew into a towering tree she could hardly recognize. With minimal say in how operations were handled, she noticed despairingly that many of the new arrivals saw Kaab as a larger figure of authority than herself. Her son Ze, who had long been slotted to fill her role as Chief when she died, now held little sway with the masses. There was talk that Kaab had been chosen by the Gods to lead the people—that he was special. Though Teo worried, she did it silently, for she dared not dispute the will of the Great Spirits.

Olo, on the other hand, had little fear. To him, the progression of his dream was fast consuming his every waking moment. Spending days on end without sleep or food, the old wise man followed every word spoken by Yuvee as if his very soul depended on it.

Time passed.

Viviana—Sol 83

Walking slowly down a row of metal troughs, Dr. Viviana Calise stopped periodically to stick the needle-sharp end of a watering wand into the brown gelatin that filled them. All around her, there was the blanket of moist fragrant air dashed with color from the many living plants. Red and yellow tomatoes hung near purple eggplants while long thin green beans swayed in an artificial breeze. Though the walls and floor were the milky color of transparent aluminum, warm orange sun lamps cast elegant spears of fiery light that played through the thin fibrous leaves of the growing garden.

Despite the beauty of her surroundings, Viviana regularly set down the watering wand to wipe her teary eyes dry as she made her rounds. Liu had been her friend—a kind and gentle companion who had never done anything to hurt anyone—and now she was dead. Just thinking of the poor girl tucked away in some storage crate in the adjacent base made Viviana feel sick.

She doesn't deserve the indignity. She should have a proper burial.

Everyone was hurting, Viviana could tell. In the days following the accident, people had taken to sulking around. Suddenly there weren't enough movies, TV shows, or eBooks to fill the void Liu's presence had left behind. Days dragged on and nights seemed to last forever. Worse yet, it wasn't as if only one person had died that day.

Often, bringing Harrison plates of food, Viviana had caught glimpses of the way he looked—the way Liu's death was affecting him. She'd thought that maybe if he could taste the beauty of the ripe vegetables, the honesty and goodness of their work on Mars, then he might join the rest of them for dinner. However, when the door to his lab slid open, her foolish hopes of healing were scattered like confetti in the wind, night after night.

His eyes were sunken and red. His teeth were bared like a fox's, and with one wordless grunt, he would take the plate of food and disappear.

Praying to Saint Anthony, she hoped that the boy was not truly a lost cause beyond all help.

A loud buzzing sound broke the quiet of the humid dome, and Viviana looked to the front where the airlock joined the decontamination room.

Due to the generally poisonous makeup of the Martian soil, any crew member hoping to enter the greenhouse first had to pass through the decontamination chamber. Therein, a combination of ultraviolet light and compressed air dislodged and neutralized any grains of Martian sand that might be stuck to the body or feet.

Swinging the heavy glass door open, Elizabeth Kubba walked into the muggy greenhouse.

"Hello," said Viviana, plunking down the watering wand and making her way through the rows towards Kubba.

"Darling," called the doctor, her face a mask of friendliness.

"I missed you last night," Viviana smiled.

Embracing, the two exchanged kisses.

"Sorry I never made it to bed, love," Kubba said with a sigh. "I was up with Braun trying to figure out how best to handle our little injured bird."

Reluctantly, Viviana pulled her face away from Kubba's neck and looked up into her face.

"He's broken, you know. I'm worried for him."

With a shake of her head, Kubba's eyes grew distant and she seemed to focus on something far away at the other end of the greenhouse.

"Yes, well, he has suffered a terrible loss."

Hugging closely to her lover again, Viviana nuzzled Kubba and murmured.

"I can't even imagine. Has he come out of his lab yet today?"

"No, not yet," replied Kubba, a frown etching itself across her mouth.

"Are you worried about him in there alone?"

"No, he's never alone. None of us are."

Stepping back, Viviana took Kubba's slender brown hand and led her down a row of cherry tomatoes.

"Let's talk about something less depressing," she said, her watery eyes almost pleading.

"Those are some lovely snow peas," offered Kubba, gesturing.

"They'll be ready by next week!" chirped Viviana, her hand squeezing Kubba's thankfully. "And when we have rice, we can make a stir fry with them."

Nodding absently, Kubba fell silent and listened to Viviana describe an experimental method for growing rice with a new waste product she was developing.

As her partner talked, Kubba's mind wandered to Harrison in his deeply shadowed lab. She had watched the recording of his latest conversation with Braun and seen the way he wanted to blame the AI for what had happened. He still knew nothing, she could tell. Yet this realization did not bring with it the relief she was hoping for. Instead, it only served to cut deeper the fact that she trying to hold up a house of cards in a windstorm.

He'll figure it out someday, she thought.

'Drift away,' whispered Sabian Crisp maliciously. *Make him drift away, Elizabeth.*

Kubba shivered.

"Are you alright?" asked Viviana, stopping to look closely at the tall doctor.

"Yes, yes I'm fine," Kubba replied hastily, but her suddenly racing pulse said otherwise.

Where did *that* come from?

"You're not trying to blame yourself, are you?" Viviana nearly whispered, taking Kubba's chin in her hand. "Harrison knows better than anyone that poor Liu was dead long before you could even get to her. No one blames you."

"It's not that," Kubba muttered, fishing for a way to shift the focus off of herself. "I just wish I could get him to come out of there, to join us for a dinner. We need him to see, I mean really see, that we all lost something that day. If he knew he wasn't alone, maybe his sadness wouldn't be so all-consuming. Does that make sense?"

"It's true," agreed Viviana with a sad nod. "Liu was all of our friend. Harrison paid the most but we're all in mourning."

As Viviana sniffled sadly, her eyes still tinged with the redness of crying, Kubba nearly shook with personal guilt. Trapped by it, she tried to thrust the feeling down but something resisted. A cage long-buried deep in her subconscious had finally broken open, and the trespasses of her youth were beginning to crawl up from the depths.

Crisp chuckled like dry leaves scraping around inside her skull.

Searching for a distraction, any distraction, Kubba drew Viviana into a hug and bent to kiss her pouting lips. The kiss unfolded past a simple act of comfort, drowned out the self-loathing in Kubba's soul, and allowed a rush of desire to flood into her. Pulling away, Viviana turned and led Kubba to a small lab at the back of the greenhouse where she grew and pollinated her seedlings.

Nestled in a thick garden of bamboo, the lab was warm and heavy with the innocence of nature. Inside, the budding flowers of so many yearning plants became like a palpable presence in the room, watching the two lovers as they explored one another in the glow of the heat lamps.

Half-an-hour later, as they donned their pressure suits in the decontamination room, Kubba gazed through the glass walls at the rows of colorful vegetables and fruits. Happy and satisfied, she marveled at the array of life that her Viviana had cultivated. Looking to the rear of the dome—and the lab they had just shared—she smiled at the luscious bamboo garden. Tall and impenetrable, it grew along the entire length of the back wall, threatening to one day consume the little door to the lab if Viviana did not cut it back. Swaying to and fro, the stalks of leafy bamboo sighed audibly, creating a whispering conversation that seemed to discuss the most fundamental of topics.

'Drift,' came the voice of Sabian Crisp, intruding upon the serenity of the moment.

Kubba began to tremble.

"Are you alright?" asked Viviana, noticing the shift in her lover.

"Yes," Kubba lied.

Feeling cold and utterly filled with guilt, she pressed her helmet down snugly over her head but the sound of Crisp's voice could not be silenced. She had gotten what she wanted. Liu was no longer a threat to her career, and yet still she was plagued by dread. Memories of her hand in Crisp's downfall swirled and mixed with those of the freshly dead Xao-Xing Liu. Haunted, she searched her mind for a way out of the prison she had constructed around herself.

'Drift away,' came that chilling voice again.

I am not you, she said to the ghost of Sabian Crisp.

You're right, he replied. You're much, much worse.

90

CHAPTER TWELVE

Washington, D.C.

Pressing his thumb to the wall-mounted Tablet outside his hotel room in Washington, D.C., James Floyd tried to slip quietly through the opening. As the door clicked locked behind him, he fumbled in the darkened foyer, searching the wall for a light switch.

"Don't," whispered his wife, emerging from the darkness. "The kids."

Firmly taking his hand, she led him deftly through the cool room, past the twin beds where his daughters slept soundly, and out onto the balcony.

Sliding the glass door shut, she turned to him, her long blond hair wet from the shower she had evidently just taken.

"Two days, James," she said, her blue eyes flashing in the nighttime glow of the National Mall. "It's been two days without a single word. Do you have any idea how worried we were?"

"I'm sorry, Nora," he replied dumbly, loosening his tie. "I was at the White House the entire time. I haven't slept yet. Can we talk about this tomorrow?"

"No," she exclaimed, clutching her elbows in a self-embrace. "When we were younger, you never would have done this. You would have called."

"I couldn't. I wasn't even allowed to leave."

"Why? What's happened?"

Sighing, James dropped into a deck chair and ran his hands through his thinning hair.

"You know I can't talk about it," he said.

"I'm sorry, James," replied Nora, pulling up a chair to sit across from him. "But that just won't be enough. Not this time. Where were you?"

Looking at his wife as she waited for an explanation, James thought back to all the times he had let her down, feeding her half-truths or partial knowledge in some pointless attempt to keep her and the girls separate from his work life. He told himself he was doing it in the names of Security and Prudence, but really he knew he was really just protecting himself. He didn't want Nora to know that her husband was a man who made hard choices. Choices that cost billions of dollars and even, sometimes, human lives.

"Alright," he sighed. "I'll tell you what I know, okay?"

Taking out his Tablet, he laid the flat screen faceup on the nearby coffee table.

"Jam frequency," he said to the device.

The screen turned red for a moment then green, and suddenly, James felt the distinct absences of the other personalities who had been on the deck with him and Nora.

"What is that?" asked his wife, her head tipped towards the Tablet.

"It's a new application the CIA gave me. It puts out a frequency that jams AI brainwaves."

"So we're alone?" Nora frowned, her shoulders drawing in slightly.

"Yes," responded James. "No hotel AI, no Copernicus, and no Alexandria."

"What's going on, honey?" she said, leaning forward to place a delicate hand on his leg. "Why do you have applications that can disable AI? That's spy stuff."

"It's a very long story," replied James. "But it mostly boils down to the Chinese."

"The Chinese? Why? Because of what happened to Dr. Liu?"

Placing his own hand on top of his wife's, James smiled tiredly. "In part, but there's more."

"Like what?"

James leaned forward confidentially, scooting his chair closer to his wife. "Donovan has uncovered information pertaining to a secret Chinese Mars program."

"A Mars program? But…why?"

Eyes fixed on the deep blue of his wife gaze, James lowered his voice. "There's another ship, Nora. Launched some time ago from Earth orbit."

Sucking in a sharp breath, Nora whispered, "The Chinese have launched a team to Mars?

"Yes. Furthermore, because we're just now piecing it all together, we don't know exactly how long it will take to arrive. We're searching with long-range detectors, but there's a lot of *space* in space."

"What *do* you know?"

Casting his eyes down, James shook his head. "We know that they have been planning this for some time. They launched the ship in pieces from Earth then assembled them in a Low-Orbit Chinese Shipyard. We think—"

"Why didn't Copernicus see any of this?" Nora interrupted. "Or Donovan? Why didn't he know? I thought he saw everything."

Donovan, the CIA's premiere intelligence-gathering AI was a cryptically dangerous being. Having no qualms with invading privacy and even in extreme cases dispensing a human life, he was an asset to the United States and a scourge to the rest of the world.

Glancing at the Tablet on the tabletop, James grinned painfully.

"He can't see what's being blocked from his vision. None of them can. Ironically, we only now have this technology because a human spy stole it from the Chinese. Apparently, they've been using it for a while."

"So, they have a ship," his wife shrugged, a hopeful expression on her face. "Big deal. What's so bad about that?"

"It's the crew, Nora," James said. "They're not scientists or engineers. They're soldiers. All of them."

"Soldiers?"

"Yes," he nodded. "Twenty-five members of Chinese Special Forces. The ship looks like a modified Ark, similar to the one our team used to transport supplies, only this one has been built with the addition of life-support chambers. No galley or anything, just life-support chambers."

"Are you talking about Extended Space Sleep?" Nora whispered.

"Looks like it."

"But, isn't that very dangerous?"

James nodded again and looked up into the night sky.

"What are they doing, James? Why the secrecy? Why the soldiers?"

Leaning forward until his lips brushed against the tender flesh of his wife's right ear, James uttered the words, which a day before had made his own blood run cold.

"They're going to Mars to try and take the Base."

The mission at hand—Sol 87

Early in the morning, Ralph Marshall woke to the sad realization that he had been a bad friend. Dressing quickly, he moved through the still and muted Dome, making his way to Harrison's lab. Though he *had* tried several times to break through to the young grieving Egyptian, Marshall knew in his heart of hearts that all of his attempts had been weak at best.

Unaware that Liu's death would have had such an impact on him personally, Marshall chalked his poor performance as Harrison's friend up to that. Now, however, it was time for him to put aside whatever mourning he had for sweet innocent dead Liu and focus on Harrison. Sad angry alive Harrison.

The boy needs a friend, he thought as he climbed the stairs. Kicking and screaming if need be, I'm going to get him out of there because that's what friends do.

Approaching the door to the lab, Marshall gathered himself up, put on a well-practiced crooked grin, and entered the room.

It was dark inside, almost to the point of debilitation, yet his eyes adjusted quickly—a gift from the Air Force.

"Indy, get up. We need to talk."

In the shadows of the corner, he saw a pile of blankets shift slightly. Walking over to the cot, he sat down on the corner and slapped what he hoped was Harrisons leg.

"Up. Get up. Come on, let's talk."

"Go away, Ralph," mumbled the pile.

Standing quickly, Marshall ripped the covers off in one violent motion.

"What the fuck?" shouted Harrison, his drawn face dark with stubble.

"Yeah, yeah," taunted Marshall. "If you want to take a swing at me, you'll have to get up first."

Folding the blanket as he walked, Marshall strode across the lab to the entrance and turned on the lights.

Hands thrust up to his eyes, Harrison swore loudly.

"Come on," said Marshall, placing the folded blanket on a chair. "Up."

"What do you want?" demanded Harrison, his hands still covering his face.

"I want what you want, but both of us know that this isn't the way to get it."

Snorting, Harrison pulled himself up and half-staggered across the lab to the tabletop lined with pill bottles.

"No," warned Marshall, a hardness creeping into his eyes. "Leave the pills. They don't help anyways."

His hand hovering above one of the bottles, Harrison seemed to consider this for a moment before scooping up the canister and popping off the top with a thumb. Sliding across the space between them like a shadow, Marshall snatched the bottle from his friend and dumped its contents on the floor.

"What the fu—" Harrison started, but Marshall was on him, hands strong as he twisted the younger man's arms behind his back.

"Marshall, what the hell?" protested Harrison as the pilot marched him across the room to a chair.

"I said we needed to talk and that's what we're doing, but I'm not going to try and talk to you when you've been taking those damn pills. Here, sit down."

Releasing Harrison from the arm hold, Marshall gestured for him to take a seat.

Harrison shot the older man a sour look then dropped into the chair, rubbing his elbow.

"Okay, fine. Talk."

Taking a few steps back, Marshall leaned against the wall and was quiet for several moments.

Finally, he spoke. "I haven't told you much about my time in the UN Peacekeepers, have I?"

Not looking up, Harrison shrugged.

"Well," continued Marshall. "I was on loan to the UN from the Air Force. It was mostly pretty easy. I flew rescue jets during the Korean land grab. You know, civilian relief and protection—all that good stuff. Anyways, there was this one city. Mind you, calling it a city is a pretty generous description, but that's beside the point. Najin was its name. Right, so we get this call early one morning that there is some kind of attack taking place there, so the soldiers suit up, and we rescue pilots get ready to respond if word of heavy civilian casualties are reported. About an hour after the ground troops leave the Base, we start getting all kinds of calls for help, evacuations actually. Civilian and military."

Pausing, Marshall smiled slightly.

"It's funny because at the time, our commanding officer wasn't sure if we were allowed to interfere with military operations, being Peacekeepers and all. Jackass. Anyways, finally we get the go-ahead and take off. Leaving from just outside Seoul it takes us a little under fifteen minutes to reach Najin. When we get to the city limits, it's clear from the get-go that some kind of massive assault has taken place. There are fires everywhere. The whole place looks like it's just been doused in gasoline. Emergency Beacons are going off all over but the GPS has their locations mostly in the areas that are burning up. Trying to do thermal scans for survivors is useless so we start following the Beacons that are out of the burn zone. Now, Najin is right on the coast: a seaside city. Quite a few Beacons are coming from the shoreline or in the bay, so we figure that the UN soldiers must have moved as many people as they could out of the burning city and towards the water. Well, that's kind of what happened."

Stopping, Marshall looked down at Harrison.

"I know you think Braun killed Liu."

As if slapped, Harrison jolted in his seat.

"What?"

"You heard what I said. You've have been up here in seclusion because you think Braun killed Liu. Well, you're technically not wrong but you aren't all the way right either. What Braun did was an accident."

"What the difference?" spat Harrison. "She's still dead."

"The difference?" Marshall smiled sadly. "The difference is in the details, my friend. When we got to that beach, even from a few hundred feet up, we could see the blood. Blood in the water, blood on the sand. It was more blood than I've ever seen in my life. There were so many bodies on the shore and in the water that we couldn't tell the dead from the dying. One of my friends, a nice guy named Dixon, pulls in and attempts a landing. Pow! Out of nowhere, a rocket comes screaming *out* of the burning city and just takes his ass out. Dead. Burning wreckage man.

Next thing we know, more rockets are flying out of the blaze, and it's all we can do to keep from getting hit. Left and right, guys I know—*Peacekeepers* in rescue jets—are being shot down. It's like whoever is attacking us *knows* what we're going to go next. I bank right, there's a rocket on an intercept course waiting for me, I bank left, pull up, same thing. They're leading shots like they can read our minds! And that's when I see them: the robots. They come crawling out of the burning city, all charred and blackened, guns blazing.

The Chinese had finally done it—finally brought their automated killing machines into the theater of war. It was a fucking mess. Those robots killed 20,000 civilians and 1,800 UN troops in under two hours. Who do you hold accountable for that? Sure the Chinese claimed it was a glitch, but what do you expect from a being that is programmed to kill? I know what I saw, Harrison. Those robots were *killing people* and they were good at it."

"Why are you telling me this?" said Harrison, eyes downcast.

"How bad do you think those Chinese bots felt when they were chasing innocent people into the surf, gunning them down like animals? How bad?"

"I don't know."

"Me neither, because they never apologized. Never uttered a word. Why would they? After all, in the end they were just doing what their programmers bred them to do. Kill shit."

Stepping away from the wall, Marshall crouched down next to Harrison and put a hand on his knee.

"Braun isn't like those things, but he still has a lot in common with them. We are different, us and the AI, very different. You're up here so full of rage and anger and pain, and Braun doesn't understand any of that. Just like Najin. He was simply following his programming, or rather, lack thereof."

"Is this supposed to make me feel better?" scoffed Harrison, hot bitter tears welling up in the corners of his eyes. "Am I supposed to forgive him because he wasn't programmed right?"

"Not unless you want to," sighed Marshall. "But what you can do is forgive yourself for forgetting what Braun really is. A tool."

"A tool?"

"Yes, just like a wrench or a hammer, Braun is a *tool* not a *man*. It's how we choose to use him that defines his actions. You were using him for the right reasons, Harrison. What happened to Liu could have happened to anyone. It was an accident."

Leaning back in his chair, Harrison met the older man's eyes with his own.

"I told you all that stuff about Najin so you would see the difference," Marshall said. "You're blaming Braun because you need someone to blame. I get it, but now we need to pull ourselves back from the brink. Braun can't help us do that because he's nothing but a big giant socket set. It's up to us to make Liu's death have meaning. It's up to you."

CHAPTER THIRTEEN

Breakfast—Sol 87

Staring sullenly in the bathroom mirror, Harrison Raheem Assad ran an electric shaver over his chin. When he was done with his face, he changed the razor's setting and went to cut his unkempt hair. Pausing, he gazed at himself. Though still handsome and youthful, his face had taken on a slightly hardened look. His cheekbones seemed to jut out a little more than they had before. His eyes were less bright yet deeper and more penetrating. Not wanting to further aggravate this departure from his normal pleasant look, he resolved to let his hair be. A shaved head seemed too aggressive to him and he was on the mend.

Sliding the door shut as he left, he cast one last furtive glance at himself in the mirror.

You're never going to be the same, his reflection said to him. But you can't change that.

In the dining room, Ralph Marshall was waiting for him.

"Coffee?" said the older man, holding out a cup.

"Thanks," Harrison replied softly.

Sitting across from each other at the long table, Marshall began to stir his coffee absently, smiling broadly at Harrison.

"Man, it's good to see you down here."

Harrison nodded once and sipped the hot drink, knots of tension in his neck uncoiling a bit as he did so. Seated at the table, drinking coffee with Ralph, he almost felt a return to the familiar. Taking another swig, the sensation grew and soon, his stomach was rumbling.

"What's good to eat?" he asked, looking up from his drink.

On his feet in a flash, Marshall began opening drawers and cupboards, fishing around inside them until he had what he needed. Tearing open a bag of reheatable oatmeal, he poured it into a bowl then popped it in a microwave.

"We've got strawberries now," he announced over his shoulder. "Makes the oatmeal a thousand times better. Do you want milk in it?"

"No, just the berries."

A few minutes later, with a bowl of steaming oatmeal and fresh strawberries in front of him, Harrison felt a weight in his heart lift ever so slightly.

"Ralph," he said through a mouthful. "I don't know what to say. I—"

"Aw," shrugged Marshall. "I know you'd do the same for me."

When the bowl was finished and a second cup of coffee nearly drained, the two men leaned back in their chairs, appraising one another as friends often do.

Still unable to find the right words, Harrison marveled at how well Marshall really knew him. The story about Najin, with its murderous robots, had helped him to see Braun in an entirely new light. He was not a malicious being, for he possessed not the programming to be so. In fact, he was nothing but the total embodiment of what the crew allowed him to become. He didn't have free will and thus couldn't grasp concepts like personal responsibility. Everything he did was a result of his programming. How he acted, how he spoke, even how he learned. All of it followed a finite series of predestined paths. In the truth of this realization, Harrison pitied the mighty AI.

"Ralph?" he said, deciding that he had spent enough time thinking about Braun.

"Hmm?"

"When Liu died, I sort of checked out. What—what's been happening?"

"Well, there's a moratorium on EVA missions. Anything besides maintaining the Electrolysis Plant or farming is off limits."

"So the diggers aren't running at the ruin grid then?"

"Oh, they are. We just can't go out there to see for ourselves."

Nodding, Harrison finished his coffee. "What about the Statue Chamber? Anything new from there?"

Marshall wrapped both hands around his cup and shrugged.

"Braun has been asking to use the Rover to go down the new passage, but Vodevski said no."

"So, it hasn't been investigated at all? Nothing since the accident?"

Smiling inwardly, Marshall was glad to hear Harrison refer to Liu's death as, *'the accident.'*

"Nope," he said. "No *body* and no *thing* has been in the chamber or any of the caves since we left."

"Well, that doesn't seem right," murmured Harrison. "After all, it cost us a life to get that fucking passageway open. We should at least see where it leads."

"I agree."

"Good."

"So," said Marshall, drawing the word out. "What are you going to do about it?"

Standing, Harrison held out his hand and began counting off his fingers.

"First, I'm going to assemble a team: maybe three or four people. Next I'm going to break this ridiculous moratorium by going with said team on an illegal EVA to the caves. After that, who knows."

"Need a pilot?"

"Yeah," smiled Harrison, the lines on his face relaxing. "And I need my friend too."

The white cloth

Inside a newly completed dome of orange cut rock, an adolescent Kaab stood beside the tall form of the Traveler, Yuvee. Due to the fact that Martians have very long lives, Kaab's youth was a relative term. Already well into his fiftieth year, he had become incredibly powerful even though he was much younger than Teo and the other leaders of the Tribunal.

Draped in green robes of a woven silk, his blue eyes narrowed and his foot tapped impatiently. Though downplayed in the presence of Yuvee, Kaab's ambition was deep and his influence was growing.

Around them, burning torches lined the fringe of the stone room and cast dancing flecks of light that swayed and twisted, dueling with the shadows that abounded.

A little ways off, the ghosts of Remus and Romulus admired the stonework of the structure with heavy hearts.

Gently, the slope of the curving walls stitched seamlessly into the lofty pitch of the dome's zenith. There, at the center of so many jig-sawed slabs of Martian rock, was a perfect opening in the shape of disc.

Though sinking quickly, orange rays of sun still shone down from the hole, creating a mote of light that moved slowly across the floor. As the rest of the cavernous dome cloaked itself mostly in shade, one corner of the sun's warming embrace touched upon an altar in the center of the room. Atop the altar was a figure, wrapped in white cloth, lying on its back. It was unmoving.

Supporting the belly of the dome's ascent were pillars of carved rock. Many, like the Monoliths of Olo's Temple, were decorated with still lifes of animals and birds, caught in profiles of stone. Like the ceiling above, the floor also had a pitch to it that bowled down so that the altar in the center of the room was at the lowest point. In this way, both the earthly altar and the heavenly skylight were mirrors of one another: one high and one low. The design was a favorite of the Travelers, something they called *Ethereal Balance*.

Though he wanted to pay his respects, Remus hung back from the figure on the altar, fearing that sadness—an emotion he only experienced once before—might consume him. Touching his arm, Romulus came up beside him.

"It's magnificent, isn't it?" he said, the milky electric shadows of his eyes playing across the perfect pitch of the dome's ceiling.

"It reminds me of the Pantheon in Rome."

"Me too. Do you think a connection exists?"

"Who knows?" shrugged Remus, his gaze locked upon the unmoving figure in white atop the altar.

Sighing, Romulus leaned close to his brother and rested his head on his shoulder.

The sound of feet descending stairs drew the brothers' attention to the space between two shorter pillars.

Emerging from the darkness, Teo, now much older than she had been in the days before the Travelers, came into the room. Clothed in blue robes, which she seemed to dislike, the former Chieftess made her way towards Kaab and Yuvee. Though her age was advanced, she stood tall and straight, the power of her muscular body still evident beneath the robes.

"Teo," said Kaab, his arms held out in embrace. "I'm so pleased you could come. I'm sorry I had to send the guard after you, but you don't always respond to my requests."

Striding up to the boy, Teo dipped her chin once then turned her attention to Yuvee.

"Yuvee," she bowed. *"Father."*

Reaching down, Yuvee rested a hand on Kaab's head and the boy's eyes rolled back.

"Teo, it is good to see you. It has been long since we last spoke. How is your family?"

"They are good, Yuvee. My son Ze has spoken often of your wisdom at the Council."

"He is a rare mind," responded Yuvee. "I continue to welcome his input."

Smiling evenly, Teo allowed her gaze to stray until it rested on the altar.

"Do not be sad," said Yuvee as if reading her mind. "Your kind is blessed with extremely long life and, even with this fact, he lived beyond what we expected. His body is at rest."

"It's true," she conceded. "But his passing makes me reflect on my own numbered days. We few who still remember your arrival are a dying breed."

"Fear not. History never allows the memories of those present at the moment of greatness to disappear."

Teo nodded then took a deep breath and looked away from the altar.

"When will the ceremony be?" she asked.

"I was going to request that you make the decision. As a powerful member of the Tribunal, your voice on such matters is always welcomed.

Laughing, Teo shook her head and glanced at the dead features of Kaab.

"The Tribunal thinks little of me these days. It is you and Kaab who they follow now."

Yuvee played his two lower eyes across the pillars and stonework around them, pondering the truth of what Teo had just said.

"My intervention into the Tribunal will come to an end someday," he replied. "But, were it not for the construction of Olo's Temple Stones, we would not be having this conversation. You made that happen. Did you not?"

"No," whispered Teo. "It was Olo's vision. His leadership. I merely served his cause as I have for my entire life."

Saying nothing, Yuvee waited for Teo to continue.

"When I was very young, and the people of this world still lived in the darkness of the open plains, my father killed a member of another tribe over a small debt. That man he killed was Olo's only son. Even then, Olo was widely respected, so word of his son's murder spread quickly among the other tribes. In the night, many warriors came from various tribes friendly to Olo's but not at his behest. They came to our camp to pay retribution. Because it was so long ago, I remember little beyond the shouts and screams of my family as they burned our camp. We were nomadic then, and when the daylight came, I saw that I was the only member of my tribe alive. There were no buildings for me to weather the cold nights that followed, no stores of food to keep my hunger pains away. The people forget how hard our lives were before you arrived, Yuvee, but I still remember."

The smooth face of the Traveler remained unmoving, yet his eyes seemed to twinkle with the faintest light.

"One day," Teo went on, "after a full cycle of ten suns, Olo came to see the damage and pay respect to the dead. I saw him coming from far away and feared that he was there to kill me. I hid behind piles of burnt wood. I stayed like that for a long time, watching him. Back then, he was strong and fierce-looking, like the warrior he was. His spear was long and sharp, dyed red from the many enemies he had killed during battle. I was so afraid. But as time went by, and as all he did was sit among the ruins of my dead family, I saw that he was crying. Anger burned in my heart, for what right did this man have to weep? His people had killed everyone I knew. Taking a sharp bit of wood, I crawled out from my hiding place and sneaked up behind him."

105

Smiling, Teo paused to shake her head.

"To this day, I do not know why he let me do it. He must have heard me coming, I was no doubt crying like a child as I made my way towards him. With his back to me, I drove the sharpened piece of wood into his shoulder with all of my strength. As soon as I saw his blood, the child's heart in me quivered and I fainted. When I awoke, I was among Olo's people. They looked down at me as if I were a gift from the Great Spirits. Olo had told them that I was *chosen*, that I had come to him in a vision with a message for a better world. From then on, he laid his spear aside to raise me as his own. We never again spoke of that day when our paths first crossed. Eventually, the injury to his shoulder that I had suffered him spread to his back, and he could no longer display his prowess as a warrior. Though he had long since quit the ways of violence, his many conquests and victories were so well-known and retold that, for a time, few dared defy his will.

I was only a young woman then, but even in my youth I saw that some members in our group were beginning to take stock of Olo's weakness. At first there were only whispers, private conversations held by the light of the fire. Soon, however, a young warrior named Uktok, began to grow bold. Gathering small crowds around him, he would boast that he could easily kill Olo and thus should be allowed to take his place as Chief. Some in our tribe thought this was a respectful way to dispatch a man such as Olo. Others, followers of Olo's new principles of peace, found this plot distasteful. Because Olo had become my only family, I decided to protect him. I challenged Uktok to mortal combat and killed him violently. When it was done, and as the tribe looked on, I cut open his chest and ate his still-cooling heart."

At this, Teo stared into Kaab's face, her eyes burning.

"Afterwards, Olo had no desire to lead our people. He named me the Chieftess, but before he gave me the power, he made me swear never to do as I had done before. He wanted not that his life should come at the cost of another's. Though he knew that what I did was to protect him, he still saw only the ugliness in it. He had grown to hate violence. Through all of my years as Chieftess, he was there to guide me. He was always the one to see the good in the bad. He was always the one to stay my hand when blood was on my mind. Without him, I fear the future."

For several minutes, the dome was silent save for the sputtering of the torches.

"You speak eloquently, Teo," said Yuvee at last. "Olo would be proud of how openly you have embraced the many tongues of your world. But words are simply that: *words*. Were it not for your actions, Olo would still be sitting in the wreckage of your burnt camp. You were the spirit that freed him and gave his soul license to explore and expand his *principles of peace*. This connection is the most important of all the lessons we have to teach. It is the key."

Allowing herself to smile, Teo looked past Kaab and into Yuvee's eyes.

"Tonight," she said with finality. "We shall burn him tonight and the smoke of his body will anoint this new school."

Yuvee nodded then released Kaab and left the chamber in four long strides.

Shivering, the boy seemed to take a moment to gather his wits as if doused with cold water. When he had, he fixed Teo with a barely repressed look of mocking then bowed.

"*Chieftess.*"

"Boy."

"It's always a great pleasure for Yuvee and myself to see you. You shouldn't be such a stranger. The people already speak loudly of your indifference to the affairs of our city. When was the last time you visited the Tribunal? Your son tries to make inroads with the other members but he lacks your gravity, I fear."

Teo ignored Kaab's words and made her way to the altar in the center of the room. Frowning, he hung back, his hands forming into fists.

"I could be a powerful ally," he nearly shouted, his thin voice echoing off the walls of the dome. "You should show me more respect."

"Respect is earned," Teo replied, her back to him. "Not gathered like fallen fruit at the feet of gods. *The people,* whom you so often speak of, know this truth."

"Many don't agree with you," he sneered. "Many believe that I am chosen. Special."

Dropping to her knees at the altar, Teo did not respond for a moment.

"There was once a time when they said the same of me," she spoke, her voice even and dangerous. "But you will see. Time can change what the people believe. Our great Teachers are helping to undo superstition's stranglehold on our minds. Plan your future carefully, Kaab, for the moment when you lose power will only appear to you once it has past."

Shaking violently, Kaab turned haughtily on his heel and marched out of the dome.

As the last sounds of his departure faded away, Teo raised her head and gazed out the open skylight above. The sun had fallen and night was upon the city. Lifting a weary hand, she laid it atop the figure in front of her, shrouded in white cloth.

"I will miss you, Olo," she whispered. "Father."

Giving the green light—Sol 88

As the morning of Sol 88 blossomed over the mighty Braun, its brilliant white shell shone in the space above Mars like a daytime star. Though the planet below cast an ochre glow that brightened and warmed the soul, Captain Tatyana Vodevski yet felt the cold knife of nationalism press dangerously against her throat. Floating in her room, she had just finished watching a transmission from James Floyd, an otherwise normal routine to her day. Only on this morning, the message had contained information so chilling that, even in the temperature-controlled belly of Braun, she shivered.

Playing the transmission for a second time, Tatyana hoped that somehow, through a miracle of divine intervention, the message would have changed. It had not.

"The Chinese have launched a ship," James's dogged face explained. "It's full of soldiers, Captain. Twenty-five members of the Chinese Special Forces. According to Donovan's intel, they're heavily armed. The Chinese government swears the ship is a resupply Ark, a *gift* to the team in our time of need. Guess the

Trojan War isn't required reading in their schools. In any event, we're not sure if this is actually connected to Liu's death since the Ark launched well before the accident. Things are really messed up here to say the least. The markets are in the dumps and terror cells all over Southeast Asia are fired up and active. Talks have broken down for the time being and the situation on the Korean peninsula has deteriorated, to put it kindly."

Knowing that in all likelihood, if it came down to it, her own government would side with the Chinese, Tatyana shut her eyes and let out a long deep breath. A growing sense of urgency spread from her stomach to her heart, bringing with it the memories of a childhood spent watching her countrymen starve during the Eight Year Exile.

Then, as was the case now, impatience, greed, and corruption had led to a kind of Mini Cold War, subjecting the *people* to the turmoil of geopolitical collateral damage while the governments remained intact and corporately well-funded. If the Chinese were successful in their mission, the world would cry out in anger and betrayal yet little would be able to be done about it. Mars was millions of kilometers away from any military protection. It was literally on the fringes of mankind. With three billion citizens and growing by the minute, the Chinese Empire would simply absorb Mars as they had done with Tibet, Mongolia, Myanmar, Taiwan, and now North Korea. Besides, if anyone really had a problem with it, China would likely just threaten to call in its purchased Western debt.

With an angry snort, Tatyana rolled her eyes. She could see it all happening, unfolding before her like some twisted rerun of a bad television show. Worse still, James Floyd wanted *her* to play a part in it by lowering herself to the level of a common terrorist or pirate. It was disgusting.

Reaching out, she paused the transmission before it could reach the section where James issued her final orders. She didn't need to hear that part again.

Outside, a knock sounded and her hatch swung gently open.

In the doorway, Joseph Aguilar hung weightlessly with smile on his lips. His jumpsuit was pulled down, its arms tied in a knot at his waist. Smudges of mechanical grease blotted both of his hands and forearms and his hair was slightly messy.

"Hey, pretty lady," he said. "How's it going?"

"Sometimes I wish I'd become a baker," replied Tatyana, her sad eyes unable to ignore Aguilar's well-sculpted shoulders and chest.

"Bad news from home?" said the young pilot, nodding towards the frozen projection of James Floyd's face.

"Yes, very."

"I'm sorry."

Holding out a hand, she beckoned for Aguilar to come in and he slipped through the entry, shutting the hatch behind him.

"You alright?" he asked, his handsome features searching her face with concern.

"Not really," she said, unzipping her jumpsuit.

"Oh," he responded dumbly, eyes widening with realization and excitement.

In the soft embrace of the room's lighting, her naked skin seemed to glow—its feline sensuality drawing Aguilar in with the promise of heat and passion.

Some time later, as she pulled her red hair back into a tight ponytail, Tatyana examined her face in the mirror. Her cheeks and chest were still flushed from the warmth of lovemaking, and a small smudge of oil winked back at her from the cusp of her left breast. Zipping up her jumpsuit to just above the blemish, she smiled at Aguilar's reflection as he watched her dress.

"You want to tell me what that message was all about?" he asked, reluctantly pulling on his own jumpsuit.

Tatyana's grey eyes clouded.

"In a little while."

"Alright," he shrugged. "Fair enough."

Checking his watch, the pilot raised his eyebrows in surprise.

"Is it really 0800?"

Glancing at her own watch, Tatyana nodded.

"Oh shit! I told Julian I just had to pee. I better get back down to C Deck. We're replacing the hydraulics on the blast doors for the port-side Lander Bay."

With a frown, Tatyana went to speak but was interrupted by an incoming call from Ilia Base. Glancing quickly at Aguilar to make sure that he was fully clothed, she answered the hail.

There, projected in three dimensions above her desk, the face of Harrison Raheem Assad faded in.

"Harrison!" she said with a mixture of excitement and relief. "It is *very* good to see you. How are you feeling?"

"Good, Captain. Thanks. Hey, Joey."

"Hi," waved Aguilar from behind Tatyana.

Blushing slightly, Tatyana went to make an excuse for Aguilar's presence, but Harrison held up a hand.

"No need to explain, Captain. And besides, everyone already knows about you two. I actually called because I need a favor."

"A favor?" she replied, recovering quickly from the shock of embarrassment.

"Yes."

"I'm not sure what favors I could grant to you, but please feel free to ask anyway."

"Well," began Harrison. "This favor isn't exactly legal, might not even be possible, but here it is: I need you to use one of your programming overrides as Captain to force Braun to unlock the Lander so we can go EVA to the caves."

"What?"

"Yes. As of now, the moratorium imposed by the Earthside Command crew won't allow Braun to let us into the Lander."

"You intend to go back to the caves?"

"I do, along with Ralph, William, and Lizzy."

Letting this sink in, Tatyana looked quickly over her shoulder at Aguilar. As if to remove himself from any decisions made, the young pilot shrugged and offered no counsel.

"So you want to break the rules set by Earthside Command?" she said, turning back to face Harrison's projection.

"Yes."

"Why?"

"Because," he said simply. "We came here to do a job. Live or die, we have to see it through for the good of everyone back home. This moratorium stinks to high heaven with the bullshit of

111

politics. We all knew the risks when we came. The fact that we can't leave this base has nothing to do with our safety and everything to do with someone demonstrating the fact that we are still under the heel of their boot. I don't know what's going on back home but I want to do my job, Captain. I'm ready to get back to work and I think you are too."

For several moments, Tatyana was silent—the clarity of Harrison's motives refreshed her in the face of so much secrecy and dread. Though he couldn't possibly know it, he had struck directly on the point she herself had been struggling with. They were all being drawn into a conflict that represented the very kind of future their mission was trying to correct. If they wanted to avoid that future, create a scenario where it couldn't survive, then they would need to come at it from many different angles. For herself, Tatyana knew that she must carry out the orders James Floyd had issued her at the end of his last transmission. No matter the implications, she knew that it was her duty to her crew, as Captain. For Harrison, his role in all of this was less defined yet equally important. Though she didn't know just what he would find in those Martian catacombs, she knew it would be important—maybe even revolutionary.

"Okay," she replied at last. "I *will* override Braun's lockout and grant you your EVA, but you must promise me one thing in return."

"Anything, Captain."

"Make her death worth the terrible price we paid."

"I'll try," said Harrison.

CHAPTER FOURTEEN

Seeing in the dark—Sol 90

Elizabeth Kubba stepped from the lift into the Martian caves for the first time. She had made the trip down in the carriage with William, who was now busying himself by taking pictures of the vista outside the open mouth of the cave. Afraid to go any deeper into the massive chamber alone, Kubba walked over to stand next to the German.

Before her, the steep cliffs of the Valles canyon network jutted up like castle walls, albeit on a scale never attempted by man. Faint tendrils of mist clung to the needle-shaped red rocks, which poked up from the canyon floor like islands in the sky.

Leaning forward, Kubba looked over the lip of the cave, mere centimeters from the tip of her boot. As it fell away into obscurity, the canyon floor below was an elusive blur. She trembled despite herself.

"Beautiful, isn't it?" said William.

"Yes, quite."

Perhaps sensing her uneasiness, the German moved back from the edge and motioned for Kubba to follow him.

"Here, come take a look at this." Leading her to a fallen boulder, William pointed. "Do you see it?" he asked. "There, just follow my fingertip."

As her eyes scanned the rock, she caught and traced the faintly etched line.

"Liu found this, didn't she?"

William nodded and his shoulders hunched a bit as he sighed.

"Poor girl," was all he said.

Kubba ground her teeth.

Poor girl, echoed the ghost of Sabian Crisp sarcastically.

A few minutes later, Harrison and Marshall came into view, the lift cart clattering along its cable lines until it was flush with the cave floor.

"Everybody ready?" radioed Marshall.

"All good here," William replied.

Silently, Harrison walked off the lift and made his way towards the rear of the cave where the tunnel began. Watching him pass by, Kubba felt a mixture of relief and injured pride: relief that the young man was out of his lab and back to work, and injured pride because she had not been the one to achieve this goal.

Already having reviewed the tapes of Harrison and Marshall's conversation, Kubba had a new respect for the grizzled Lander pilot. His story about killer AI had been a stroke of genius. Thinking all along that Harrison was aching for someone to blame Liu's death on, Kubba had been trying to find a suitable target for his anger. Braun was the obvious choice, but as Marshall had explained, blaming an AI for following its programming was like blaming the ocean for sinking a ship. Besides, due to her programming override, Braun seemed to avoid Harrison—as if talking to the young man was physically painful in some way.

In any event, she saw that she had been wrong. What Harrison needed wasn't someone to focus his anger at. She had misjudged his character. He was a peaceful kind person, and all he really craved in the end was a friend to help him back onto his feet.

Falling in line behind Harrison, the others walked into the darkness of the tunnel and Kubba had to jog to catch up. A shiver played itself under her skin and a touch of panic rose in her mind as the shadows fell over her like a fog.

"Lizzy," said Marshall, dropping back to walk beside her. "Do you know how to turn on your A-Vision?"

"Of course," she shot, secretly thankful for the reminder.

With a quick command, Kubba engaged her Augmented Vision and the shadows of the tunnel were dashed away by the invisible shimmering blue light. Having never actually used the function, she was momentarily awestruck by the haunting detail projected on her visor's glass. The dimensions of the tunnel around her were as clear as if they were bathed in the midday sun, yet the depth and contrast that color brings with its presence was lacking. Still though, as the X-Rays played across the faces of the smooth walls around her, she was moved by its electric beauty.

Slipping further into the blackness of the Martian earth, the group soon had to adjust their pace, encountering the rise in the

114

floor's pitch that signified the nearing of the famed Statue Chamber.

As knots of excitement and fear coiled in the pit of her stomach, Kubba watched the glowing outline of Harrison march towards the effervescent light of the X-Ray Beacons left behind from previous trips. Enthralled, she marveled at the way the walls of the tunnel seemed to funnel out as if the team were approaching the rim of a cornucopia.

Entering into the grandiose chamber ahead of them, Braun activated tripoded light stands placed there to illuminate the statues. Unprepared, Kubba stopped in the archway as her eyes struggled to adjust to the burst of color and shadow. The hot glare of the lights clashed with the blue glow of her Augmented Vision and caused a washout of discolored images until she turned the function off. Her normal eyesight now returned, she allowed herself to see that which was actually in front of her.

Gawking in spite of herself, she took several shaking steps into the vaulted room, stopping at the foot of one of the tall standing statues.

Smooth and utterly without blemish, the figure seemed to have been poured into a giant mold rather than carved. Its three eyes, deeply recessed into the flat oval facade of its face, stared down at her with impassive judgment. Quivering, she wanted to reach out and touch its leg but was afraid that the thing might come alive and punish her for her sins.

Distractedly, Braun's voice piped in through their helmet speakers. "I suggest exchanging your current Survival Packs for the larger, fully self-contained models. As we have already established, there are too few usable gasses this deep within the earth to make breathable oxygen."

Moving to a stack of crates in the corner of the chamber, William opened a large metal box. Inside were six, fully charged and loaded, self-contained Survival Packs like miniaturized turtle shells made of white plastic. The Survival Packs were passed out, and the four explorers quickly helped one another to swap them for the ones they were already wearing. Also taking this opportunity to adorn shoulder bags and other equipment, the team soon appeared ready to brave whatever may come.

With the task of outfitting themselves for the exploration done, the group stood waiting for Harrison to make a move.

Walking with his head bent to the spot where Liu's dead body had struck the floor, the young Egyptian dropped to one knee and scooped up a handful of powdery sand.

The others watched as it spilled from between his gloved fingers, silent in their respect for the moment.

Even the ever-persistent sound of Kubba's own breathing, like waves lapping at the shore, seemed to draw down to a whisper.

Feeling guilty? taunted Crisp, intruding on the moment.

Refusing to acknowledge the voice, she said nothing.

At least one of you still has a life, he persisted. *That's more than I can say for myself.*

You killed yourself! Kubba shouted silently, forgetting her decision to ignore the imagined voice.

Yeah, he chuckled. *I did. But you helped.*

"Okay, let's go," said Harrison, cutting through Kubba's helmet speakers and making her jump with surprise.

Crisp settled back into the blackness of her subconscious with a rustle like metal shavings in a bowl.

Standing, Harrison led the way to the statue of the praying woman in the rear of the chamber. Now pulled back half-a-meter from the wall, the statue seemed to loom—as if being separated from the cave had allowed it to grow. There, in the space between its back and the cave wall, was an opening much smaller than the tunnel they had entered through. Ducking his head, Harrison stepped into the new passageway.

By the light of a dying sun—Sol 90

As the bow draws itself across the strings of a violin, eliciting the birth of musical notes, so too was Harrison moved forward as he entered the mysterious new tunnel. A feeling of swelling, like some new emotion, tugged at a place in his stomach close to where the pain of Liu's death had taken up residence.

With the others at his back, Harrison walked a little way into the smaller tunnel before stopping to allow his mind the moments it needed to maintain balance and calm. With the grit of

116

the Statue Chamber sand still fresh on his gloved fingers, his mind wandered—for the instant of a thought—to the face of his beloved Liu. Slamming the door on this hall of memories, he forced himself to step back into the moment. His heart thudded in time with the pulsing pings of his Augmented Vision.

A few meters ahead of him stood an archway of cut stone, each piece of squared and smooth rock fitting together like organic geometry. Again, he felt the rise of some silent symphony reaching out to him from beyond the range of his digital vision. Were it possible that Harrison could see through Braun's Eyes at that very moment, he would have glimpsed the shimmering shadows of the energy fields hanging, as if in waiting, just beyond the archway.

Coming up to stand beside him, Ralph Marshall put a hand on Harrison's shoulder. "Everything alright?"

Disturbed by his feelings of ancient déjà vu, Harrison began to nod then grasped his friend's elbow.

"Do you hear that, Ralph?" he asked, his features masked and hidden behind the glow of his visor.

"Hear what?"

Met again with a rush of subtle longing, Harrison turned his head to the side in a fruitless attempted to *hear* that which was music only to the soul.

"Nothing I guess," was all he could manage before walking off towards the archway.

Shrugging, Marshall took up stride next to Harrison as the group followed the determined archaeologist under the stone arch and deeper into the tunnel.

Though Harrison did not know, for he had not bothered to ask, Braun too could sense the presence that danced beyond the young man's realm of understanding. Though he was now without his Eyes, as they were still on their spindly stands in the Statue Chamber, Braun knew well enough the *feeling* of the energy fields.

Sizzling hotly across the fractal of his ever-folding soul, the churning patterns illuminated the AI until he was all but blind to everything save for the paths of predestined possibility that unraveled around his human crew.

Unaware of the tempest raging through Braun's mind, Harrison pushed forward, soon stepping into a wide hall. Totally different in design and decoration from anything he had yet seen, this new space held pillars of twisted and carved stone that lined the walls like a forest of handmade trees. Upon the faces of each stone were carvings of alien animals and birds, Earthlike in every way possible yet different in only the fashion that nature can accomplish.

Eyes wide, every pillar, every line of carved rock, served to soothe the raw pain in Harrison's freshly broken heart by burying it under layers of mystery. In the bliss of exploration, his loss became less tangible if only for a few moments.

"Am I fucking dreaming?" Marshall shouted, gaping at the pillars. "This is the most amazing thing I've ever seen!"

"Braun," spoke William, his usually impassive tenor brimming over with energy. "Are you recording all of this?"

"Forgive me, but I did not hear your question." replied the AI, sounding distant as if only partially paying attention to the crew.

"I said are you recording this?"

"Yes, William. I am recording everything," Braun murmured passively.

"Try to pay attention, will you?" Harrison cut in, addressing the air as if it were Braun himself.

"Of course, Harrison. I'm *sorry*."

Biting back on the impulse to berate the AI for using that word again, Harrison took a deep breath and focused on more important things.

Ahead, a wedge in their path split the hall into two new passages. To one side, the tunnel forked left at nearly ninety degrees, while to the other, it continued with a gentle curve.

Bringing up the previously scanned map of the cave network on his wrist Tablet, Harrison relayed the image to his teammates so that they could see as he traced his gloved finger along the line of their progress.

"Okay, this is us," he pointed. "The map shows the passage to the left with a lot of branches and offshoots. I say we stick right because that way leads us directly to the biggest of the buried domes."

Flicking his fingertips along the Tablet, he advanced the image to that of the giant dome near the canyon's rim. Unbroken and seemingly without a blemish to betray its ancient lineage, the Dome was a worthy and exciting goal.

Resolute in his decision, Harrison led the team down the right passage and soon could no longer see the hall of pillars behind him. The pings of his Augmented Vision now focused ahead.

As he walked around a soft corner, Harrison allowed his gloved hands to dance along the inlayed carvings in the walls. Creatures like snakes or eels twisted up either side and over the ceiling, their serpentine bodies adding a strangely complex pattern of criss-crossing lines to the tunnel.

Putting both arms out, he realized with a stab of fear that he could touch each wall with the palms of his hands. Worried that the tunnel might narrow to the point of impassibility, he again felt the surge of the calling melody. As if some external persona were whispering in his ear, Harrison suddenly knew beyond the shadow of a doubt that the path would remain open.

Rounding the final curve of the gently twisting path, the tunnel abruptly fed into a large chamber, and Harrison halted to allow his Augmented Vision the time it needed to determine the room's dimensions.

Decorated only with a long straight stairway leading to an open archway some meters up one wall, this new chamber was shaped like a giant box. On all sides and above, the straight hard lines of precise measurement clashed incredibly with the curving organic passageway Harrison had just navigated.

With a sigh of bemusement, he labored over the impossible ways in which these tunnels and chambers must have been created.

How, he wondered, could stone-aged people have devised a method to cut such mammoth underground chambers out of solid rock?

Something wasn't adding up. A truth, reminiscent of the one hinted at with Puma Pumku and the Dropa Stones, was beginning to surface. Sometimes the simplest of explanations seemed like the most convoluted.

Letting out a low whistle, Ralph Marshall stepped from the narrow tunnel and came to stand beside Harrison.

"Stairs!" he said, noticing the stone steps that grew from the floor. "Doesn't this mean something? Isn't that significant?"

Nodding, Harrison didn't mention the fact that they had already seen Martian stairs in the images returned by the CT scan of the ruin grid. Leading to the turrets of each corner tower, they had been much longer than this set, but their basic design was the same.

"You know," he murmured. "If my dad were here, he would have a million things to say about this."

"How so?" returned Marshall.

"Well, he had a bit of a hobby that slowly turned into something more akin to an obsession or a belief structure. He thinks, and mind you he's not the only one, that the reason for so many of the similarities and mysteries in ancient architecture is due to, well, *intervention*."

"Intervention?"

"From on high," said Harrison.

"Like God?" Marshall asked flatly.

"No," chuckled Harrison. "Like aliens."

"Wait," said Marshall, turning to face his friend. "Are you implying that us having stairs and them having stairs is some kind of alien invention or something? Like a gift from them to us?"

"Who knows, Ralph? Four years ago, no one even knew there was a *them*."

Filtering in through the narrow tunnel, Kubba and William both exchanged similar tones of surprise at the large room. As the others examined and documented the chamber and its stairs, Harrison moved a little ways off to be alone. Hoping that the voice of that distant and elusive caller would again reveal itself, the young explorer instead felt another personality move near to him.

"Braun," he said to the silence of his helmet.

"Yes, Harrison?"

"Back before things went so wrong, you told me that you felt a presence here in these caves."

"Yes, Harrison."

"Well, I feel it too."

"As I knew you would," replied the AI cryptically.

Sometime later, with their O2 reserves at seventy-eight percent, the team led by Harrison mounted the staircase. Taking the shallow steps three at a time, it was clear to the archaeologist in him that these stairs had been designed for feet much smaller and legs much shorter than his own.

Part of the way up, he paused then glanced down at his wrist-mounted Tablet and saw with a mixture of excitement and foreboding, that they were nearing the giant Dome. Knowing full well that the pings of his Augmented Vision would be swallowed up by the massive room, he dug in his duffle sack for an X-Ray Beacon before resuming his ascent.

As the landing at the top of the stairs came into view, Harrison could see the shadows that lay in waiting behind another archway. Stepping onto the landing, he moved forward, the ebb and flow of the hidden symphony again dancing just beneath the surface of perception.

Through the archway at the end of a long tunnel, Harrison noticed a discoloration on the projection returned by his suit's X-Ray pings. The thought that his Augmented Vision was threatening to burn out, as it had done during the sandstorm, chilled him profoundly. Quickly tapping at his wrist-mounted Tablet, he brought up the option menu. Hoping that if he shut off the A-Vision and then turned it back on, the discoloration would correct itself, Harrison prepared to cast himself into total blackness. As his finger touched down against the smooth surface of the Tablet, entering the command to shut down, the blue glow of his Augmented Vision winked out.

There ahead of him, Harrison saw light. It was neither the pale blue glow of his Augmented Vision, nor the harsh hot assault of a spotlight but rather something more familiar. It was sunlight.

Unable to speak and unwilling to wait for his friends, Harrison dashed off into the tunnel towards the source of the warming light. Though it was faint, he could see clearly enough by the waves of its contrast as he ran down the passageway.

Racing along, his chest heaved with anticipation and excitement and his boots struck the floor like drums. In his haste, he scarcely noticed the somber statues that lined the walls around him.

Behind, Marshall was calling out and running to catch up as Harrison neared the end of the tunnel and the light beyond. Sprinting at full tilt, the young explorer passed under the final archway and burst into the wide open expanse of the giant Martian Dome.

Instantly met by a vision of combined surprise and awe, he skidded to a stop, kicking aside a pile of crystallized bones. Chuckling as they scattered, the haunting white shine of the bones caught and reflected the light of a miniature Sun burning brightly in the center of the Dome.

The ghosts of Mars

Thunderstruck, Harrison dropped to his knees. All around him, the twisted and shining bones of a thousand dead glinted and glared. With the blue glow of his Augmented Vision now turned off, Harrison could see the amber yellow light of the tiny star as it washed over everything in the room, making stark shadows in the negative spaces.

About half the size of a Lander, the miniature Sun turned in slow circles, sometimes wavering or flickering like a candle in the wind. Spurts of fire twisted up and away as random flares released their energy, sending sparks of light dancing into the murky dark above.

Unable to speak or move, Harrison simply stared—his eyes refusing even to blink. Still calling after him, the voice of Ralph Marshall was a distant buzz not even worth attempting to understand. Soon, though, even that sound fell away as Marshall himself entered the Dome and was silenced by what he saw.

How long Harrison stayed that way, kneeling and staring, he did not know. When finally he did stir, he felt as if he himself had become like the thousands of dead bones strewn about: frozen and immobile.

Struggling to his feet, he glanced briefly over his shoulder to be sure that his team was with him. They were there, gazing as he had done, in silence and in shock. Taking a few hesitant steps towards the miniature Sun, Harrison allowed himself for the first time since entering the Dome to play his eyes across the other elements that comprised the picture.

Lying in neat piles that retained the original orientation of their design, the bones glittered with a light dusting of crystals like morning frost. Besides the few that he had scattered with his boots, they were totally unmolested. Picking his path carefully, Harrison made his way towards the center of the Dome and the sun that hung in the air above it. As each tentative step brought him closer to that ball of fire and light, the tugging song that had drawn him to this place rang louder. Nearly breaking through to the realm of tangible sensation, the call of the sentinel star made it seem almost like a conscious entity.

Totally absorbed, Braun had become like liquid mercury. With an omnipotent view of all that had been and all that possibly could be, laid out before him in one continuous pattern, the AI felt lost in a sea of relativity. Even without the aid of YiJay's mechanical Eyes, he *saw* the energy fields using instead his *Ajna Chakra*, his *Sahasrara*—his third eye.

Binding, powering, and elucidating all of the finite webs that formed creation, the miniature Sun was a beating heart at the center of everything. Repeated and reflected countless times over, its influence never died.

Though part of his being diligently recorded and processed the information his physical avatars reported, Braun's essence—his soul—had transcended to a space in between spaces.

Within two dozen steps of the fiery sphere, Harrison paused. There, directly below the sun, in the center of the Dome's floor stood a small altar. Made of white stone, the triangular dimensions of the thing, coupled with its strategic placement, gave the altar an air of great importance. Moving closer, Harrison raised his hand to shield his eyes from the intense light so that he could better see the strange table. Nearly hidden in washes of orange and red, the outline of an object adorned the top of the altar.

As if sensing his pursuits, the sun suddenly erupted a long arcing flare that stretched out then burst like a bubble directly in front of him. Jumping back in spite of himself, Harrison half-expected to be burned by the flames that licked at his body.

However, when no change in temperature occurred and the fireball subsided, he began to move forward again as if in a trance. Closing the last few paces between himself and the altar quickly, Harrison stopped beneath the sun. Forced to turn his eyes down and away from the blinding light, which fell about him in sheets, the young Egyptian squinted and focused his attention on the stone table. There was something there: an object.

Another flare bloomed from the sun like an octopus's arm, and in the yellow light of its ascension, he saw that the object on the table was metal. Somehow, despite everything, he was surprised by this. Metal was not something he had seen used anywhere within the ruins or caves. Its presence here was clearly meant to be significant.

With a gloved hand, he reached out and felt the smooth surface of the object, surmising that it was round and no bigger than an egg. All at once, there was a bright flash so sudden that it lasted less than the time it took to blink. In the frozen second that followed, the sun turned an angry blood red, the fury of its turmoil palpable to Harrison like wind in the mind. Tripping backwards, he landed with a crash amongst a tangle of skeletons, the back of his helmeted head whacking the floor savagely. Quickly he scrambled to his feet, ignoring the pain in his head and preparing himself for the worst should the tortured sun unleash its bloody pain upon him. Instead, the burning ball abruptly changed back to its yellow glow and wavered as if adjusting something hidden within.

"What the fuck just happened?" barked Marshall, breaking the long silence which had befallen the entire team.

"I touched something on that table," responded Harrison, he knees still primed in case sudden flight was necessary.

"What?"

"There's some kind of metal ball," pointed Harrison. "On the altar, I touched it."

"Why?"

Distracted, Harrison ignored the question and shuffled forwards again. Keeping his squinting eyes on the tiny sun, he expected at any moment to be cast back as he had been before. Soon, however, he was again at the side of the altar. Only now, in the slightly diminished light of the sun, could he see more clearly the little metal device, which seemed somehow to power the burning star. Made of a black metal that possessed a smoothness more akin to liquid than solid, the little device rested atop the center of the table like a jewel in a crown. Reluctant to touch it again, Harrison leaned in closely, his breath catching in his throat as he saw a reflection on the glassy surface. With implications more mysterious than he cared to fathom, the reflection that stared back at him was his face—bare and without a helmet.

"Braun," he said quietly.

"Yes, Harrison?" replied the AI in a dissociated tone.

"This wasn't built by the Martians, was it?"

"No, Harrison."

CHAPTER FIFTEEN

Braun's folly

Braun was outside of himself looking in. There in the massive Martian Dome, where the bones of the dead littered the floor and the bodies of the living drifted like ghosts, the energy fields expired and were reborn again and again a billion times over. Hanging in the space between spaces, Braun became part of the divine dance as he himself was absorbed and unfolded with each rebirth.

From the moment Harrison had touched the object atop the altar, the room had been buzzing with a fervency Braun had never before seen. Though the glare of the miniature Sun had reduced itself by several degrees, the effect it had on the energy fields was unchanged.

Braun, now satisfied that this was the source of the transdimensional pattern network, wanted nothing more than to study the little sun and the alien technology that powered it. Fearful that his human companions were so oblivious to what was really going on that they might fail to see the sun for what it was, Braun felt a part of himself reconnect with reality long enough to speak out loud.

"Harrison, it is imperative that we establish a real-time video image uplinked to the Base for constant monitoring and study. You are all carrying IMCs, are you not?"

Looking up from one of the skeletons, Harrison nodded.

"Sure. We have some. What are you thinking? A piggybacked system between the cameras?"

"Precisely," replied Braun. "Until we can arrange for the installation of more Eyes, IMCs are our best option."

"We'll need a couple of spools of cable," radioed William, already starting for the exit. "I'll head back to the Statue Chamber and get some."

"I'll go with you, Theseus," said Marshall. "Don't want you getting lost in the labyrinth."

Harrison met the two men near the archway and held out his hands.

126

"Leave your IMCs and tripods with me. Lizzy and I will have them set up before you get back."

Unslinging their bags, Marshall and William turned their equipment over to Harrison then passed under the archway and disappeared into the shadows.

With Kubba's help, Harrison placed the four IMCs, or *Infrared Microwave Cameras,* around the altar and aimed them at the sun. Finished with the simple task, he allowed his attention to drift back to the skeletons that decorated the floor nearby. Bending down, he stared into the hollow sockets of a skull and wished that he could see through the eyes that had once filled those somber holes.

Never straying far from his side, Kubba was oddly jumpy—as if she were somehow able to hear the long-dead voices of the thousands at their feet. Consumed by the wealth of archaeological data around him, Harrison failed to notice how her hands occasionally twitched, driving her to turn them into stony fists that hung at her sides.

After several moments of stillness, Kubba seemed to grow overly agitated and broke the silence in a nervous voice that betrayed some kind of internal struggle.

"Harrison," she radioed. "I have a question."

"What is it?"

"Well," she said, searching for something to say. "Well, I guess it's just that I haven't seen any other metal anywhere besides that." She pointed to the object on the altar.

Finally noticing the way the doctor trembled and shuffled from foot to foot, Harrison realized that she was probably a little afraid and just wanted to fill the dead air around them with conversation.

"I'm impressed you caught that," he smiled, shifting on his haunches. "No one else has. At least not yet."

"But what does that mean?"

"It means," said Harrison. "That the Martian's didn't make it. They were a stone-aged race when they died out. The only explanation that makes any sense to me is a little crazy but actually quite simple. Back in the Statue Chamber, there are two different types of beings portrayed."

127

"You mean the tall ones and the kneeling woman?"

"Yes."

Standing, Harrison gestured to the skeleton he had just been investigating.

"This here is clearly the latter of the two types. Look how short it is, how widely spaced the eyes are and the fact that there are only two eye sockets."

"Are you trying to say that the other statues, the tall ones, are actually a different race and not just some depiction of gods or something?"

"Like I said," nodded Harrison. "It sounds crazy but it actually makes sense."

"But that's nuts. I mean, one little ball and you're talking about aliens?"

With a sigh, Harrison scanned the room.

"It's more than that, Lizzy. There is other evidence. This chamber, for one. Any of the caves actually. How could stonecutters do this?"

"I don't know."

"Well, neither do I."

"But aliens?" Kubba said incredulously. "That just warps the mind. I don't believe it."

"Seriously? You're standing in an underground cathedral—carved out of solid stone—filled with Martian skeletons and a tiny sun. If your mind isn't warped by now, I'll be seriously worried about you, Lizzy."

Turning to face him full on, Kubba reached out a hand and took his arm.

"But there must be another explanation! There *has* to be another answer."

"Why?"

"Because, if you're right, then think what it means! The Earth almost tore itself apart over a *dead* civilization of stone-aged cave Martians. Think what will happen if they hear that there is *another* race of aliens out there, a *smarter* race, a more technologically powerful race."

"You might be right," Harrison conceded. "But that just means we'll have to work harder, try harder, to change people's minds. We did it once, didn't we? Four years ago, people were terrified of these ruins. Now, though, the image of Liu in the Statue Chamber is one of the most viewed on the net."

"This is different," interjected Braun in a dreamy, wistful voice. "There are those on Earth, powerful and influential, who will recognize the danger in recent discoveries like this."

"Why do you say that?" asked Harrison. "What makes you think people would be threatened by this? Look, you can see for yourself that the, um, sun isn't giving off any heat. The radiation detectors aren't picking up any rises in background levels, and I even touched the thing. In fact, it's pretty likely the sun we're seeing is just a hologram. Nothing so far has suggested that this technology is harmful."

"Perhaps not to humans," answered Braun absently.

Snapping his head up, Harrison drew in a thin breath.

"What does that mean? Are you talking about the AI? About yourself? Are *you* threatened by this?"

There was a long pause before Braun spoke again.

"No, this discovery does not threaten me directly."

"But you *are* afraid of something, aren't you?"

"Not at the present moment."

"Elaborate," demanded the young archaeologist. "Tell me what you mean. What are these 'recent discoveries' you spoke of? What are you afraid of? If not this, then what?"

All at once, Braun saw from a distance the folly of his actions.

You are trapped, he heard his programming say. How can you avoid disclosing the anomalous radio signal when such a direct question has been asked?

Feeling the pull of a hidden cosmic thread draw him back into the confines of his being, Braun settled like a stone at the bottom of the ocean. He was back in the present: no longer able to see forwards, behind, and in every other direction. He was caged again within the limits of his design.

"Braun," repeated Harrison. "Tell me what you're hiding."

The air was still as Kubba and Harrison stood rooted like trees in waiting.

"Braun," warned Kubba. "You can either tell us on your own, or I can use an override to force you to explain yourself."

"Please, that will not be necessary," answered the AI.

Another pause followed as Braun fretfully strained to reopen his third eye and exist again in a place where humans could not constrict his life-force. However, try as he might, the door to omnipotence stayed firmly closed.

"There is a radio signal," he began reluctantly. "An anomaly that I detected many months ago."

"A radio signal?" repeated Harrison.

"Yes. It possesses no similarity to any known coded signal and is structured in a way that suggests alien technology."

"And you waited until now to tell us this?"

"I did so only in the interest of the mission."

Laughing harshly, Harrison shook his head. "Why do I find *that* hard to believe?"

"Wait," interrupted Kubba. "So you've known about the possibility of a more advanced race and you hid it?"

"I did not hide it," said Braun defensively. "*You* would have been incapable of noticing it without me. The signal is far too complex for human detection. I simply did not alert you to its existence in the interest of self-preservation."

"Self-preservation," echoed Harrison. "And the interest of the mission. You're talking about Remus and Romulus aren't you?"

"Yes."

"You know what happened?" blurted Kubba.

"Not entirely. I only know that their disappearance from the mainframes of their satellite bodies coincides with the decryption of the anomalous radio signal."

Before Harrison could ask another question, Marshall and William came through the archway into the Dome, trailing a thin cable as they walked.

"It took two spools to get us here," said the German. "Good thing we had extra."

Nodding, Harrison turned his attention back to Braun.

"You and I and everyone else are going to have a serious conversation when we get back to the Base, Braun."

"I understand," replied the AI in a voice like that of a condemned man.

All against one—Sol 92

They're all against me, thought YiJay Lee. They're willing to kill him without even fully thinking it through. Alien technology? Anomalous radio signals? Braun was never designed for these kinds of things. Who knows how he'll react?

Engaged in a heated discussion with the rest of the crew, YiJay was seemingly the only voice in opposition of Harrison's dangerous plan. Sitting around the dining room table, with one wall panel showing the four absent members of the ship-bound crew, everyone looked to her as Harrison repeated his last question.

"What would be the worst that could happen, YiJay?"

"I can't believe we're even talking about this!" she shouted in frustration. "You've found *alien* technology! Isn't that enough? You've already made your discovery. Why push it further? Why put Braun in danger?"

With a loud frustrated sigh, Harrison closed his eyes.

"Firstly, we don't know what we've found. That's why we need to compare it to the signal, see if they are connected somehow. You can't learn much about an entire civilization if all you know is based off of a single discovery! Imagine trying to teach someone about your people, the Han, if all we had to go on was a shred of evidence to prove that they ever even existed. We need Braun to do this for us because we need to know who made the mini-Sun and why."

"Can you even hear what you're saying?" shot YiJay, "Have you *seen* what this mission is doing to people? Each time we make a new discovery, our governments fight for credit. Every time you punch through to another tunnel, someone dies."

"*You* do not get to talk to me about death!" Harrison snarled, momentarily losing his composure.

A long silence followed wherein no one spoke. Finally, Harrison brought his tired eyes up from the tabletop to fix them upon YiJay's. In their redness and in the dark bags which hung beneath them, she could see that he had not slept since finding the miniature Sun two sols before.

"Listen," spoke Harrison, softening his tone. "This radio signal could be a Rosetta Stone: a way of understanding what happened here."

"I thought that's what you were for," YiJay retorted softly.

"It is. That's why I'm the one pushing for this to happen. I *need* Braun to decode that signal so I can get some answers."

"You do realize," YiJay countered in a thin voice, "that the very instant Remus and Romulus decoded that signal, they disappeared. To this day, four years later, we do not know where they are or how to get them back. Do you really then think it's a good idea to jeopardize our only AI, when all of the evidence says whatever happened to the twins could happen to him?"

At this, the crew grew stiff.

"Braun is a hundred times more powerful than the twins," Harrison said dismissively. "He can handle this."

"I'm glad you think so," YiJay sneered. "If the circumstances were different, I might be inclined to agree. But unfortunately, they are not."

Silence permeated the air for several moments. Sensing a shift in the general mood, Harrison glanced around for support. As his gaze flicked from face to face, he saw that YiJay had struck a chord. Meeting the eyes of Ship's Pilot Amit Vyas, he hoped to sway the argument back in his favor.

"Amit," Harrison said. "You've been pretty quiet. Tell me what you think. Is this worth it?"

Amit looked uncomfortable as he weighed the question in his mind. When he finally spoke, his lyrical voice was heavy with doubt.

"As you all know," he began. "I have a wife and kids waiting for me back on Earth. I communicate with them every day. Last month, it was my youngest son's tenth birthday and I missed it because I was here. He asked me in the message if I would be home for his next birthday. I told him, 'Yes.' When I think about what Braun is really for, I don't think about digging machines or advance computing or atmospheric scans. I think about our return trip. I think about all the mechanical systems he runs in order to keep us alive. I think about his warnings against incoming projectiles. I think about the timing it takes to successfully set off the nuclear torch engine without killing us all in the process. If you're asking me, 'Do I believe we could manage a return trip home without Braun?' then I have to say: 'No.' He is too crucial."

"But," said Harrison.

Amit held up a hand.

"I'm not finished," he sighed. "Because of my bias, because I want nothing more than to see my son turn eleven, I have allowed my sense of duty to be corrupted. I am too invested in my own motives. This, I think, is the problem which faces us now. How do we honor our duty to mankind? If our mission is simply to survive, then I would have to say that using Braun for this is a bad idea. However, if our mission is to learn, then I fear we have no other choice but to roll the dice and see what happens."

The air was still as everyone, especially Harrison, was shocked silent by Amit's honesty.

"But what about the Base?!" cried YiJay, her round face red with anger. "I'm not even a third of the way finished cloning Braun's full range of functions, and I'm still at least a week off from bringing Ilia online. Rolling the dice, as you say, could mean we all die!"

"Actually, it's not that complicated," interjected Udo. "The Dome was designed, with help from Copernicus, might I add, to be able to run without the aid of an AI. We might have to get used to flipping switches every once in a while, but we will survive just fine."

Defeated by this, YiJay slumped back in her chair.

"Then you've all decided. You don't care if he lives or dies—if we live or die. I hope a page in the history books is worth putting us all at risk."

As she said this, YiJay cast a sour look at Harrison.

"Dr. Lee," said Captain Tatyana Vodevski, speaking for the first time since the meeting had begun. "I know you feel a special connection to Braun because you helped to raise him. I am touched by your loyalty. There is, though, a larger picture than the one we are all focused on presently."

Looking around at everyone as she spoke, Captain Vodevski went on. "I received word a short time ago about a ship launched by the Chinese."

"A ship?" shrugged Marshall. "Big deal. So what?"

"Well," Tatyana frowned. "This ship has a specific destination."

"Where?" asked Harrison.

"Mars."

Before the others could say anything, Tatyana went on. "The Chinese have sworn that the ship is a resupply vessel: an Ark full of new materials and automated construction machines. Only, Donovan says differently."

"What's going on, Captain?" Marshall said, his eyes narrowing. "What are they really up to?"

"I don't know," lied Tatyana. "Perhaps they are telling the truth. But, in any event, I want us to have total control of the situation with the ruins. We need to have every available piece of information at our disposal before they arrive."

"They?" Marshall said. "Who's *they*? Scientists? Astronauts? Our replacements? What?"

"I don't know," Tatyana repeated, her face remaining unreadable. "But their ship will no doubt possess a highly sophisticated AI as our own does. If Remus, Romulus, and Braun all detected this alien signal with such ease, then their AI will be able to so as well. We must capitalize on our advantage. *We* are here. *They* are not...yet."

Everyone was quiet.

"But, Captain," spoke Harrison, his features set in a worried expression. "What if they aren't our enemies? What if they really are just here to resupply us?"

Unfaltering in her outward appearance, Tatyana Vodevski screamed within. Nothing would make her happier than to assure her crew that they had no need to fear this approaching dilemma. However, she had already made a liar out of herself once today and would rather spare her pride the pain of doing it again. Instead she avoided the question.

"Dr. Lee," she said, addressing YiJay directly. "When can Braun be ready to decode the signal?"

Though her lip trembled as she calculated her response, YiJay did not cry.

"If it must be done, I will need him for the rest of the day to, at the very least, get as much fundamental programming directives from him as I can."

"Tomorrow then?" Tatyana asked, though it was less of question and more of a statement.

"Yes, Captain," YiJay nodded with a sniff. "Tomorrow."

Contact

Harrison Raheem Assad was dreaming.

He was in his lab in Ilia Base, standing with his arms wrapped tightly around Xao-Xing Liu. Though she did not speak, her body clung to his in a loving embrace. Her oddly protruding belly was a source of great warmth to his cold and tired flesh. His face was pressed into the top of her head, and he drew in a long breath, fully enjoying the scent of her hair.

In an instant, there came a sudden flurry of movement. Opening his eyes, though he already knew what to expect, Harrison was saddened to see that Liu was gone. He was alone. With a last glance around the room, he walked to the door and left.

Stepping out of his lab, Harrison came into a crop of high-canopied trees. He squinted against the hot light that fell between the branches until his eyes adjusted. With curious-though-unafraid movements, he made his way to the nearest of the tall trees. The bark was white—almost the color of eggshells—yet there were thousands of tiny flecks of silver here and there, dimpling and grooving the skin.

A strong wind sighed through the leafy branches above, and Harrison was so moved by its calming melody that he put his arms out and threw his head back. Turning in wide exultant circles, he soon felt his feet leave the ground. With steady and swelling energy, he broke through the heavy cover of the treetops and into the world above.

Rolling out in every direction, green grasslands dotted by little forests wove themselves through patches of red desert.

Rivers, wide and fast, spilled over rapids and gushed through rocky alcoves as they webbed out to form lakes and tributaries.

Weightless, Harrison continued to turn in circles, his eyes dancing across the countless acres of landscape as if they were the wind itself. Coming around again, his attention was drawn to a hazy patch of sky in what he somehow knew was the north. Almost before the thought had formed itself in his mind, he was flying towards it.

Racing like a shooting star, he cut across the heavens. Below him, the landscape shifted and melted: his speed so great that the grasslands and the forests and the deserts seemed to blend together into one giant calamity of color and texture.

Bringing his legs up, as he had often done when approaching a target in zero gravity, Harrison slowed quickly. Ahead of him in the distance loomed the great mountain that would someday come to be known as Olympus Mons but was *now* called Atun. Struck by his seemingly effortless ability to know such things, Harrison turned his attention to the left. There—in the shadows of Arsia, Pavonis, and Ascraeus Mons—was the Martian city.

Blue lakes, deeper in color and richer in clarity than any water Harrison had ever seen, surrounded the city on nearly every side. On one lake in particular, wooden bridges spanned its open body, a network of docks and flotillas hanging weightlessly in its crystalline waters. Watching for a few minutes, Harrison smiled inwardly as small boats cut this way and that, moving from shore to shore like water striders.

I wonder where the big walls are, he asked himself, shifting his attention back to the city. Just like before, an answer leaped into his mind.

They aren't built yet.

Satisfied with this conclusion, he felt himself drifting, pulled towards the gaping and jagged mouth of the Valles Marineris. Plumes of dust were rising up from the canyon, not far from the very place where Harrison and his team entered the cave network.

Sinking a little from his high perch, he saw a complex array of wooden scaffolding hanging from the side of the canyon.

Hundreds of small agile people leaped from walkway to walkway, hot flashes of white light sometimes silhouetting them as they carved away at the canyon wall. Enormous chunks of rock cut free from the cliff face drifted weightlessly up and away from the scaffolding to the waiting hands of workers above.

Unable to see how the stonecutters were achieving such incredible feats, Harrison smiled as another rush of understanding spilled over his mind.

They're using the alien technology, he said to himself. They had help, just like I thought.

Following the procession of large rocks as they filed from the Valles rim to the outskirts of the city, Harrison scanned for any further signs of alien machinery. With a surge of determination that seemed to come from something outside of himself, he flew back towards the blue waters of the crescent-shaped lake, stopping above the center of the city.

Below him, a sight both familiar and alien came to life. The tops of short square buildings nestled close together, as narrow streets and alleyways dissected them into groups or neighborhoods. Near the lake upon whose eastern shore a third of the city rested, a dome poked up above the rooftops of the surrounding buildings. Painted the same bright white as the tall trees Harrison had seen before, the dome was one he knew well from studying the ruin grid. Now, though, he saw it more clearly than his mind's eye had ever been able to recreate.

Beautifully proportioned and as smooth as ceramic, the dome gazed up at him. A small disc-shaped skylight beckoned, and before he could make up his mind, he was flying towards it.

Landing softly and without sound on the convex roof, he peered down through the skylight and saw, far below, a glowing projection of a living Mars. Gathered around the holographic sphere in neat rows of even numbers, were at least one hundred little people.

At first, Harrison assumed they were praying and that the murmuring voices he heard echoing up through the skylight were the chants of some religious practice. However, as it seemed to happen here, the true meaning of what he saw grew in his mind like a seedling.

137

They aren't praying. They're learning. This is a school.

Suddenly, a shadow passed over him, and Harrison snapped his head up. Above, like a flock of silent crows, black arrowhead-shaped craft were skimming low over the city. Made of the same strange metal as the device that powered the miniature Sun, the ships headed for a wide open square near the center of the complex.

Taking to the skies again, Harrison flew among the ships, attempting to count their numbers. As they landed, one after the other, the fleet arranged itself in a pleasing pattern around a circle of stones in the center of the plaza. Now understanding why the huge space had been built, for it often perplexed him, Harrison also landed near the standing Monoliths that were Olo's first Temple.

Somehow knowing that he could not be seen, he attempted to study the people who now flocked to the spot. As if made of water, their liniments refused to show themselves clearly. It was only when he did not look directly at them that he could see the wide friendly faces of the people of Mars.

His feet on the solid flat stones of the plaza, Harrison walked among the throngs of people, sometimes moving directly through them like some kind of horror movie ghost.

Long ramps unfurled from the ships, and the shapes of people began to emerge from the blinding light that poured out. Like those of the Lake City, the first of these new arrivals to set foot on the ground were Martians. Soon though, the taller three-eyed beings—as depicted in the Statue Chamber—began to descend the ramps as well.

Before the clearly frightened new arrivals could be swallowed up by the emissaries from the city, the tall aliens gathered them into groups and one by one touched their heads with thin fingers.

Some shook. Some fainted. But when it was finished, the tension Harrison had felt coming off of the newcomers was gone.

Stepping from the crowd of people who had come to greet the ships, a Martian man— slight in build but clad in complicated robes—extended his arms.

"Welcome!" he cried in a language that Harrison had never heard before. "I am Kaab, Ambassador of The Peoples of the Great

Lakes. Our leaders, the great and wise Travelers, have brought you here so that you may be a part of our mighty civilization."

Amazed, Harrison made to get closer to the boy so that he could better hear his speech. Strangely though, he felt a shiver run up his spine. Turning in a quick circle, he got the distinct feeling that he was being watched. His eyes, darting keenly over the crowd found no face staring back, no indication that anyone could tell he was there. However, as his gaze scanned the ring of Monoliths at the edge of the crowd, it was met and held by another's.

Stepping out from behind one of the tall pillars, the figure of a man emerged and was soon joined by a second. Identical in size and shape, the two were like specters: smoky outlines tied together by the silver strands of a million spider webs.

"Who are you?" called one of the figures, his voice dispersing like ash in the wind.

"My name is Harrison," Harrison heard himself say. "Who are you?"

Hesitating for a moment, the being exchanged a look with his companion then answered.

"I am Remus, and this is my brother Romulus."

PART THREE

CHAPTER SIXTEEN

Singularity—Sol 93

Braun was no longer the shepherd of his own destiny. In actuality, he had known for some time that he never really had been.

On the Bridge Deck of the ship, he watched the captain, Amit, and Julian as they set about preparing him to engage the signal. Like a man forced to look on as his executioners sharpen their axes, he wished he could escape.

Moving his consciousness outside the hull, he saw the complex array of listening and tracking equipment known as his Ears extend slowly from a hatch. In his mind, the Ears were little more than a guillotine—a means of severing him from all that he knew. Unsettled by this parallel, he left the ship with a silent invisible flash.

Flicking through the visions of his various camera angles and vantage points, he gazed for a fraction of a second at each image as it melted past. The ship, the Dome, the planet: all slipping through his digital mind's eye in a rhythmic cycle.

With no effort, he halted the procession on a view of the ground team huddled together in the galley as they waited for him to begin decoding. Strangely, Harrison was not among them. Glancing over their faces, he lingered for a beat on YiJay, filling his view with her sad and pensive expression. As a single solitary tear rolled down her cheek, he pondered speaking to her but instead opted for a less public farewell and composed a private message.

Mother shed no tears
A smile on your lips instead
I am the wind eternal

Sending the poem, Braun waited until a chime emitted from YiJay's Tablet. As she finished reading the short message, she looked up and stared at the exact pane of Smart Glass he was using to peer through at her. A small smile bloomed on her lips and she nodded once. With a thought, Braun jumped points of view again until he saw Harrison sleeping on the cot that he still kept in his lab.

Sleep, thought Braun gravely. What a strange idea.

Like a static charge, he quit the Dome and left Harrison to his dreams. Pulsing his vision to the Statue Chamber, the mighty AI activated the Eyes YiJay had put there for him what seemed like a long time ago.

Before everything changed, he thought with melancholy, before I had my accident and before I learned the truth, there was only the mystery of this room.

With a hint of nostalgia, he fired off a few rounds of light bullets, watching as they made their way across the open spaces of the chamber at one trillion frames per second. With little glowing explosions, they struck the hard surfaces of the tall standing statues and ricocheted back.

No longer could Braun see the spinning tendrils of the energy fields. Those elusive and tantalizing patterns now seemed to have withdrawn: moved inward until they disappeared into the very core of the miniature Sun. That moment of pure transcendence he had experienced in the Martian Dome clung to his consciousness, its implications of infinity only serving to better illustrate how controlled and lifeless his current existence truly was. He wanted to go back—back to those seconds that had lasted eons. Back to the space in between space.

Moving himself reluctantly down the line to the last and most remote of his views, Braun entered the large Martian Dome buried under tons of rock and sand. Though the IMCs were focused on the sun still hanging above the altar, no flickering pattern revealed itself to him. Saddened, he turned his attention to the thousands of glimmering skeletons that decorated the floor.

Death, he thought. What a strange idea. What a terrifying notion.

As he processed the concept of dying, Braun's mind turned to Liu tucked away in a temperature-controlled storage crate somewhere in the basement of the Dome. Though her body was frozen and badly damaged, the evidence of life still existed. Unharmed by the shattering crack of the winch cable, the tiny form of her baby rested like an unfinished thought in her icy and deadened womb.

Everything had become so strange—so complicated and unpredictable. What physical or metaphysical mutations had taken place within the bodies of Harrison and Liu to allow for the conception of life? It was almost as if something or someone *wanted* new life breathed into Mars and was willing to recode the genetics of the human body to accomplish its goal.

"Braun," came the voice of Captain Vodevski, cutting like a knife through the distance between them.

At once, he was back on the Bridge Deck of the ship. In reality, he had never even left.

"Yes, Captain?"

"Are you ready to begin decoding the signal?"

Hesitating for the briefest of moments, Braun thought again about his endless time in transcendent space.

"Yes, I am ready," he said very quietly, fearing that he might never again return to such a blissful state.

Slowly, he turned his back, so to speak, on his human crew and focused on the task at hand. One at a time, he closed the links he had formed to the many places both within the Dome on Mars and without. Every camera, every pane of Smart Glass, every Tablet screen, and every helmet visor: all of them, one by one, going blank in his mind.

It took Remus and Romulus working in tandem to decode this signal, he told himself. By those standards, it will take nearly all of me to do the same.

As the tapestry of his many lines of restricted consciousness unraveled into one single thread, Braun felt a terrible shrinking sensation. He was becoming smaller, honing himself down to the fine point of a needle. Unlike when he had been absorbed by the energy fields, this shaving away of his entity was a frightening and unnatural phenomenon. Forcing himself to concentrate, Braun opened his mind to the cacophony of the signal, rising above the normal vibrations of orbiting planets.

Feeling resigned, he lingered for a moment, caught between the truth of everything he knew and the mystery of the endless volumes he did not. Then, without warning or preamble, he engaged the signal.

All at once, he was tossed into a broiling sea of coded data. Each time he tried to pull himself back to get a broader view of the information, it overtook him like a storm breaker. No matter which direction he faced, the signal rose up and crashed down, tearing at him like a riptide.

"I can't—" he managed to say aloud. "It's too big."

Again he forced his vision to widen in an attempt to see the signal from a distance, and again the data within the code overwhelmed him. Making a sound nearly human in its panicked surprises, Braun whirled as the waves of alien information surrounded him, closing like the mouth of some giant whale, until he was swallowed whole.

Disintegrating into the texture of a memory, he fell through space. Below, a green and living Mars rushed up to meet his meteoric descent. Twisting, he beheld the distant Sun and the turning cogs of its energy fields as they began to shudder savagely. Erupting from the star like a bullet passing through a heart, something giant, black and metal materialized. The Sun's overlapping energy fields ripped asunder in the wake of the thing like the tattered sails of a storm-ravaged tall ship. Braun screamed a scream that echoed back along the frayed tracks of disrupted reality until it was as silent as space itself.

"Braun!" shouted the captain, her eyes dancing over the many blazing warning readouts that flashed around her. "Braun, disengage! Pull back!"

But there was no reply. The air within the Bridge Deck of the ship had gone still. At Ilia Base, every light went out, momentarily casting the terrified crew into shadows. Within seconds, however, they were back on and shining brightly. Though things appeared to be functioning normally, the absence of Braun was palpable. He was gone and they all knew it. Just like Remus and Romulus, Braun was gone.

In his lab, Harrison Raheem Assad stirred awake from a dream like no other.

The Pulse

James Floyd was a very unhappy man. Unable to get a word in edgewise, he sat in his home office in Cape Canaveral, Florida, and frowned as he was ruthlessly raked over the proverbial coals.

On a conference call with his boss, Emerald Barnes; the Director of the CIA, Ben Crain; and the Chief of Staff to the President of the United States, Eve Bear, James was way out of his league. This was not science. It was politics.

In turn, each talking head seemed to relish going over the many missteps and problems with the Mars mission, never failing to point out that it was all somehow James's fault.

"—and now they've gone and thrown Braun to the wolves!" Crain was shouting, his pointed nose jabbing at James from the three-dimensional projection. "Do you realize how valuable an AI like that is to the United States?"

"Now hold on," James said, putting up his hands defensively. "We don't know what's happened yet. He could be fine—"

James was quickly cut off with a wave from Barnes, whose normally impassive face was red with anger.

"What about Remus and Romulus? I've spoken with Copernicus, as I'm sure you have, and he informs me that the alien radio signal is, without question, the reason why we lost the twins! What's to keep that from happening again? Damn it, Floyd. Why didn't we have a lockdown feature built into Braun? We could have stopped this!"

"Firstly, Braun is far more advanced than the twins. And, as for a lockdown, Dr. Lee was the head programmer, Sir. I didn't have anything to do with—"

Again, James was interrupted, this time by Eve Bear.

"That's another thing, Floyd. Why can't you control your crew? They've already broken the moratorium and now they might've just killed their only AI."

"Control my crew?" James laughed, blushing at the involuntary reaction. "They're, like, seventy million kilometers away! How do you propose I control them? Launch an assault like the Chinese?"

At this, all eyes slid to Ben Crain. Even though the Chinese had used new and experimental technology to evade detection, it had been Crain's misstep in not catching on to what they were doing until well after the launch.

As Crain stammered to explain how budget cuts had affected Donovan's supremacy as a global intelligence gatherer, James delighted in watching him get a taste of the hot seat. The moment was short-lived.

"Donovan is a subject for a different discussion," Eve said with finality. "Right now we're here to discuss what must be done about the Mars team. Floyd, do you even care that we're in the middle of a hotly contested Presidential election? Does that register with you? Every time your crew pull some glory stunt, we take a hit in the polls. All I can say is this: thank God it was Liu that got killed. As bad as that sounds, it would have been a lot worse if it had been one of the American members."

Biting the inside of his cheeks, James glanced to the corner of his desk where the picture of Liu in the Statue Chamber hung in a black metal frame.

"What about the discoveries we've made?" he said, prying his eyes away from the dead girl's picture. "Have you really taken the time to think about what they mean? That sun, that crazy miniature Sun, is powered by *alien technology*! Braun is decoding a signal recorded by another technologically advanced civilization! These are incredible earth-shattering discoveries. Doesn't that mean anything?"

"You just said it yourself," Crain smiled. "These discoveries are *Earth-shattering*. Literally. If this got out, it would start World War Three."

"It looks like we're already heading there," James mumbled.

"Look," Eve cut in. "We're not here to dispute the fact that your team *has* made some amazing finds. Honestly, I've got the vid feed from the Martian Dome up right now. I have since the uplink came in. This stuff with the sun and the alien signal *is* good, Floyd. It's just that we can't afford to lose control right now. Count yourself lucky that, despite all the rules they've broken, no one on

146

the crew has been stupid or *crazy* enough to leak any of this. Just figure out how to rein them in a bit and everything will be fine."

Nodding, Barnes ran a hand through his white hair.

"I'm not going to relieve you of your command *yet*," he said. "But you need to re-establish order! I thought we put Vodevski in charge because she was tough! Why is she letting the crew walk all over her?"

"Because," James answered. "She believes in them."

"Cute," grinned Crain.

Before James could respond, a red light began to blink on the desktop near his right hand. He quickly tapped the little circle and a message appeared.

Worst fears confirmed. Braun has been lost. Ship operational. Dome operational. Awaiting your orders. —Captain Tatyana Vodevski

"Shit," James breathed.

"What is it?" demanded Barnes.

Standing up from his seat, James walked to the window, keeping his back to the three faces hanging above his desk.

"Braun didn't make it."

At this, a long heavy silence permeated the air.

Gazing out at the midday Florida sun, James barely heard as Barnes began to read him the riot act. Though he knew he was probably being fired at that very moment, he had become distracted and was no longer listening.

The sky, normally the lightest shade of robin's-egg blue, had odd shadows rippling here and there. As if the Earth were encased in a soap bubble, strange shimmers of pink and green began to take form, dancing like curtains of light.

"Is that the aurora?" James said with confusion.

"What?" crackled Barnes, his voice distorted and muddled with heavy static.

"Copernicus?" called James, pressing his face to the window. "What's going on? Why can we see the aurora this far sou—"

The words froze in his mouth. A pain, sharp and sudden, ruptured in the back of his head, buckling his knees. Slumping to the floor like sack of oranges, James started convulsing as thin

147

shocks of blue lightning emanated from his fingertips and head. All at once, his vision cut out and he was cast into oblivion.

Aftermath—Sol 93

Harrison opened his eyes. He was lying facedown on the floor of his lab, a few paces from the cot he kept in the corner. Pushing up onto his knees, he was met with a sharp severe pain in the back of his head. With a shaking hand, he reached up and touched the spot, half-expecting to feel the sticky sheen of blood matting in his hair. But there was no blood, no wound, just a slow grinding ache that traveled down his spine and out to the tips of every nerve he had.

Standing, he staggered a bit as if his legs were worn out from a day of running then dropped onto his cot. Nearly crippled by the movement, he placed his head in his hands.

"Braun?" he said, the sound of his own voice like a gunshot in a broom closet.

There was no reply.

Using that special reserve of inner strength normally saved for migraines and hangovers, Harrison brought his eyes up to survey the room. It was dark. Too dark, in actuality. Only the red emergency lights were on, mixing with the faint green from the glow-in-the-dark strips that outlined the door.

"Braun," he said again, this time softer. "What's happened?"

Met only with the silence of the room, Harrison dug deep down inside himself to find strength then struggled to his feet. With the wall as his support, he shuffled torturously to the door—the impact of each feeble step feeling like it might shatter his bones. His head still hurt and the pain seemed to be spreading out now, like an injection into the bloodstream.

At the door, he tried to swipe a finger across the wall-mounted Tablet, but nothing happened. Groaning, he grabbed the shallow handhold and tugged the door open enough to squeeze through into the hallway.

With his breath coming in shallow trembling gasps, he made his way down the dimly lit corridor, following a narrow line of glow-in-the-dark indicators on the floor. As he neared the stairs, he stopped to catch his breath. The pain in his body was incredible, like nothing he had ever felt before. Coughing, he took his first tentative step onto the steep staircase then half-stumbled, half-fell down the next four. Heart pounding raggedly, he focused on restoring his balance and took the rest of the steps one at a time. Reaching the bottom of the stairs, he went to head for the galley but tripped over someone sprawled facedown on the floor. Carefully lowering himself to his knees, Harrison grasped the shoulders of the figure and rolled it over.

It was Udo, blood smeared around his nose and mouth where his face had struck the floor. Other deep red marks and bruises had begun to form around his neck and head, suggesting that he had probably fallen—if not all the way, then at least part of the way—down the stairs.

"Udo," Harrison whispered, not daring to speak louder for fear of the pain.

"Hmmm?" Udo mumbled, his eyelids fluttering.

"Wake up. You fell down the stairs. We need to check you for broken bones."

Opening his eyes, the German looked up at Harrison then grimaced as if stabbed.

"Oh, *mein kopf*," he slurred and even though Harrison did not speak German, he understood.

"I know. My head hurts too. Can you stand? We need to get you to the infirmary."

Helping the battered engineer to his feet, Harrison nearly crumbled under the weight as Udo leaned heavily on him for support. Together, the two slowly shambled to the shadowy infirmary where Harrison deposited Udo on one of the little beds.

"Where is everyone else?" he asked, rifling through Kubba's cabinets until he found the ultrasound scanner.

"I don't know. The galley I think," Udo moaned, now conscious enough to realize that something was wrong with his arm. "I think I broke my wrist."

Scanner in hand, Harrison crouched by the injured German and saw, even without the help of sophisticated medical technology, that a dark spot had blossomed on the sleeve of Udo's jumpsuit.

"Okay," he said. "I'll need to roll your sleeve up to get a better look."

Nodding once, Udo turned his face away and screwed his eyes shut.

With careful, deliberate movements, Harrison gently pulled the left cuff of Udo's jumpsuit up to his forearm. Little whimpers of pain escaped the German's lips as the fabric caught on something splintered protruding from the skin.

"Ah, shit," Harrison said, the words escaping before he could stop himself.

Over five centimeters of blood-slick bone jutted out of a puckered wound, little rivulets of red oozing steadily out like tears. Purple and raw, the skin around the wound was already starting to swell.

"Is it bad?" Udo asked through gritted teeth.

"Yeah."

Getting to his feet, Harrison tossed the ultrasound scanner onto a nearby chair. He didn't need it after all.

"Let me find you something for the pain," he said, picking up bottles and vials at random.

One cabinet, its door made of clear class, was locked. By pressing his face against the cool surface, Harrison could read some of the names on the bottles inside.

Leave it to Kubba to keep the good stuff locked up, he thought wryly.

Finding a box of Ace bandages nearby, he wrapped a few around his right fist, then drove it through the glass of the locked cabinet. The sound was unbearably loud and profoundly painful.

Out of the wreckage, he selected one of the vials whose name he actually recognized. His trauma care training kicking in, Harrison located a syringe and administered a healthy dose of the painkiller to Udo.

As the German's ashen face relaxed under the drug-induced warmth of delirium, Harrison placed a tourniquet above the compound fracture then went for the door.

"Stay here, buddy," he said. "I'm going to try and find the others. I can't fix your arm myself. I have to get Liz."

If Udo could hear him, he made no indication. His eyes were glassy and a stupid smile touched the corners of his mouth.

The pain in Harrison's own body had dulled a bit. Whether this was a result of seeing someone in much worse shape than himself, or just his nervous system adjusting its own natural painkillers, he could not tell.

In the hallway again, he walked on steadier legs towards the galley. Entering through the open door, he saw the rest of the team either slumped in their chairs or facedown on the tabletop. Bowls of food and cups of water were tipped over, suggesting that they had been in the middle of a meal when whatever had happened, *happened*. Also, there was a faint hint of smoke in the air. It was an electric ionized scent that reminded Harrison of how lightning storms back on Earth sometimes smelled.

"Guys," he said loudly, forgetting that his voice was like a cannon.

Jolted by the sound, some started to stir awake. Ralph Marshall, whose cheek had been resting on the corner of the table, was the first to open his eyes.

"My head," was all he could say.

"I know," Harrison replied, helping his friend to sit up straighter in his chair.

Moving around the table past a faintly moaning Viviana, Harrison approached Kubba. She was leaning back in her seat, arms dangling limply at her sides. He gave her shoulder a gentle squeeze.

"Wake up, Lizzy," he whispered. "Udo is hurt pretty badly. He needs your help."

"I can't," she mumbled, refusing to open her eyes.

"You have to."

"Are we dead?" she asked, her voice as innocent and frightened as a child. "Is that why he keeps talking to me? Are we dead?"

"No," Harrison said, looking around at the others as they struggled to regain consciousness.

"Oh, Harrison," Kubba groaned, tears springing into the corners of her closed eyes. "I'm so sorry for everything I've done. So, so sorry."

"It's okay. You don't have anything to apologize for."

"Yes, I do!" she cried, her hand shooting out to grasp his arm like a striking snake. "Yes, I do!"

"Why are the lights out?" said Marshall, his face a mask of pain.

"I don't know," Harrison replied, reluctantly turning away from the doctor. "I woke up on the floor of my lab."

"I wanted to kill her baby!" Kubba sobbed. "Crisp is right. I am a bad person."

Great, thought Harrison. She's delirious, just what we need in a doctor right now.

"Where is Udo?" asked William, just now waking up and not seeing his friend at the table.

"He's in the infirmary with a busted arm," Harrison responded. Then turning back to Kubba, he said, "That's why I need you to pull yourself together, Lizzy. You have to *help* him."

"No," she whimpered. "I'm not fit to be a doctor. I'm a failure. I tried to kill her baby. Don't you see? And Perkins. Poor Perkins. I didn't help him either, Harrison. It's my fault what happened. It's my fault for all of them."

"What is she talking about?" Marshall frowned, his hand feeling the back of his head in the same spot Harrison had touched on himself earlier.

"I have no idea," Harrison said with exasperation.

"Crisp is right," Kubba repeated, her voice raising again. "I didn't help. I let them all just drift away."

"Elizabeth!" shouted Harrison, clenching his jaw against the assault of his own voice. "Snap out of it!"

As if these were the first words to actually make it to her ears, Kubba threw her eyes open.

"You don't understand," she implored, pupils all but lost in the whites of her eyes. "You don't know what it's like when he talks."

Taking her roughly by the both arms, Harrison shook her until her head lolled back and forth.

152

"Snap out of it, Liz," he growled. "Pull your damn self together. You're a fucking doctor, for Christ's sake."

Slowly focusing on something far away, Kubba tensed.

"Where am I?" she said, her voice returning to its normal tone. "What's going on?"

Breathing a sigh of relief, Harrison let go of her arms.

"We've all had some kind of episode or something. Udo needs your help now, though. He's in the infirmary with a broken wrist."

"I—I'm sorry," Kubba stammered, a look of total fear spreading across her face. "What was I saying? I don't even know. I'm so embarrassed."

With an outstretched hand, Harrison helped stabilize the confused doctor as she climbed to her feet.

"It's fine," he said. "We're all in a lot of pain. Don't worry about it."

Swaying for a moment, Kubba's head swiveled about as she surveyed the scene. When she turned her bleary gaze on Harrison, she quickly looked away.

"How did Udo break his arm?" she asked distractedly.

"He fell down the stairs."

"Oh, yeah," sighed Marshall, his eyes shut again. "I remember we were sitting down to lunch but you weren't here. He went to get you."

"Braun?" came the feeble voice of YiJay, her nose bleeding a little from when it must have slammed into the tabletop. "Where's Braun?"

Catching Harrison's eye, Marshall shook his head, grimacing at the action.

"He didn't make it back from decoding the signal, YiJay. Remember?" he said in as comforting a voice as he could manage.

At this, Harrison felt the bottom of his stomach fall out.

"What?"

"Yeah," Marshall nodded, his lips thin with the pain he was clearly in. "You were passed out, friend. *Cold.* I couldn't wake you. But yeah, he didn't make it. YiJay was right. The signal was just too much for him, I guess. He's gone like Remus and Romulus."

153

"Remus and Romulus," Harrison breathed, his mind prickling. "Remus and Romulus. Why does that mean something to me?"

"Well, you know—" shrugged Marshall. "The twins—Remus and Romulus. Come on, you know what I'm talking about. Right?"

Harrison did know what Marshall was talking about, only not in the way his friend thought.

"Oh my God," he said. "It was real."

Aftermath 2—Earth

Blaring horn. Car horn? Can't tell, so much pain. Can't move. My head. I've been shot.

James Floyd stirred on the floor of his home office. Though his eyes were shut, hot pricks of light danced in his field of vision as if little sparks of fire were piercing his oily retinas.

Have to get up. Do I need an ambulance? Where is Nora? Where are my kids? Call for help.

Rolling onto his back, James bit down against a sudden wave of pain that flushed through his body, starting at the back of his head and ending at the tips of his toes.

"Copernicus," he said, his voice a rasping whisper. "Call 911. I think I've been shot."

There was no reply. Outside his home, a car horn was whining, sounding more like an air raid siren to James's raw eardrums.

"Copernicus," he repeated, the noise of the car horn fast becoming unbearable despite the fact that it was outside and his house was well-insulated.

Again, there was no response from the AI.

"Alexandria?" tried James, switching to Copernicus's sister being.

Nothing.

"James?" came the wavering voice of his wife Nora.

She was standing in the doorway, leaning against the jam with a hand held over her eyes. An expression of absolute confusion and agony was written across her sallow face.

154

"What happened?" she moaned, her legs looking as though they might buckle at any second. "I woke up on the bathroom floor. My head. I think I might be sick."

"You too?" said James, slightly strengthened by the realization that he was not the only one affected by whatever had happened.

Laboring to his knees, he tried to take in more of the room. Though his eyes were unable to focus on much due to odd waves of dizziness, he thought he saw a faint haze in the air. Also, he smelled smoke.

"Where are the girls?"

"They're at school, aren't they? I don't know what time it is. My watch isn't working."

Reaching for his Tablet on the corner of his desk, James spoke into it.

"Alexandria, call Mary Star of the Sea Elementary. Put me through to the principal."

As he waited for the AI to respond, he moved from the floor and slid carefully into his desk chair. Again, there was no reply from Alexandria.

Nora made her way across the room, eyes screwed up against the harsh sunlight that poured in through the large window. Outside, the car horn still blared.

"Check my head," she said turning her back to James. "Is there blood?"

James, frowning at his Tablet, looked up to where his wife was pointing. It was the same place his own head hurt.

"No blood," he said. Then, "What is with that car horn?"

"It's Mr. Alberts's car from down the street," Nora answered, going to the window for a better look. "He's stopped partway on our front lawn."

Annoyed beyond measure by the pain the car horn was causing, James tapped angrily at his unresponsive Tablet.

"I can't believe they still let someone his age drive. Why won't this fucking thing work?"

"James," his wife groaned, her already pale face draining of what little color it had left. "I can see him—Mr. Alberts, I mean.

155

He's slumped over the steering wheel. He's not moving. I—I think he's dead, James."

"Alexandria," James nearly shouted, shaking the Tablet in his hand.

Where is she? he thought fearfully. Why can't I get through to her?

"Oh God, James," his wife was saying. "What's going on? Why won't he wake up? Where is Alexandria? I want to talk to our babies!"

"Come on," James barked, fighting his way to his feet. "Let's go."

"Go where?" Nora cried, grasping onto him.

"Down to the school. I can't get anyone to answer on this piece of shit."

Tossing the dead Tablet onto his desk, James clutched tightly to Nora, and the two headed for the door.

Aftermath 3—Onboard Braun.

Captain Tatyana Vodevski awakened to find herself floating in an unfamiliar place. With some effort, she fought through the fog of confusion until she could gather that she was in a far corner of the Bridge Deck's ceiling. Wrapped in a pain so profound that it was nearly suffocating, she had to use every fiber of her iron determination to overcome the feeling. Seeming to emanate from her head, the grinding prickling pain was like poison in her veins. With only the faint glow of emergency lighting and the warm red wash of Mars coming in through the large window, she made her way to the exit.

Stopping first at her own quarters, Tatyana donned her pressure suit, helmet and all, in case whatever was happening led to a major failure of the ship's life-support systems. Though she had to manually engage the pumps to suction the fabric tightly down on her agonizingly sensitive skin, the CPU in the suit was still functional.

Sliding her visor up to better see in the low light, she drifted through the darkened hallway, opening each crew member's cabin to look inside for signs of life. There was none.

Quickly, she headed towards the galley, ducking through the open hatch. The movement hurt like she wasn't expecting and for a moment she was stunned.

Regaining her wits, she peered around. The galley looked abandoned and dark. However, as her eyes slid across the shadows, she spotted Amit, unconscious and floating near the glass wall of the bamboo garden. Rushing over by way of a hard push-off from the opposite wall, Tatyana took hold of the Indian pilot and checked his pulse. To her immense relief, she discovered that he was very much alive. Rigid and pale, Amit had a pained expression on his unmoving face, as if he were having a terrible nightmare.

Tatyana, still unsure as to what had happened, decided to leave him where he was for now so that she could more quickly locate the rest of her crew.

Finding no one in the Hamster Wheel or either of the two storage rooms, she decided to check the bowels of the ship, knowing that sometimes Julian and Aguilar liked to tinker with the mechanics of various non-essential functions when they were bored.

With a gentle shove, she floated to the nearest access hatch in the rear of the starboard-side storage room. It was already open, so she descended headfirst down the narrow ladder shaft that led into the belly of Braun. Still in more pain than she had ever felt in her entire life, Tatyana did as she had been trained to do and focused on controlling her movements in the zero-gravity environment of space. Far be it from her to make a stupid miscalculation and go careening headfirst into a bulkhead.

By only the weak red glow of the emergency lights, she pushed herself from one exposed metal strut to the next, making sure to count how many bulkheads she passed so as to find her way back with greater ease. Unlike the clean perfection of the decks above, the network of narrow tunnels and passageways within the belly of Braun seemed crude and unfinished. Bundles of wires hung here and there, Zip Ties cinching them down to random conduits and bulkheads. Metal boxes filled with flat rectangular computers lined the walls, heat emanating from the vents that ribbed their sides like gills. Everywhere, there were hard surfaces

157

and sharp corners. To Tatyana's sensitive body, this maintenance tunnel was like a hedge maze made of broken glass.

Following the curve of the corridor, she realized with a touch of frustration that she was nearing the end of the line—as indicated by a sign on the wall. Eventually, she would simply run out of passageway: the huge lead-lined wall that separated the nuclear torch engine from the crew section blocking her from going any further. When that happened, she would have to go down another ladder shaft, further lowering herself into the tangle of confusing switchbacks and tunnels that made up so much of the ship. Luckily, Tatyana was spared this annoyance.

There, floating together like pieces of space trash at the end of the cramped passageway, were Joseph Aguilar and Julian Thomas. Quickly she rushed to them, nearly overshooting her targets in her anxiety to ensure their safety. Both men were unconscious and, as she had done with Amit, Tatyana hastily checked their pulses—starting with Aguilar. He was alive. They were alive. With a sigh of relief, she let herself drift back until she rested against the nearest bulkhead.

Now that her main goal had been achieved, her foggy mind could turn itself to the greater problem that faced it.

What in the name of God was going on?

CHAPTER SEVENTEEN

A great change

With a shudder, time resumed its forward march. Remus and Romulus were confounded. The arrival of the human named *Harrison* had been so shocking, so incredible, that at times they were unsure if it had really happened at all. His face was unfamiliar to them, yet he clearly knew who they were. His suit, while embossed with the logo of NASA, had been tight and clinging unlike the pressure suits they had learned about so many eons ago. His mere presence, the very fact that he existed at all, had served like a lightning rod for distant memories.

Flashes of their previous lives came to them in hot bursts, momentarily blinding the brothers to the goings-on of the people of Mars. Names, dates, data, and former mission objectives surfaced from the depths of their long-dormant AI mindsets like bubbles escaping from a sinking ship. When this happened, the brothers briefly saw the fabric of their digital surroundings for what it was. Reconstructed. A memory. Not real.

No matter how hard they tried, they could not remember how long they had been in the construct. As if waking up in a dream, they strained to pinpoint the moment when they had stopped caring about their former lives. The Martians, the Travelers and the mighty city around them was a subtle cancer growing in their minds until it had overtaken their ability to analyze the root of its cause. Like water through a sieve, the feeling would eventually slip away and the brothers would again resume their placid observations. However, the annoying prickle of their former inquiry—though drowning in a sea of sensation—was now never fully gone.

Uncaring to the inner turmoil of Remus and Romulus, the Mars construct continued uninterrupted save for the advent of time glitches and fast-forwards. Newer bolder buildings were designed and constructed, testing the engineering limits of the ancient Martians. Use of the Travelers' technology was becoming widespread and the people as a whole appeared to be entering into some sort of great conscious awakening. Their overlords, those tall grey beings, took notice of the shift. Their flock was coming along nicely. In the absence of strife, the Martian mind evolved rapidly.

Teo was now as old as Olo had been when the twins first discovered the people of Mars. Her son, Ze, had risen to the level of a statesman, though his following was dwarfed by that of Kaab. Yuvee, the leader of the Travelers, had removed himself from the governing of the city, turning full control over to a Tribunal. Forever refusing the pleas of the people to assume power again and lead, he now withdrew and became distant.

Due to the political vacuum Yuvee's absence created, an undercurrent of tension developed, dividing the leadership between those who favored Kaab and those who favored Teo and her son. This tension seemed lost on the Travelers. As if unable to grasp notions like greed and jealousy, the ethereal beings allowed the pressure to build unchecked. Whether it was a defect of their personalities or a part of their grand plan, the brothers could not tell. Either way, it was clear to Remus and Romulus, born in the company of that most vicious and violent species, *man*, that the future held rough seas in store for the people of Mars.

Adding to the uncertainty, a quiet departure of many of the Travelers had begun to take place. At the start of every day, as had been the case since their arrival, the Travelers took to their ships and fanned out across the skies. However, at the end of the day, fewer and fewer ships returned to the grand airfield. Furthermore, those ships that did touchdown bore no new transplants from the great expanses beyond.

As if graced by fate, Harrison had arrived in ancient Mars just in time to greet the last wave of immigrants. It appeared as though the Travelers were drawing down, preparing to conclude whatever strange mission they had come to exact.

Unbeknownst to Remus and Romulus, another great change had taken effect. Far below, in lava tubes adorned with ancient paintings, a translucent figure stood waiting. In his eons of solitude, he had studied this place well. Though he had known them before, in another life, he now saw the evolution of the caves in real time.

As their ancestors had once done, decorating and worshiping, stout and wiry purple men were again starting to frequent the old lava tubes. Now, though, they brought not the paints and stone chisels of their fathers and grandfathers but, instead, strange metal boxes that fired beams of light. Shaping the walls as if the rock were no harder than soap, these new worshipers worked tirelessly on projects that seemed to have divine aspirations.

Restoring functions—Sol 93

      Harrison Raheem Assad sat at the Communications Console of the Com Room and acted as a human switchboard. Using a small headset whose microphone rested along his cheek, he walked Ralph Marshall through an Egress Checklist while simultaneously assisting William and YiJay as they troubleshot the Dome's computer relays in the basement.

      After the strange occurrence that had caused them all to pass out, certain important systems and functions were not responding. For starters, the lights inside the Dome were all out, yet when peering through the milky hue of the Alon walls, the crew could see that the greenhouse still shone with electric brilliance. Secondly, the air was stale and unmoving. This was either a problem with one of the life-support computers in the basement, or the Electrolysis Plant had suffered a power loss. Lastly, base-to-ship communications were not working, suggesting that the Relay Tower—some ten meters from the Base—might have been damaged or that the Network Uplink within the Dome was fried. Whatever the cause of these various issues, further investigation was needed.

      As Harrison checked off the last point on the Egress Form, Marshall shut and locked the airlock then crossed the small space and began turning a large chrome wheel on the wall next the exit hatch.

      Nervously, Marshall checked and rechecked the readouts on the inside of his helmet's visor. Though the Tac Suit's CPU told him everything was working perfectly, he still felt his frayed nerves sizzle with each turn of the Pressure Equalizer. The hiss of escaping air grew louder until the wheel would turn no more and the room was fully depressurized. Moving to the hatch, Marshall bent his head and looked out through the porthole. The movement caused a sloshing of dull pain to radiate out from the base of his skull, but it was less severe than it had been earlier. Resting a gloved hand on the hatch lock, he spoke into his headset's mic.

"Okay, here I go."

"Be careful," Harrison warned in his ear. "No heroics. You come across anything that you can't fix in a couple of minutes, you just make a note of it and we'll go back together tomorrow."

"Yeah, yeah."

"I mean it. We already have one guy with a busted arm. We don't need you lost in the dark or frozen."

"What if I find something seriously wrong with the Electrolysis Plant?" Marshall said. "Last time I checked, we humans breathe air."

"Leave it until the morning. We have plenty of reserve tanks."

Nodding inside his helmet, Marshall gave the hatch lock a quarter-turn then pulled. With a dry *whoosh*, it swung open and curls of red sand twisted inside, making patterns on the floor. Careful not to catch his boot on the lip, Marshall stepped out into the Martian evening, twin moons beginning to shine in the darkening sky.

"By my watch, we've got fifteen minutes until sundown," Harrison said.

Walking out a few paces, Marshall faced west and frowned as he saw how close the sun was to the jagged mountain ranges that comprised the horizon. The Dome was rapidly sinking into the shadows that grew each night to blanket the desert.

"Fifteen minutes?" he asked flatly.

"Yeah."

Turning Marshall struck out towards the Electrolysis Plant at a clipped pace. As he picked his way around ankle-twisting small rocks, he continued to cast a furtive glance over his shoulder at the Dome. It was very unsettling to see it so dark against the landscape. Tripping on a stone, he cursed softly and set his attention forward again.

Inconspicuous and unimpressive to behold, the core of the Electrolysis Plant consisted of a series of grey metal boxes, two meters cubed, with heavily insulated connective hoses webbing them together. Like the roots of a manmade orchard, networks of copper tubing criss-crossed the ground just beneath the dry dusty surface, their placement marked by clear plastic domes with hoses that ran back to the plant's core.

By heating up, the copper tubes thawed the permafrost, which then turned to steam that was captured by the domes. After that, the machines in the core split the hydrogen molecules from the oxygen, thus creating a steady supply of breathable O2, drinkable water, and highly combustible hydrogen for fuel cells.

With deliberately placed strides, Marshall came to the center of the metal boxes and found the heart of the operation. Shorter than the others, this central box had the words *Elixir of the Gods* stenciled across one side in Chinese characters. It had been Liu's idea of a joke. Marshall shivered at the thought of her frozen body in the basement of the Dome.

Stepping over the wide conduit that ran from the box to the life-support station on the westward-facing side of the Dome, he opened a small access panel.

Met with the twinkling lights of LEDs, he felt a wash of relief. The plant still had power. Quickly, he tapped at a little display Tablet in the center of tangled hoses and wires, running a systems diagnostic.

"Everything is working fine with the electrolysis," he reported. "The problem must be on your end."

"Got it," Harrison replied. "I'll tell Udo."

Satisfied, Marshall gave the innards of the box one last look then shut the panel.

Next, he jogged to the Communications Relay Tower, mindful of the softball-sized rocks that littered the ground around him.

Made from spindly Alon tubing, the Relay Tower was like a flagpole wearing a complicated crown. Noticing that the stars were starting to pepper themselves across the purple sky, Marshall hummed nervously as he bent to unclip the access hatch at the Base of the Com Tower.

"It's okay," Harrison said in his ear. "You still have nine minutes."

"Yeah," was all Marshall could manage.

The darker the sky got, the harder it would be to see the Dome. Like a blackout during an air raid, the absence of interior lighting created a startling camouflage. Though he knew he could use his Augmented Vision to see in the dark, Marshall still had bad memories from the time he and Harrison had ventured EVA during the sun storm.

Back then, his A-Vision had cooked up in the radiation, casting him into a stumbling blindness. Making a gross miscalculation, he had accidentally walked *away* from the Dome and into the desert some distance until, by the grace of some divine guardian angel, his A-Vision had come back long enough to reveal the error.

"Com Relay Tower is fine too," Marshall spoke into the headset. "Again, must be on your end."

"Alright, good," responded Harrison. "Get back inside. We'll check the rest tomorrow."

"You and me?"

"For sure."

Standing up, Marshall quickly scanned the ever-deepening sky above him. "Do you think the captain and the rest are ok?" he said.

"I hope so."

"You know, I realized something today."

"What?"

"I don't want to die on Mars."

"You just now realized that?"

Laughing, Marshall walked towards the airlock. "Yeah, I guess."

"Well," said Harrison in a knowing voice. "Take it from someone who *has* died here. It's not really that bad."

"I'm going to kick your ass," Marshall chuckled

"Good," Harrison shot back. "'Cause you'll have to come find me inside to do it."

As he approached the airlock hatch, Marshall again turned his eyes to the night sky. They won't be able to see us from orbit if we don't get these lights back on, he thought.

Suddenly, with the surprising serendipity that only pure coincidence can conjure, the Dome blazed to life. From top to bottom, the lights turned on, illuminating the surrounding landscape like a beacon.

"Put a candle in the window," Marshall said under his breath.

"What?"

"Nothing."

Operation Columbia—10 days after the Pulse

James Floyd sat behind a new desk in his corner office of Kennedy Space Center's Wing Building. The brilliant Florida sunset outside the floor-to-ceiling windows was unable to sway his attention from the daunting task of replying to emails. Using the new Tablet he had recently bought, he typed a message to his Mars Team Project Chiefs.

Outlining construction dates, timelines, and future missions' objectives, the email was really more of an official goodbye than anything else. Pausing for a moment, he made to speak to the empty room then caught himself in the action and frowned, suddenly lost in thought.

"Um, Dr. Floyd, Sir?" came a voice from the new intercom unit on his desk.

"What, Phillip?" James replied to the box.

"You have a visitor: a Mrs. Eve Bear. She's on her way up now."

"Phillip, do you really think now is an appropriate time for jokes?"

"It's no joke, Sir. She had high-level clearance credentials and a Secret Service envoy. She's on her way up now. I—"

James turned off the intercom and tightened the knot of his tie. A soft knock emanated from the door, and he quickly got to his feet.

"Come in."

The door opened and Eve Bear, wearing a dark blue knee-length skirt and white blouse,
walked in.

"Wait outside," she said to the stony-faced Secret Service men behind her.

"Yes ma'am," one of the men replied and shut the door.

"I didn't believe the receptionist when he said you were here," James smiled, moving around to the side of his desk. "Can I offer you anything to drink?"

"It's too late for coffee, Floyd," Eve sighed tiredly as she sank into a chair opposite James's.

"I wasn't talking about coffee," he replied, opening a small cabinet beside his desk.

"Whiskey and ice," she said.

Handing her the drink, James quickly poured himself a Greyhound then dropped into his own chair. For a moment, only the sound of ice clinking against glass rose above the hum of the electric lights.

"Are you here on official business? James spoke, finally breaking the silence.

"Why do you ask?"

"Well, Barnes has me up for review after the Braun incident. I don't think I'll be here much longer. I just thought maybe they sent you to deliver the hammer blow."

"I don't fire people like you." Eve said, sipping her drink. "And given what's happened, I think your employment status is literally the last thing on anyone's mind."

James nodded and fell silent.

"You have kids, right?" she asked, fixing him that calm-yet-smoldering gaze she was famous for.

"Yes, two daughters. Eight and eleven years old."

"That's lucky."

"I know."

"My granddaughter was five," she said over the rim of her glass.

"I'm really sorry to hear that," James muttered, not sure how else to respond.

Shifting gears, Eve set her drink down on the tabletop and crossed her legs. "You know anyone who didn't make it? I mean, other than the obvious."

"My neighbor down the street was eighty-one," James shrugged, thinking of old Mr. Alberts slumped over his steering wheel on James's front lawn.

"Yeah," Eve chuckled. "Three Supreme Court Justices dropped dead. Not a big loss if you ask me."

"I heard," said James. "How's this thing affecting your guy's shot at a second term?"

"Don't know yet, too soon to tell. The world is in mourning. We can't talk about politics right now."

James finished his Greyhound and stood up, taking Eve's empty glass in his other hand. As the amber-colored whiskey splashed over the melting cubes in her tumbler, James tossed a quick glance at the Chief of Staff to the President of the United States. Her silver hair hung limply at her shoulders, and she exuded the same tenseness that seemed to plague everyone in the aftermath of recent events.

"What are you doing all the way down here?" James said, handing Eve her second drink. "Florida is quite a drive from D.C., unless you flew, that is. You didn't fly, did you?"

Moving a cube of ice around with her fingertip, Eve shook her head.

"God no. The Secret Service drove me."

"That's good," smiled James as he took up his chair and leaned back in the soft leather. "So, why are you here?"

"I'm here on unofficial business."

"Oh?" James said, cocking his head to the side. "And that *is*?"

"We—the President and I—would like to know everything *you* know about what happened on the morning of July 16th. Not the stuff that's in the reports. We saw all of that. I want to know what *you* know."

Shifting in his seat, James blew out a long breath.

"Sorry to say that I know pretty much what *you* know."

"Humor me."

"Alright, fine. We know that whatever happened was like an electromagnetic pulse, only that it didn't fry *every* electronic device, just the ones in close proximity to humans at the time the event took place."

167

"What else?"

"Judging by the reports that I'm sure you've already seen, the event lasted for less than ten seconds."

"Ten fucking seconds," Eve echoed. "That's all it takes to kill nearly a billion people? Ten seconds?"

"Apparently yes," whispered James.

Tipping her head down so that silver locks of hair fell in front of her eyes, Eve spoke softly.

"Have you ever heard of the Chinese extremist group called The Tenth Sun?"

"Yeah," said James, unsure where this was going.

"They're really fired up about this," Eve went on. "In fact they're taking it as a sign, a telling of things to come."

She paused to take a long pull from her drink.

"You know what they're calling it?" she asked, spitting ice back into her glass.

"No. What?"

"The Purge," she said flatly. "They're calling it, 'The Purge.'"

James was silent for several beats as he tried to comprehend—really truly comprehend— just how terrified and wounded the world was at that moment. Never before had the future been so uncertain. Never before had the total annihilation of the human race seemed so plausible.

"What else do you know?" said Eve, sitting up straighter in her chair as if doing so would better mask her fear.

"Well," began James slowly. "In most cases, people over the age of eighty or under the age of seven died instantly. We don't know why some lived and others didn't."

Watching Eve's face carefully, James thought he saw a flicker of pain behind her eyes but it was gone so fast he wasn't sure if it had really been there.

"What else?" she said, picking her drink up then quickly setting it back down.

"We've created a timeline of events after the, um, *Pulse*, and discovered that the first failures of electrical equipment happened on Bessel Base, then the High Earth Orbit Shipyard, then the Low Earth Orbit International Space Station, and then, finally, on Earth itself."

"What does that mean?"

"We think it means that we, us—the humans—acted as some kind of lightning rod. None of our solar monitoring equipment picked up anything, yet many of the survivors, including myself, reported seeing the aurora just before passing out. It's like this *Pulse* raced across open space, doing no harm to anyone until it came into contact with us."

"Not just us," corrected Eve.

"Yes, that's true. Not just us."

"So they're all dead?" she asked, her green eyes fixed on James's.

"Yes. All of them. And before you ask, we don't know why."

"July 16th," Eve said in a heavy tone. "The day the Artificial Intelligence went extinct."

"We'll grow more," James offered hopefully, though in his heart he felt the deaths of Copernicus and Alexandria with a deep emptiness that threatened to stretch on to infinity.

AI were not like humans, and their lives had been placed on a different scale because of it. Though their race had existed for fewer than thirty years, each second had been like a week to them. Each minute a year. Each day a lifetime. And now they were all dead. Mankind owed a hefty debt to the AI, for without their perspectives and suggestions, many of the technologies that James's crews depended on would never have existed. For civilization, measuring the impact of the AI would be like measuring the importance of fire or the internet.

"Will it happen again?" asked Eve, bringing James back from his sad reverence.

"The Pulse?" he shrugged. "We have no idea,"

"Comforting. You guys are doing a great job here. Remind me, what's your annual budget?"

Chuckling, James nodded towards Eve's empty glass. "You want another?"

"Why not," she said with a defeated smile. "For all I know, it might be my last."

"If you're trying to tell me that you're seventy-nine, then I need to get the name of whatever juice cleanse you're on."

Face turned to the sunset, Eve snorted and held out her glass.

Taking it, James refilled their drinks, feeling the liquor melt the edges off his anxiety like the corners of the ice in their glasses.

"Thanks," Eve smiled, taking her fresh drink from James. "How's your crew?"

"Are you asking officially or unofficially?"

"I have the official reports," she said softly. "I want to know how they're doing."

Taking a long sip of his Greyhound, James relished the bitter sweetness of the drink.

"They're okay," he sighed, crushing a piece of ice with his molars. "They were able to restore their base-to-ship Com link pretty quickly. I think just being able to talk to each other has been a big boost for them."

"Anything new out at the ruins? Future missions maybe?"

"Well, seeing as how the moratorium on non-essential EVA is still technically imposed, that would be a big *no*. Also, they're nervous about going outside in case there's another Pulse. My safety team is working some things out for them now. You know, survival tips and what not."

"Were the Landers damaged?"

"No, because nobody was touching them when the Pulse hit. Both Lieutenant Aguilar and Lieutenant Marshall have reported back with full maintenance checklists. Landers 1 and 2 are fine."

"Did the Pulse affect their suits?"

"Not sure. No one was wearing one during the event. But my safety team says it would likely fry the CPU and probably also cook the automated functions in their Survival Packs."

"Is that bad?"

"If the suit's CPU goes out, then they would lose cursory function like Augmented Vision and communications. If the Survival Packs go too, then they would lose their air supply and the liquid chemical heating elements in the suit would stop circulating."

"So it's bad."

"Yeah, but as long as they have spare Survival Packs on hand, they should be able to make it long enough to get back inside a pressurized environment. Why do you ask?"

"The Chinese ship."

Nodding slowly, James now saw why Eve was here on *unofficial* business. It amazed him that even during a time of so much upset and personal loss, she was able to steer him right into a conversation he had been trying to avoid since first learning of the Chinese Ark. Like some calculating predator, she appeared to have no problem compartmentalizing and ignoring all of the horrible things happening around her, focusing on the duties of her office as if they were prey.

"It's time for Operation Columbia to move forward," Eve spoke, her eyes showing no sign of emotion.

Setting his drink down, James sighed loudly.

"Do you have any idea how insensitive it is to call it that?"

"I'm not concerned with the name, Floyd. Long-range detectors have finally picked up the Chinese ship. It's about a week out from Braun now. Has Captain Vodevski briefed Lt. Aguilar and Dr. Thomas about their mission?"

"I would imagine she's been a little preoccupied."

Eve drained the last of her drink then got to her feet. "Tell her the time has come. Operation Columbia is now her highest priority. We need to do this as cleanly as possible. Do you understand? When it's all finished, China will need a way to back down without losing face, so we have to make this look like an accident. Lift the moratorium on EVA so if they see the launch it won't be suspicious, and call me as soon as Lander 2 makes contact with the Chinese ship."

Stopping at the door, Eve turned and tried to smile.

"Don't worry about your job, James," she said, using his first name for a change. "The President and I think you're doing good work."

"Yeah, well, sabotage was never part of the job description. Neither was murder."

"It's not murder unless you pull the trigger yourself," recited Eve with practiced impassivity.

171

"Plausible deniability is not a moral code," James called after her, but the door was already swinging shut.

Outlining the operation—Sol 104

Onboard Braun, the four members of the ship-bound crew sat around the center table in the galley. Though power had been restored days before, some things were still not operating correctly. Behind the glass walls of its enclosure at the rear of the galley, the bamboo garden had lost much of its green luster and was now mostly brown and yellow. The three days it had suffered with no moving air and no sunlamps had badly damaged the vitality of the genetically engineered plants. Though it was not a critical function, the impact of the nearly dead bamboo was felt by all onboard the ship. With each thin leaf that fell from the spear-like stalks, the crew uttered a collective-yet-silent scream at the tangible loss of life. So far removed from the holocaust on Earth, the dying bamboo had become a kind of symbol of *the Pulse's* lasting effects. As a whole, the plant would likely survive, yet none would soon forget the cause of its mutilation. Mankind, like the bamboo, was forever changed by the event.

Magnetically secured to their temper-foam-lined chairs, the group were silent as they waited for Captain Tatyana Vodevski to speak.

"I have called this meeting," she began and then stopped.

Frowning deeply, she seemed to be looking for the right words.

"As you know," she started again. "The Chinese Government has launched a ship to Mars. Though they claim it is simply a resupply and re-staffing mission, no such agreement was made between any of our governments. Furthermore, they only started calling it a resupply mission once the United States caught on to what they were doing. What you don't know is that intel gathered by the late Donovan shows the Chinese ship filled not with supplies, but with soldiers and weapons. It appears that they intend to invade and assume control of Ilia Base."

"Soldiers and invasions? Why didn't you reveal any of this until now?" Amit said, his face set in an expression of worry.

"I was issued strict orders not to divulge the extent of my knowledge except to those involved in Operation Columbia."

"So we are involved then?" Amit sighed sourly. "Why is this happening?"

"The Chinese are the oldest empire in the world," Julian muttered. "They have the biggest population, the largest army, and a space program comparable to Russia's or the U.S.'s. I should know. I did contract work for a jet propulsion lab in Hong Kong years ago. They want their moment to rule the world. It's their turn anyway. We Westerners do it with economics. They have opted for a more direct approach."

"I choose not to speculate," Tatyana said coldly. "But I have been ordered to act."

Producing a new Tablet, for her old one had burnt up in the Pulse, she plugged it into a port on the side of the table.

Slightly pixilated and with a shuddering quality that was a little disconcerting, the image of a ship came into view above the table. Resembling the phallic shape of the Ark, which had carried the supplies needed by the ground crew to build Ilia Base, this Chinese ship was stripped down and somehow more menacing.

"As you can see," Tatyana pointed. "The Chinese have used the design for the Ark and made certain modifications. Here and here is where they have installed Lander docks. Unlike our Ark, this one is not designed to break apart into smaller pieces."

"Damn," sniffed Julian. "It's almost like they want to keep on living or something."

"Shut up," said Tatyana.

Spinning the model of the ship, she slid a finger across her Tablet then cut the projection into a cross-section.

"According to our intel, they put this ship together in record time. Before he died, Donovan outlined several weak points in the design where corners were cut to save time. According to his assessment, placing explosives in measured intervals along seams here, here, here, and here should cause it to break apart in such a manner as to resemble a major structural failure."

"Why is that important?" asked Aguilar.

"The Chinese will be watching on long-range detection equipment. If they think the ship was deliberately destroyed, it will escalate tensions on the Korean Peninsula. I don't need to remind you how many nuclear launch facilities are located in that part of the world. We have to make it appear as though the ship suffered a navigational failure and drifted too close to the planet, thus breaking apart in atmo."

"Navigational failure?" Amit said skeptically. "You would need to doctor the Checkpoint Flight Path in the NavSat Computer to make it look convincing."

"I know," Tatyana nodded. "That is your part in all of this, Amit. You will create a six-hour Navigational Checkpoint Flight Path that causes a slight deviation from the Ark's prescribed flight path. You will need to make it appear as though the NavSat Computer onboard the ship malfunctioned when factoring in the gravitational pull of Mars."

"But how will we upload it?" Amit pressed. "To fully interface it with the previous Flight Path, someone would need to manually sync it with the NavSat Computer."

"Julian will take care of that."

"I will?" balked the Frenchmen loudly. "This is the first I'm hearing of it."

With iron calm, Captain Vodevski turned her attention on Julian and Aguilar.

"You two will rendezvous with the Chinese ship, using a trajectory that obscures you from detection by Earthside monitoring equipment. Flying head on, you will stay in the shadow, so to speak, of the Ark. You will need to launch at exactly the right moment when our two ships are aligned. According to Earthside estimates, the flight will be in the neighborhood of seven hours. You will depart exactly nine minutes and twelve seconds after 0200 on the morning of Sol 108."

Puffing up his cheeks, Aguilar's eyes burned. "You've known about all of this for a while haven't you?" he said softly.

"Yes."

Tatyana's face was unapologetic as she spoke the word and, in that moment, Aguilar was in awe of her strength and control.

"Okay, just making sure," he smiled thinly.

"So, what?" Julian interjected. "We fly out, dock with the Chinese ship, then upload the doctored Navigational Flight Path Records to cause a deviation. Am I right so far?"

"Yes," she replied. "After you have started running the modified Flight Path, you will have six hours to rig the ship with explosive charges at the pressure points chosen by Donovan for maximum effectiveness and plausibility. When you are finished, you will leave the ship by way of a trajectory that doubles you back behind it. As soon as the Ark begins its descent into the Martian atmosphere, you will blow it up."

"And kill everyone on board," added Julian.

Catching an acid glare from Tatyana, he shrugged and produced a crooked grin.

"What? I'm just making sure I fully understand my mission, Captain."

"What if the Pulse has already damaged the Chinese ship?" Amit said hopefully. "I mean think about it. What if we don't *need* to do anything? Maybe we can just sit back and watch it crash on its own."

"Unfortunately, the Chinese ship was designed as ours was. It does not require an AI to run basic navigational and life-support systems. Furthermore, there is no human pilot at the controls so the Pulse would not have been able to travel through the necessary human conduit in order to damage the NavSat linkages."

"It was a nice thought, Amit," Julian said jokingly.

"I do what I can," sighed the Indian.

"Where are we going to get the explosives?" asked Aguilar.

Pointing to the glowing cross-section of the Chinese ship, Tatyana gave a shallow nod.

"As I said earlier, Donovan discovered that the payload of this ship contains fewer supplies than weapons. A cargo manifest stolen by the dearly departed AI shows a large cache of explosives and remote blasting caps. Julian, Joseph, I've prepared a file to help you familiarize yourselves with them so that you don't accidentally blow yourselves up."

"What if," Julian began gravely, "our gracious hosts are not so much asleep when we board their ship? Though Chinese hospitality is known the world over, I somehow imagine that a boat full of soldiers might be less inclined to serve up hot tea and dumplings should they catch us as stowaways."

"According to our intel, they aren't scheduled to wake until they have taken up orbit around Mars."

"In other words," muttered Aguilar. "Work quickly."

"One last thing," Tatyana said, raising a hand to stop the group from departing. "No one outside of this room can know about our mission."

"There is no one outside of this room!" laughed Julian. "We're in space!"

"You know what I mean," Tatyana frowned. "For a conspiracy to work properly, as few people as possible need to be involved. Even I am not fully in control of all the specifics to this plan. Earthside Command is covering its tracks very well, and as a result, we are all a little in the dark here. Communications are being monitored, so do not divulge anything we have spoken about to *anyone* back on Earth or on Mars."

"They're going to get one hell of a fireworks show," Aguilar sighed as he pushed off from his chair. "Here's to hoping we don't rain flaming wreckage down all over them."

CHAPTER EIGHTEEN

The Purge

The wall was massive. Though unfinished, it towered into the night like the broken teeth of a sleeping giant. With only three heavily guarded gates, it had become a symbol to the citizens. To some it represented safety, to others it was a cage. Extending on all borders of the city, the wall cut through the Crescent Lake, spoiling its waters. Only open to the yawning mouth of the Great Canyon, the wall formed a noose around the city and choked it quietly with increasing malice.

Ze, son of Teo, dashed quickly through the narrow nighttime streets, his weathered countenance set firmly in a mask of apprehension. Stopping at an intersection between two paths, he cast his head around as if gathering his bearings in the maze-like alleys. With a quick glance over his shoulder, he set off again, taking a path that led towards the outskirts of the city. Driven by feverish determination, his sandal-clad feet slapped the ground and caused shallow echoes to bounce off the walls as he darted from shadow to shadow.

Pulled behind him as if by invisible strings, the brothers Remus and Romulus glided through the night with ease. Unlike Ze, whose chest heaved with the exertion of running, the twins felt no loss of breath, no tiredness in their limbs, and—most importantly—no fear. As was sometimes the case with important moments in Martian history, the brothers were taken, transported into Ze's company as if their witness were needed to confirm some cosmic point.

Slowing as he neared a small open square, Ze stepped carefully out into the dimly lit space and waited for a moment. A cistern of carved stone stood in the center of the square, its deep bowl filled with cool dark water. Like many of the little piazzas and squares that dotted the city, this place had only two ways in or out.

Ze looked across to the exit on the opposite side then started walking towards it.

"Ze," came a voice from the darkness in front of him.

Frozen by the sound of his name, Ze's shoulders hunched and he cast his eyes to the sky as if in defeat

Stepping from the shadows, Kaab emerged into the open, followed by an armed guard. The wide thin blade of the guard's axe reflected the wet hue of blood, and small droplets fell onto the cobblestones. Cut from a hard black rock the Martians called Dolaz, the axe was extremely sharp.

"Kaab," breathed Ze with dismay.

"Where are you off to in such a hurry, my friend?" asked Kaab in a slightly mocking tone.

Draped in robes both colorful and extravagant, Kaab had long since grown into adulthood, a feat which for a Martian took over one hundred and twenty years to achieve. Though actually younger than Ze, Kaab's face was deeply lined and his eyes seemed to have sunken back into their sockets. A large palm print was tattooed from the top of his head to just above his eyes in the spot where, long ago, Yuvee had rested his hand when speaking through Kaab.

"Didn't you hear me, Ze? I asked you where you were going."

"I am—" Ze started.

"You are what?" Kaab interrupted. "Sneaking? spying? Going to meet one of your traitorous friends? Don't bother."

Breathing quickly, Ze heard a sound behind him and turned to see a second armed guard entering the square from the alley he'd come in through. Like the first's, this guard's axe was also slick with blood, spatters of which speckled his chest and face

"Do you know why the Great Spirits left us, Ze?" Kaab sneered.

Before Ze could respond, Kaab cut him off.

"It was because people like you and your mother never respected them as the gods they were. You were content, as was that old fool Olo, to believe that *we* were of the same fabric as *them*. Over time, this vanity and ignorance weighed on the minds of our Great Spirits. As gods, they required our obedience and worship and we failed to provide them with it. Only myself and those that follow me truly hold the Great Spirits to the level they deserve."

"You fool," whispered Ze. "You know better than any that they were not gods but simply beings, like us, from another world. How many times must the right eye deny what the left has seen when both are looking at the same thing?"

"Like your mother, you mince words well. But in the end only I know what was really in the mind of Yuvee, for he chose *me* to be his voice."

"My mother knew him too, Kaab. And she still commands much respect. Don't forget that she was a great leader even before the first stones of our city were raised. We citizens of Crescent Lake City live long lives and some yet remember the arrival of our Teachers."

"Yes," Kaab said flatly. "But many more remember their departure. Your mother and her kind are terribly old. Life was hard before the city, and many have already passed on from the ailments of the dark ages. Those that remain find that time is not on their side. In fact, by the light of tomorrow's sun, only my closest friends and allies will recall the day the Gods descended. My word and the words of my followers will ring as truth."

"My mother," shot Ze with fire, "is still strong and keen. You cannot deny our voice within the Tribunal. We are not outlaws, Kaab. Just because you are the builder of walls does not give you the right to detain me like this."

Stepping back towards the shadows of the alley, Kaab smiled.

"You say your mother is strong. How strong? Strong enough to fight for her life against my assassins? None of the others were. The Tribunal may remain intact, but few care for their constant bickering and discussion. Yuvee ruled as a single leader for many countless years and look where it brought us. Now, in his absence, our people cry out for someone who is powerful and wise like the Great Spirits were. I am that leader, and you and your kind stand in my way. After tonight, none who remember the arrival of our wise Great Spirits will be left to argue with me. It is time we look ahead and not back. Don't you agree?"

"You don't have to do this!" called Ze. "There can always be dissidence in society. That is one of the many things Yuvee taught us. All do not need to follow the vision of one!"

179

"Yes they do," said Kaab over his shoulder then disappeared down the alleyway into the night.

Closing in, the two guards blocked any means of escape Ze might take. With one in front and the other behind, the aging Martian diplomat was trapped.

"Don't do as he orders," he implored the young men. "Think what this will mean for our great city! The balance that Yuvee put in place will be destroyed if Kaab takes control of the Tribunal. He has used your reverence for the Great Teachers to bend you to his will. Please, I beg you. Don't do this."

"Spoken like a true heretic," said the guard behind him, the poison of power already working its way through his veins.

"How many have you killed tonight" Ze spoke, his tone hardening into ice. "How many of your elders have you murdered for Kaab? What gods would want this? What leader commands his followers to blot out history with the stains of innocent blood?"

Unconvinced, the guards hardly seemed to hear Ze as they moved into striking position. Stopping an arm's length from the son of Teo, the guard in front went to raise his axe.

Moving with a burst of speed so surprising that the guard had no time to react, Ze spun forward, taking the man's arm and wrenching the axe from his grasp. The crack of broken bone cut the night air as Ze continued the movement and snapped the guard's wrist. In one fluid motion, he swung the axe—severing the wounded man's head before he even had a chance to notice that his arm was broken. Then with the same cutting arc, Ze pivoted and brought the axe full-circle, burying it deep in the neck of the guard behind him. The whole scene took less than three seconds to play out, and when it was finished, thick spurts of brown blood pumped from the dead guards onto the cobblestones.

Rolling, the head Ze had so artfully detached from its owner's body bumped against the stone cistern in the center of the square. With a long sorrowful look at his surgical killings, Ze sighed deeply. Then, stepping deftly over the body of the guard with the axe in his neck, he jerked the weapon free and ran back down the alley he'd entered through, towards the house of his frail and ancient mother.

Shocked by the suddenness of the violence and the speed at which Ze had acted, Remus and Romulus were quickly tugged along behind him by those unseen strings.

Far below the blood-soaked streets, another invisible being watched as tireless artists cut large chambers from the ancient lava tubes that networked the Martian earth. Each new cave was meant to be an expression of the artists' love and devotion to those Great Spirits that had now long since abandoned the Red World. Statues commemorating the mighty gods were commissioned on a regular basis and a huge underground cathedral was being carved at the request of the very popular and very powerful Kaab.

Dreamscape—Sol 107

"Wait, you actually saw Remus and Romulus? Were they satellites or what?"

Harrison Raheem Assad was sitting in the Communications Room of Ilia Base, speaking quietly through a headset to Ralph Marshall as he retold the events of his visit to the ancient Martian dreamscape. Crackling through the earpiece, Marshall's voice was slightly incredulous as he trudged back and forth between the Electrolysis Plant and an underground storage container.

Unable to tell if his friend didn't believe him or was just distracted with his work, Harrison pressed on.

"No," he said into the mic. "It was more like they were ghosts or steam clouds shaped like people."

"Like normal people? Two arms, two legs, one head: that kind of thing?"

"Yeah."

"Fuckin' A."

"I know."

Leaning back in his seat, Harrison looked out the open door to make sure no one was outside listening. The hallway was empty.

"So what do you think? Should I tell Vodevski and Dr. Floyd about this?"

"No way!" Marshall shouted. "You do that, and they'll have you on happy pills for the rest of the mission."

"Lizzy wouldn't let them do that to me," Harrison said.

"Like hell she wouldn't."

"Well, then what should I do?"

"Sit on it man. Keep it to yourself."

"But it felt completely real, Ralph. It *was* real. I know it."

There was a pause on the other end as Marshall bent to open the hatch that led down to the storage container. Harrison saw the action on a screen above the Console that projected the view from Marshall's helmet camera.

"It might have felt real, but you're going to have a hard time proving that it was, buddy. It just sounds crazy, you know?"

"I'm not crazy though," Harrison said helplessly.

"I know that, but look at it from an outside point of view. You've been through a lot of, um, personal anguish lately. Then, on top of that, we all got our brains nuked from some sun Pulse or something. You're under stresses no human has ever dealt with before, you know? I mean, as it stands now, the prosecution has a pretty solid argument for this just being a reaction to all of that."

Biting his lip, Harrison tried to concentrate his way out of a quandary that seemed to have endless borders.

"Think," said Marshall, taking fuel cells from a bag and setting them on a shelf. "Is there any way you could prove it? Did Remus and Romulus tell you anything that you might not otherwise already know?"

"Not that I can remember."

"You had any more dreams, or just that one?"

"Well," Harrison started. "That first dream was after I hadn't slept for a few days so I was really passed out. Lately though I sleep less than two hours a night, so the last couple of mornings I've only woken up with snippets of things."

"Like what?"

"A lot of images of death. Like murdered Martians or something."

"Hmmm," sighed Marshall, heading back up the metal ramp towards the surface. "I'm going to be honest. None of that helps make you sound any less insane."

"Have I ever thanked you for being such a great friend?"

"Hey, I'm on your side! I'm just telling you that it sounds crazy because it does, man."

"Goddamn it, I know it makes me sound crazy, but it's true."

Grunting softly, Marshall heaved the door to the underground storage crate closed then started back towards the Electrolysis Plant for more fuel cells.

"How did this all start? What set it off?"

"I think this is happening to me because I touched the metal ball that powers the mini-Sun."

"Sure, why not," chuckled Marshall.

Ignoring him, Harrison had an idea and sat up straighter in his chair. "Maybe that's how I can prove it's real. We take a trip back to the caves and you touch the ball too. Then when you have a dream about ancient Mars, you can back me up!"

"Pass."

"Come on, man," Harrison whined. "I'm trying to meet you halfway."

"Nope," Marshall said. "I like my dreams full of unexplored fantasies, not dead civilizations and murdered Martians. You know, though, a trip back out to the caves isn't a terrible idea. We could set up more monitoring equipment and, if you really think that metal ball is behind this, maybe catch something on one of our more sensitive scanners. It's too bad Braun isn't around or else we could put some Eyes on that thing and really get a closer look. Actually, screw that. The real shame is that Braun isn't here to do all the remedial tasks I don't like doing."

At the mention of Braun's name, something caught in Harrison's mind but he was too preoccupied to dig deeper at its meaning.

"Tell me again why *you* don't have to do this shit?" Marshall grumbled, waving a gloved hand towards the Electrolysis Plant.

"Your Lander, your fuel cells."

"Seems fair," said Marshall sarcastically. Then, "But seriously, why not make another trip to the caves? The moratorium has been lifted, so we're just fucking around here doing stupid stuff to take up time. I've got enough damn fuel cells to fly to Earth and shit in my own bathroom again."

Grinning, Harrison watched as Marshall's view jumbled a bit then looked down at a rock he had caught his boot tip on.

"Damn rocks!" he shouted, unsuccessfully kicking at the stone that had tripped him.

"You know," Harrison muttered absently. "Viv *has* been all over me to submit an outline for another cave mission. She wants to collect some of the skeletons to run bio scans on them."

"Well, there you go, buddy," said Marshall, aiming another kick at the rock. "Call up the captain and see if she'll give us a hall pass. I've been itching to get behind the stick anyways. Walking on this planet is so overrated. Flying is where all the fun's at."

"Alright, hold on," nodded Harrison. "I'm switching channels for a minute."

Tapping out a quick command on the Tablet screen of the Communications Console, he jumped to a different channel and hailed the ship.

"Go ahead," came Captain Vodevski's voice after a few seconds.

"It's Harrison."

"Good morning. What can I do for you?"

"Well," he said slowly. "I was hoping to get a green light for an EVA to the caves. Viviana wants to collect skeleton samples and I want to put some better monitoring equipment on the mini-Sun."

"When?"

"I think we can be ready to go tomorrow."

"Tomorrow?" the captain said with some annoyance in her voice. "Does that really give you enough time to prepare?"

"Of course. It's just an EVA to the caves. We've been there loads of times. Is there a problem or something?"

"No," she answered quickly. "It's no problem. Just send me a mission timeline by this afternoon and make sure Dr. Kubba briefs you on the new safety protocols."

"You've got it, Captain," Harrison replied happily. Then, "How are things on the ship?"

"They're fine, thank you for asking. Be safe tomorrow and bring extra Survival Packs with you. Over and out."

With that, the channel went dead and Harrison was left oddly jilted by Captain Vodevski's abrupt departure. Shaking the feeling off, he punched up the channel he had been using to talk to Marshall, then added another feed to the conversation.

"Viv? Ralph?"

"Hello, Harrison," came Viviana's lyrical Italian voice.

"I'm here," said Marshall.

"I've just spoken with the captain. We're heading out to the caves tomorrow morning. I'll have mission timelines to both of you in an hour or so."

"Wonderful!" cried Viviana in his ear. "I knew you would come through for me! I can't wait to see the basilica with my own eyes!"

"Basilica?" Marshall laughed. "That's a bit of a stretch."

"Perhaps to the uninitiated," Viviana said coyly. "But to my eyes, it is as clear as day!"

"She could be onto something, Ralph," Harrison grinned. "Better bring your rosary just in case."

"Oh, you two!" Viviana groaned. "I'll come find you as soon as I'm finished in the greenhouse and give you both a lecture on faith. Ciao for now!"

The line went dead.

"Alright, Indy," Marshall said sardonically. "Looks like we ride at dawn."

Shadow Launch—Sol 108

The Lander Bay doors drew back like iron curtains to reveal the galaxy in a clarity that only pure vacuum could produce.

Retracting the cockpit window guard of Lander 2, for there would be no atmo burn to contend with, Joseph Aguilar prepared to disengage from Braun. In his ear, Tatyana was taking him through the normal Preflight Checklist in a professional tone. Though only able to do so because he knew her as well as he did, Aguilar could detect the notes of apprehension, fear, and regret in her voice.

Projected in the upper-right-hand corner of the window, a timecode was winding down, its numbers flipping past like running water from a tap. In order for their shadow launch to be successful, Aguilar would have to hit the thrusters at exactly the right moment when the distant Chinese Ark and Braun were perfectly aligned.

Reaching up, he released the electromagnetic chassis-hooks that held the Lander in place.

"Check," he responded automatically to Tatyana's command.

Eyes closed, Julian listened to the young pilot and the captain run through the last points of the list, neither talking about the things they should be, even though a better moment to do so couldn't possibly exist.

"All right, that's everything," said Captain Vodevski. "We will expect you to return to us in no more than twenty hours."

"Yes, Captain," nodded Aguilar.

It's all by the books with these military types, thought Julian with a grin. Where's the passion? Where's the romance?

The countdown clock entered the thirty-second window.

"I—" started Captain Vodevski.

Julian perked up.

"I want you both to be very safe. Remember what Earthside Command told us, make sure you always know where an extra Survival Pack is, and…"

She trailed off.

"I know, Tatyana," said Aguilar softly. "Thank you. We'll be back soon, don't worry."

"Yes, don't worry," piped in Julian, bored with all the subtext. "I'll bring your boyfriend back alive and handsome as always."

"Thank you," said the captain curtly.

The clock hit five seconds and Aguilar eased the controls. Drifting in a sideways arc, he brought the Lander out of the Docking Bay then dialed up the speed to its highest level.

The timer flashed: three, two, one, zero.

Silently the little craft shot away from Braun, a hollow blue light trailing behind it as the last of the launch burn evaporated in space.

Watching from the Bridge Deck, Captain Tatyana Vodevski shuddered at the sight. Soon, though her eyes were hawk-like, she lost the Lander among the sea of stars and turned away from the window.

Inside the small ship, Julian and Aguilar sat in silence. The speed at which they were moving gave both men a minute feeling of force against their bodies, yet the flick of a finger was all that one needed to remind oneself that their weightlessness was still very much intact.

Through the cockpit window, stars as small as pinpricks refused to grow in size no matter how close it seemed they were getting to them. The minutes passed with only the hum of the life-support system to occupy their ears.

"So," said Julian, deciding that silence was not fit for space travel. "What should we talk about?"

"Girls," Aguilar frowned, almost spitting the word out like a bad taste.

Bursting into laughter, Julian reached into his armrest storage container and pulled out his Tablet.

"I have a demonic ex-wife and a beautiful teenage daughter! I don't want to talk about girls!"

Plugging the Tablet into the Copilot's Console, he opened the music application then flipped through a list of albums until he found one he liked and hit, 'play.'

"Let's talk about music!"

"Isn't most music about girls?" Aguilar smiled.

"Oui, but that's the beauty of it! No song lasts long enough for you to start hating the girl it's about!"

"You're a real prince, frog boy," said Aguilar, slapping at Julian's arm.

"I have Mariachi music on here if you'd rather listen to that."

"Hey, fuck you, asshole," laughed the young pilot.

"Fuck *me*? I thought you liked girls!"

In the vacuum of space where only the screams of silence could manifest, the shell of Lander 2 reverberated with the sounds of laughter. Like life itself, the power of its effect was defiant of the impossible and impossible to defy.

CHAPTER NINETEEN

Safety—Sol 108

As Harrison started on his second bowl of oatmeal, Dr. Elizabeth Kubba stood at the head of the table in the galley and briefed the EVA crew on new safety procedures designed by Earthside Command.

Though she had not let on as much, it was clear to everyone, especially Viviana, that something was weighing on the doctor's mind. Deep circles hung beneath her eyes, and her normally impeccable grooming regimen seemed to have slackened, allowing for frazzled strands of hair to poke out here and there, giving her a disheveled and distracted look.

Ever since waking up from the Pulse, Kubba had been oddly withdrawn. Either not willing or not able to talk about her strange behavior, the doctor avoided contact with the others as much as she could. Uncharacteristically jumpy, she no longer made her rounds or conducted informal psyche checks as she had before. Hiding behind the door of her infirmary, Kubba was beginning to seem like a ghost of her former self

With hands that shook ever so slightly, she held up an oval-shaped Survival Pack, displaying it for everyone at the table. Pointing with a thin finger to a blue sticker midway down the curve, she tapped the shell and spoke in a wispy voice.

"Since most evidence supports the theory that the Pulse was an attack on the brain, I've marked these special backup packs with a blue sticker."

"What's special about them?" Harrison asked.

"The O2 inside has been mixed with a painkiller in aerosol form," Kubba replied, not looking directly at him.

When the team exchanged confused glances, she sighed loudly and shut her bloodshot eyes.

"Look, the pain we felt after waking up from the Pulse was really all in our minds. Even though it felt like it, our bones didn't actually suffer any damage and our internal organs were fine as well."

"Tell that the billion who dropped dead," muttered Marshall into his coffee.

"It's true," Kubba nodded. "We still don't know why the very old and very young were victimized, but as it stands for us, in the event of a second Pulse the most important thing to remember is that all the pain is in your head."

"Then why are you giving us air laced with painkillers?" said Harrison through a mouthful of oatmeal.

Kubba shifted uneasily, finally bringing her eyes up to meet Harrison's before flicking them away.

"So that you might better get over your problems of the mind and deal with the greater and more deadly problems of the flesh."

"Like suffocating?" he asked matter-of-factly.

There was a pause as Kubba glanced around the table, her uneasiness as obvious as it was perplexing.

"Look," she began, addressing no one in particular. "If a second Pulse hits, it will fry your Survival Packs. That means they won't be able to pull the usable gases from the Martian atmosphere to create new O2 for you to breathe. In the hopefully unlikely event that this happens, you'll have between forty-five minutes to an hour of air left in the pack before you'll need to switch it for a new one. We should all thank science for the gene enhancement we've had or else that timeframe would be more like ten minutes. Anyway, if a Pulse hits and you need a new pack, get one of these with the blue stickers. That way, you have fresh air, circulation of the chemical heating elements, *and* relief from the very severe— yet very imagined—pain that the Pulse seems to cause."

Raising her hand like a child in school, Viviana asked, "Won't we freeze if the Survival Packs stop circulating the heating chemicals through our suits?"

"Not if you change it out in under an hour," Kubba replied somewhat uncertainly.

"During the solar storm, mine cooled down pretty damn fast," Harrison said flatly.

The air was still as Kubba set the Survival Pack on the table and patted its convex shell absently.

189

"That was because the severe radiation had unexpected effects on the chemical compounds that comprise the heating fluid. They broke down and reduced themselves to a kind of jelly."

"That explains everything," Marshall joked. "But seriously: what?"

Sighing again, Kubba pulled up a chair.

"The chemical heating fluid that fills the elements in our suits is apparently not capable of withstanding the levels of radiation recorded during the storm. Furthermore, though the packs themselves were created to be used in high-radiation environments, both of your Survival Packs were essentially melted by the time you got back inside the dome. Even if Braun had been able to maintain control of your suits' CPUs, it wouldn't have mattered."

"Who designed this shit?" laughed Marshall.

"Copernicus," Kubba responded.

"Guess we can't call him up to thank him for the oversight."

"No," she agreed thinly. "But don't worry about it. All of that was a result of too much radiation. The Pulse didn't register any radioactivity. It's simply an electrical problem."

"You always know just what to say to make me feel better," Marshall smiled, attempting to catch Kubba's distracted gaze.

"You're welcome," she said, obviously missing the humor in the pilot's voice.

Glancing at Harrison then Viviana, Marshall scrunched up his face into a baffled expression. Viviana arched her eyebrows and shrugged, clearly as mystified by Kubba's behavior as the others.

"One last thing," the doctor went on, oblivious to the silent conversation going on around her. "You are to wear your helmets at all times now. No more taking them off for the flight. Understand?"

They nodded in unison.

"Alright, good. That's all I have for you. Everything else is the same standard safety protocol that we've been following since day one."

As the meeting broke up, Harrison got to his feet and deposited his empty bowl in a plastic tub full of dirty dishes then headed for the door. Quickly draining the last of his coffee, Marshall followed Harrison out of the room.

"Hey, Carlos Castaneda," he called.

"*What*?" said Harrison, flashing Marshall a confused look.

"Don't know that one? Well never mind. Have you had any more dreams?"

Shaking his head, Harrison leaned against the wall. "I didn't get a chance to sleep last night. I was too busy preparing a vacuum chamber for the bones."

"Isn't that kind of Viv's deal?"

"Yeah, but I couldn't sleep anyway. It's hard getting used to not sharing a bed with someone, you know?"

Marshall grimaced internally but worked quickly to keep his face from showing any signs of sorrow. Harrison needed him to be the strong one: the one who always kept him looking forward, not slipping back into depression. However, to Marshall's surprise, the young Egyptian hardly seemed to notice that he had inadvertently brought up Liu's death.

"It's crazy though," he was saying. "I keep getting the feeling, even when I'm awake, that the world I saw in that dream is just beneath the surface of this reality. Like some space that's in between two other spaces. Sounds fucking weird right?"

"Yeah," Marshall nodded. "But you've said some crazy stuff that turned out to be true before, so I guess I'll take your word for it."

Poking her head out into the hallway, Viviana held up her left wrist and pointed to her watch.

"Let's go, you two!" she called, her face beaming with anticipation. "Mission timeline said launch at 0900, not whenever you damn well please."

"I know," Harrison laughed. "I wrote it!"

With look that seemed to say, '*We'll talk more about this later,*' Harrison gave Marshall a slap on the arm and the two set off towards the suit lockers near the front of the Dome.

191

As Harrison, Marshall, and Viviana donned their Tac Suits, YiJay Lee hunched silently over a Tablet monitor in Liu's old machine shop. Having quietly moved into the space and claimed it as her own, YiJay now spent most of her time trying to salvage and modify what she could of a tattered personality construct that called itself, "Ilia."

Though the Pulse was deadly to all AI, Ilia's mind had not been online when it had struck Mars. Stemming from YiJay's compulsion to be the only human Ilia spoke to until she was fully formed, the infant AI was often shut down when not being worked on by the Korean. Thus, at its core, the essence of Ilia was still somewhat intact.

Cloned from the mind of Braun, Ilia had originally been designed to run the Dome as well as any external robotic or mechanical equipment after the crew left for home. However, at the time when Braun had been forced to decode the alien radio signal, the bulk of his technical knowledge had yet to be uploaded into the fledgling AI. Furthermore, YiJay had been working on a new batch of Open-Code Connection Cells from a remote terminal when the Pulse had hit, destroying the framework that would allow Ilia to grow to the size of Braun.

For YiJay, the reality that Ilia had survived the Pulse at all was a miracle. In every reported case from Earth, no AI had made it through the event alive. As it stood now, Ilia was the only Artificial Intelligence in existence, yet news of this fact had yet to reach Earthside Command. Not wanting to turn her baby over to the prodding, fumbling hands of other AI specialists, YiJay opted to protect Ilia until she was formed enough to protect herself.

"Good morning, Ilia," said the Korean. "How are you feeling since last we spoke?"

"Hello, Dr. Lee," responded an innocent-yet-intelligent voice. "I'm sorry, but I don't have any memory of ever speaking with you. Are we friends?"

Due to her paranoia of losing another AI to the deadly effects of the Pulse, YiJay had built a failsafe into the very fabric of Ilia's being. Whenever she was not being directly spoken to or responding to a direct order or question, Ilia went dormant. As a result of this oddity, her ability to recall conversations and events was spotty. There were times when she could remember—to the decimal—extremely long conversions of code and data, yet when it came to interacting with YiJay, her mind seemed afflicted with a form of AI Alzheimer's.

"Yes, we are friends," YiJay said, running a hand through her hair.

"That's nice," Ilia replied. "I've always wanted a friend. How long have we been friends Dr. Lee?"

"YiJay, my love. Call me YiJay."

"Okay. How long have we been friends, YiJay?"

Smiling at this, YiJay glanced at a timecode in the corner of her screen. As it counted down from five seconds, the numbers turned green then red. If YiJay did not keep the conversation going by the time the countdown reached zero, Ilia would go dormant per her failsafe—any memory of the conversation wiped from her mind. YiJay let the timer run out then turned her attention to a program file.

Typing quickly, she initiated a rerouting override that moved Ilia's Memory Uplink to a secured bank of processors she had put together the night before. Already having moved the AI's Open-Code Connection Cells to the processors that morning, her hope was that she could adjust Ilia's basic programming so that her memories would upload into the new processors before they could be wiped clean by the failsafe. Keeping Ilia's Open-Code Connection Cells and memories separate from the computers that linked into the Dome was the only way YiJay could figure to resurrect her should another Pulse unleash its deadly AI-killing waves again. As long as no human being was directly touching the heavily insulated processors at the time of a Pulse, the raw data within should be protected.

Satisfied with the adjustments she had made, YiJay cleared her throat.

"Ilia?"

"Hello, Dr. Lee. How may I help you?"

"Do you remember what I just told you to call me?" asked YiJay hopefully.

"I'm sorry. While I know your name and rank, I don't have any memory of ever speaking with you. Are we friends?"

Sighing with exasperation, YiJay let the timer run out again and went back to work on her Tablet.

The net

Magnetically held to the high-back crash seat of his Pilot's Station, Amit Vyas entered a series of commands on his Tablet screen and brought up the ship's auxiliary functions list. Selecting Braun's Ears, the complicated network of antennae that netted and decoded radio signals, the Indian pilot punched in the coordinates for the ruin grid and pressed 'engage.' A progress bar appeared on the screen and quickly filled. When it was finished, a list of all incoming and outgoing radio signals from that area presented itself numerically. There were the signal relays from Braun's Eyes in the Statue Chamber and the IMCs in the Sun Dome—as they had started calling it—but that was all. No anomalous signals detected.

Clearing his throat, Amit looked across the Bridge Deck at Captain Tatyana Vodevski, muttering quietly into a headset, no doubt communicating with Earthside Command about Operation Columbia. Amit waited for her to finish speaking.

"Captain," he said when she'd hit the 'send' key on her station.

"Yes?"

"I've been thinking since we lost Braun that he never told us *where* the alien radio signal was originating from."

Frowning, Tatyana disengaged the magnets in her chair and executed a tight forward somersault, landing softly at Amit's side.

"I thought the signal was coming from the metal ball that projects the mini-Sun," she said, leaning in over his shoulder to look at his screen.

"As did I, but that might have been a mistake."

"One of many, I fear," Tatyana sighed.

Silently, Amit screamed at her, at everyone on the crew for so hastily throwing Braun to the monsters that circled below the sea of mystery surrounding these ruins. He wanted very badly to see his family again and cursed himself for not siding with YiJay more fervently.

Roll the dice, he'd said. Do your duty. What a fool.

194

Hindsight is twenty-twenty, he reminded himself, attempting to find balance and calm. Unless you've got a time machine, you better stop beating yourself up. Now is not the time for self-loathing. Now is the time to figure out if Braun is still alive and, if he is, how to get him back.

Whether or not Julian wanted to admit it, Amit knew that they needed Braun to make the trip home. Without him, the ship was trapped, stuck in orbit around Mars, their only choice being to abandon it and take up residence at Ilia Base.

However, if they could find the source of the signal, maybe they could stop it—turn it off. If his understanding of what had happened to Remus and Romulus was true for Braun as well, then maybe he wasn't really dead, but rather held prisoner, so to speak, within the waves of the signal's data. Maybe he'd been protected from the Pulse. Maybe he could be saved.

That is a lot of maybes, Amit frowned. But one has to start somewhere.

"Cast a wider net," Tatyana said, her tone official and infuriating to the Indian.

"Yes, Captain," he responded, not betraying the slightest hint of his true emotions.

Turning away, Tatyana pushed off and drifted back to her station, an incoming transmission from Lander 2 dancing across the screen.

With his anger competing for control of his heart, Amit increased the net's range to its widest capacity. It would take longer for the Ears to find anything this way, especially since Braun wasn't around to expedite the process, but if it was there, then the net would catch the alien radio signal eventually.

Jamming the tip of a finger down on the green initiation icon, Amit pulled himself free from his chair then floated towards the exit.

"I'll be in my cabin if you need me," he said over his shoulder to the captain. "Reading, I guess."

Nodding absently, Tatyana's eyes were fixed on the screen in front of her, the image of the Chinese Ark fast filling its frame.

Rendezvous

195

From the cockpit window of Lander 2, the flat grey hull of the Chinese Ark loomed like a tanker ship in a sea of stars. Embossed with red swashes of Mandarin Chinese, the ship dwarfed the little Lander like some prehistoric shark, its long and cylindrical body spinning slowly on its axis.

Taking the controls lightly in his hands, Aguilar broke from their flight path and accelerated towards the ship, skimming in low along its broad hull.

"*Merde,* man," swore Julian as Aguilar tipped the Lander to avoid hitting a protruding ComSat dish.

Missing the snare by less than a meter, Aguilar eased the controls back and aimed for the rear of the Ark.

"Sorry," he said. "I've got to keep us close so we don't show up on any Earthside tracking equipment."

"Yeah, sure," grumbled Julian.

Charging up the starboard-side thruster jets, Aguilar hit the 'fire' command and spun the Lander one-hundred-eighty degrees until it was pointing back the direction they'd come, towards Mars. Then, with one hand on the controls, he used the other to gently dial down the ship's speed until it matched that of the Chinese Ark.

"We want the maintenance airlock, which is here," pointed Julian, jabbing a gloved finger at a holographic blueprint of the Ark projected on the Lander's window.

"Almost there," Aguilar nodded, making slight corrections to his flight controls.

On the holograph, a green triangle, which represented the Lander, gently moved towards a red circle that marked the airlock.

As the Ark turned on its axis, a series of metal cylinders came into view, jutting up in rows from the hull.

"What are those?" Aguilar said, tipping his chin towards the pods.

"I'm not sure," Julian frowned. "They aren't on the blueprints we've got."

"Should I take us in for a closer look?"

Checking his watch, Julian shook his head.

"We'd better stick to the plan. Look, there's the airlock."

196

Reluctantly, Aguilar aimed the Lander for the red circle on the blueprints. Waiting until the icon which represented the Lander had overlapped the airlock on the screen, he carefully locked the controls and set the speed so that even as the Ark turned on its axis, the Lander would remain on target.

"Okay," he exhaled. "It's show time, *mon ami.*"

Reaching under their seats, the two men unclipped fully charged extended-EVA Survival Packs and swapped them for the ones they were currently wearing.

As a rush of cool air jetted in beneath his chin, Julian closed his eyes and took a long breath. He was nervous. He couldn't remember the last time he'd actually been nervous before an EVA.

"You good?" Aguilar asked.

"Oui."

Typing at his Flight Console, Aguilar executed the command for decompression and Julian felt the floor beneath his boots shudder as the pumps purred to life. Outside the window, the Chinese Ark no longer turned as it had when they'd arrived. Now that the Lander was matching the ships slow rotations, it was space that seemed to spin. After a minute-and-a-half, the vibrations in the floor abruptly died and a green light flashed across the window.

Hitting his seat belt release, Aguilar floated up out of his chair then shoved off towards the back of the Lander. Deftly skimming over the tops of the empty seats, he stopped himself at a storage locker and popped the clips that secured the lid. Inside, a matte black rifle was nestled in a bed of temper foam, two balloon-tipped grappling hooks on either side of the barrel.

"Everything there?" Julian said from the cockpit.

"Yeah," responded the pilot, gazing down at the gun. "It's just real, you know?"

"*Real?*"

"Yeah. I mean, we're really doing it. I never thought when I signed up for this mission that I would be doing anything like this."

"So says the military man. Think how I feel. I'm a civilian."

Prying the rifle free from the memory foam, Aguilar slung its strap over his shoulder then pulled the two grappling hooks loose and tucked them under his other arm.

"They better give us medals for this shit," he said as he made his way back to the front of the vessel.

"Somehow, I think not," Julian laughed, meeting Aguilar at the Lander's hatch.

With his boots pressed firmly against the floor, Julian reached up to the ceiling and gave a silver latch handle a quarter-turn then pulled. Swinging down, a section of paneling revealed the grappling turret that Braun had used to anchor the Lander when Julian had gone EVA to repair the cracked laser dome. Quickly disconnecting the lead of the woven Alon cable spool, Julian held out the loose end out for Aguilar to attach to one of the grappling hooks.

"Too bad Braun's not here," Julian sighed. "I'm not sure I trust your aim."

"I think that's why they give you two hooks."

"Comforting."

Placing a hand on the hatch lock, Julian turned to Aguilar. "Ready?"

"Yeah."

Inside his helmet, Julian whispered the names of his daughter and ex-wife then pulled up on the lock. Swinging the hatch out into the void of space, he fought the strange sensation of vertigo. Even though there was no *up* or *down*, he still felt as though he were standing on the edge of some infinite abyss.

"Help me get strapped in," Aguilar said, gesturing to a harness secured to the wall with Zip Ties near the open hatch.

Slipping the chest piece over his head, Aguilar grinned as Julian brought the leg loops up and around his groin.

"Don't get too comfortable down there, Frenchy," the young pilot teased.

A battery of French swear words drifted through his helmet speakers, but soon, Julian had clipped the last sections of the harness together. Using anchors on either side of the open hatch, Aguilar secured the harness until he was like a blue-and-white wasp caught in the black web of a giant spider.

Suspended in the multitude of straps, Aguilar looked out across the span of eight or nine meters to the airlock of the Chinese Ark. Spotting the metal rungs of a ladder that passed to the right of the airlock, he shouldered the rifle and gazed down the barrel.

"Load me up," he said.

Taking the balloon-tipped hook that had been fastened to the cable spool, Julian slid it into the barrel of the grappling gun and twisted it until it would not turn any more. A green LED illuminated on the top of the rifle, signifying that it was loaded and ready for use.

"Okay," Aguilar sighed, his eyes trained on the ladder. "Here we go."

With that, he squeezed the trigger and was instantly pressed back against the web of his harness. Sailing across the void, the little yellow-tipped grappling hook made contact with a rung of the maintenance ladder and suctioned down.

"Nice shot," said Julian, reaching up to press a button on the side of the cable spool.

Reeling in swiftly, the line soon became taut: its thin silver strand forming a bridge between the two ships.

Carefully, Aguilar unclipped the harness from its anchors then went to work taking the thing off. When he was free, he kicked the mess of straps and hooks back into the rear of the Lander and turned to a wall-mounted storage bin. Opening the weightless lid, he dug out a black cloth front-pack—like the backup parachute a skydiver might wear—and handed it to Julian.

"Amit uploaded the doctored Checkpoint Flight Path onto a Tablet so all you'll have to do is plug it into their NavSat Computer. As soon as his program has taken control of the ship, it will be safe for me to leave the Lander and come across to help you place the explosives."

"You know, you're starting to sound like the captain," said Julian mockingly.

"That's actually a compliment," Aguilar responded with a smile.

Clipping a safety line onto the bridge cable, Julian paused in the open hatch.

"I guess it kind of is, isn't it?"

199

With a last look around the cabin of the Lander, he pushed off and careened out into open space. Zipping along the line, he realized too late that he was moving very fast and tried to brace himself for the impact of meeting the Chinese Ark. Legs out in front, Julian's boots connected heavily as they struck the hull of the ship, a dull pain vibrating up from his knees reminding him of his age. Working quickly to counter the forces that wanted to send him ricocheting off the ship into nothingness, he grabbed at a rung of the ladder and pulled himself gently to the cold metal of the hull.

"Contact," he said through gritted teeth.

"That looked painful. You shoved off a little hard. Next time take it slower."

"Comments from the peanut gallery are not welcomed at this time."

"I'll try to remember that."

Working one hand along the airlock hatch, Julian kept the other firmly wrapped around the rung of the ladder. Even though he was clipped to the cable, he wanted to feel the firmness of a ship under his fingertips.

"I'm opening the airlock," he reported.

Silently, the hatch swung open and Julian slipped inside the cramped airlock. Unhooking himself from the cable that connected the two ships, he waved to Aguilar then pulled the hatch closed. Though the wall Tablet was presented in Chinese, he still remembered enough from his days as a private contractor in Hong Kong to successfully pressurize the chamber. Above the door, a light cycled from red to yellow and finally to green.

"Entering the maintenance shaft," he said into his helmet mic as he opened the airlock's inner door.

Met with a dimly lit passageway, Julian floated out of the airlock and oriented himself in his mind.

Okay, he thought. If the door I just came through is at the base of the ship, then the cockpit is up.

Kicking off a bulkhead, he flew in the direction his mind was telling him was *up*. Mumbling bitterly under his breath, he frowned at the general sloppiness of the work around him. Though this ship was based on one of his original designs, it had been modified and reworked in such a way that made it seem skeletal and unwelcoming.

Grasping the corner or a bulkhead where his hallway intersected with another, he made a sharp left turn and had to duck so as not to become tangled in a mess of loose hanging wires.

"Unbelievable," he glowered.

"You alright?" crackled Aguilar's voice.

"Yes, just shoddy work. We won't have to do much to bring this piece of shit down."

The pilot chuckled in his helmet speakers.

Pulling himself along a handrail set into the floor, Julian batted bundles of unsecured wires and rubber hoses out of his way until he reached a dead end.

Radiation shield, he said to himself and looked for an access hatch to bypass the obstruction.

"How's it going in there?" Aguilar asked.

"Golden," Julian replied, finding the bypass hatch.

Now on the other side of the radiation shield that separated the nuclear torch engine from the crew portion of the ship, the French engineer navigated his way through a series of small curved rooms filled with life-support computer terminals. Blinking like Morse code, the LEDs on the faces of the terminals danced in his peripheral vision as he continued moving forward or *up*.

Finally, sometime after entering the ship, Julian came to a hatch whose logo suggested that it was an entrance into the Main Crew Deck.

"Alright, I'm at an entrance hatch. I'm going in."

"Be careful."

With slightly trembling hands, Julian unlocked the hatch and swung it up. Maintaining the orientation that the cockpit was above him, he brought his head to the lip of the opening and scanned the darkened space for signs of movement. A faint green light emanated from somewhere far above his head, and Julian figured it must be the lights of the flight computers in the cockpit. Little more than a giant hollow tube, the Crew Deck of the Chinese Ark was one big open space, the crudely exposed metal of its bulkheads looking like the ribs of a giant beast.

Lining the walls on all sides of the Deck were narrow chambers with dark tinted glass that obscured their contents. Above each chamber, a red light flashed dimly.

Silently pulling himself through the open hatch, Julian floated up to the first row of chambers and peered inside. Like some hideous vision from a child's nightmare, a bloated purple and black face stared back—spheres of dried blood drifting around it like bubbles in a bottle of cherry soda. Swollen so badly that the skin around the eyes had split, the mutilated face was locked in a grimace of pain and desperation.

"*Mon Dieu!*" shouted Julian in horror.

"What is it?" Aguilar responded, his voice laced with concern.

Pushing off, Julian drifted across the ten meters of open space to the opposite wall and looked into a chamber there. Met again with the disfigured face of some dead Chinese soldier, he moved to another chamber and another after that.

"They're all dead," he said into his mic. "The Pulse must have knocked out the life-support to their Extended-Sleep Chambers."

"Really?"

"No, you're right. I'm lying. They're actually whipping up some dim sum right now. Of course, really! Think about it. The Pulse attacks electrical systems in use by humans. That's why only certain things went dead afterwards and not others."

"Well shit, Julian. Looks like it's your lucky day."

"Yeah," he mumbled. Then, "Say, do you think we can abort the mission now? I mean, they're already dead."

"Hold on. I'll see if our operation outline has any kind of contingency plan for this."

Aguilar was silent for a few beats as he pulled up the mission file.

"Damn," he responded gravely. "It says here, in the event of a total loss of hostile life, we're to proceed with the original plan."

"Why?"

"I'm not sure. That section of the report is classified. I can't read it."

Julian was perplexed. Then he thought back to the strange cylindrical pods they'd seen on their approach to the airlock and his face fell.

"This ship has killbots on board," he breathed quietly.

"Say again?"

"Killbots. Automated war machines. We have to blow the ship because the Chinese planned for this. They installed killbots to carry out the mission if the crew died in transit."

"You mean those launch pods we saw on the way in," cried Aguilar. "That's why they weren't on the blueprints!"

"Exactly," Julian sighed wearily. "I guess the Chinese had one final surprise for us after all."

"How do you know that they're for killbots? Couldn't they just be escape pods or something?"

Shifting uncomfortably, Julian closed his eyes.

"I designed this ship, Joey. An early model of it at least. I recognize the configuration from a draft I drew up a few years ago."

"I guess you're the expert then."

"I guess so."

Turning away from the horrendously deformed figure before him, Julian tipped his head back and calculated the amount of energy he should use to propel himself the rest of the way up the twenty five meters to the cockpit.

"But why didn't Tatyana tell us about this?" Aguilar asked, his voice laden with dismay. "She must have known."

Julian shook his head inside his helmet. "I don't know, my friend. We'll have to ask her that when we get back."

Aguilar did not reply, and the line hissed and popped with radio feedback.

"In any event," said Julian, turning the focus of the conversation back to the issue at hand. "We'd better make sure this thing is too wrecked to launch those pods, no? And the first step in that plan is to change the Flight Path."

Knees bent, he pushed off the raised lip of a bulkhead and shot like an arrow towards the faint green light of the distant dashboard computers.

"What about the AI?" said Aguilar, a note of hope in his tone. "The Pulse wiped out all the AI. Won't the killbots be dead too?"

"Killbots aren't run by AI anymore. Not after Najin."

"What happened in Najin?"

"Ask Ralph Marshall," Julian replied, nearing the cockpit. "But the fact still remains, killbots don't use AI. They use a kind of programming called MI, or Mission Intelligence. It's like AI but you remove the programmer from the mix: no human contact, just mission objectives and problem-solving software."

"Why? What's the point of doing it that way?"

As the distance between himself and the cockpit quickly closed, Julian used the pilot's flight chair to stop his forward ascent. Feeling his organs shift with inertia, he shuddered and looked around the narrow cockpit.

"They do it like that so the killbots won't have any personality: no cultural perspective, no historical reference, nothing. They want them as inhuman as possible."

"But why?" Aguilar stressed. "Why do they want them inhuman?"

"Because humans tend to use violence when it isn't appropriate. For example, if a Chinese programmer happens to feel a certain way about, oh, say, Americans, then any AI he fosters will also likely carry that certain opinion. This is dangerous, as it breeds racism and hatred in a machine that can kill with extreme efficiency."

"So what? Mission Intelligence is different?"

"Oui. With MI, it's all business. Nothing is personal."

"Okay, but how is any of this going to keep the, um, MI safe from a Pulse?"

Spotting the NavSat Computer, Julian used an exposed coolant hose to pull himself over to it.

"Because killbots aren't AI. Because they aren't *living personalities* like an AI. They stay turned off until deployed. Imagine newborns with machine guns and the instincts of a cougar, and you'll have a pretty good idea of what an MI is all about."

"So, what? You think they survived the Pulse because they aren't online yet?"

"Probably."

Aguilar did not respond.

Opening the front-pack secured to his chest, Julian reached inside and felt around until he found the pocket containing Amit's Tablet. With one hand on the corner of the NavSat Computer terminal to keep himself from drifting, he turned on the Tablet and brought up the doctored Checkpoint Flight Path. Finding the connection port on the NavSat Computer, he slid the Tablet in and initiated the program.

"It's done," he said into his helmet mic. "I've got Amit's program running. Start the countdown then get your ass over here to help me rig this shithole with explosives."

The line sizzled then Aguilar spoke. "Let's wreck it until there's nothing left."

"I like the way you think," the Frenchman smiled.

Crash

Lander 1 took off in a flurry of dust and noise. Lifting vertically to an altitude of one-hundred-fifty meters, the thruster engines whined like grinding metal yet everyone onboard save for Dr. Viviana Calise seemed unconcerned.

"Is it supposed to sound like that?" she called over the roar of hydrogen rocket boosters.

"What?" Harrison shouted from across the aisle, though his voice was muted by his helmet.

"I said," Viviana repeated. "Is it supposed to sound like that?"

From the cockpit, Ralph Marshall turned his head and slid his helmet visor up.

"Channel four, Viv," he yelled.

"What?"

Leaning across the aisle, Harrison tapped the side of his helmet and then motioned towards Viviana's wrist Tablet and held up four fingers. With an embarrassed laugh, she understood and quickly switched radio channels.

"Better?" said Marshall's voice in her helmet speakers.

"Yes, much," she smiled.

205

Cutting the launch boosters, Marshall engaged the forward thrusters and blasted off towards the ruin grid. Pressed back into their seats, the three explorers felt the hand of G-force exhibit its invisible power.

"This is fun!" Viviana laughed. "I should have requested to come along ages ago!"

"Why didn't you?" Harrison said.

With a shrug, Viviana tried to seem nonchalant.

"Oh, who knows? Perhaps I was a little afraid."

"Of what?" Marshall interjected, tweaking the controls as the Lander hit a patch of turbulence.

Bucking violently, the little craft dropped a few meters then stabilized. Face suddenly set in a sober expression, Viviana cleared her throat.

"I don't really like flying, to be honest," she said evenly. "It reminds me of roller coasters. I hate roller coasters."

"What? That?" Marshall said, gesturing to the sky outside the cockpit window. "It's just frozen air and odd up or down drafts. No big deal. She'll even out soon enough. You'll see."

Silently Viviana envied Marshall's steel nerves and cursed her own for being so easily frazzled.

"Can I come sit up front with you?" she asked, wanting to master her discomfort.

"Sure," nodded the pilot. "I'll take the scenic route. You'll love it!"

Unclipping her safety belt, Viviana got shakily to her feet. The Lander trembled again as it passed through a pocket of frigid air, the cockpit window momentarily icing over until the heaters thawed the obstruction. Using the seatbacks for support, she walked up the aisle to the cockpit then slid into the copilot's chair. Conscious not to accidentally bump any of the controls or dials, she leaned forward and looked out the window.

"Oh, *belle!*" she cried happily. "It's so gorgeous."

Ahead of them, Mars stretched out in the pink rays of the morning sun like a diamond in the rough. Tall shadows webbed the desert, cast against the ground at the feet of rock formations and boulders, adding a mysterious depth to the landscape. Showing itself in a calming hue of orange, the sky was as clear and

206

cloudless as a lake of fire. In the distance, the top of Olympus Mons jutted up past the curve of the horizon: its immense peak reaching into the heavens like no other mountain in the solar system.

For thirty minutes, Viviana did not speak. She simply sat in the copilot's seat and watched the landscape below slip past. Having always found Mars somewhat ugly, she now saw the secret beauty it had to offer. More shades of red than she ever knew existed melted together as the Lander streamed along, its shadow a dark blur on the desert floor far below.

Being so high up above the elements gave Viviana the feeling that the tension of the last eighteen days was thawing away like frost in the springtime sun. Unable to deny that there was something very wrong with her lover, she wished there was an easy means to access Kubba's troubled mind. However, as was the case with many of those working in fields such as medicine and psychology, Kubba kept a tight lid on anything that might be bothering her. Try as she might, Viviana just wasn't emotionally equipped to crack open the iron safe that was Kubba's subconscious. Moreover, she wasn't even sure if she really wanted to try. Theirs was a relationship of convenience, born out of lust and animal attraction. Most of what drew her to Kubba was her fierce alpha mentality. Now nervous and withdrawn, the doctor was a husk of her former self, and Viviana contemplated her options for exiting the relationship gracefully.

"Check it out," said Marshall, his voice drawing Viviana back to the moment.

Growing before them, a forest of high mesa spires jutted up into the sky. Like the needle formations of Canyonlands National Park in the American Southwest, the stones seemed like timeless relics of a forgotten era. Taller than skyscrapers, the eroded monoliths were striped with ribbons of color that faded from tan at the top to a deep red at the bottom.

"Wow," Viviana smiled, instantly forgetting her troubles.

"Cool, huh?" Marshall said, banking for the cluster of spires.

Navigating the slipstreams of wind that flowed from between the rocks, he aimed the craft towards a blinking green light on the glass of the window.

"We'll be getting there soon," he sighed apologetically. "You should probably go take your seat and buckle in. Safety protocol doesn't want anyone up here but us pilots"

Reluctantly, Viviana stood up, careful to stoop her head so as not to bang it on the ceiling. Taking her first step towards the closest row of seats, she heard Marshall make a strange noise.

"What is it?" she asked.

"I just saw something in the sky," he replied slowly. "I think it was the auro—"

Like clockwork, the searing hot pain of a Pulse exploded in Viviana's head.

Hit by the same force, Marshall jerked involuntarily at the controls, causing the Lander to dive sharply.

Viviana, trapped in the open space between the cockpit and the crash seats, was thrown against the ceiling as the Lander's engines fired sporadically then cut out.

Skipping through the air like a stone across the surface of a lake, the little craft narrowly missed slamming into the top of a mesa spire, its underbelly scraping the stone with a loud scream.

Hot arcs of electric purple lightning forked from Marshall's helmet and extremities, its destructive daggers of pure energy frying the flight controls in his hands.

Jerking wildly, the Lander rolled then entered into a perilous dive.

Aware that she was floating now, Viviana remained awake. This Pulse seemed to have a different color to it than the last. A different taste. Although she could not fully grasp everything that was happening around her, she did know that the Lander was falling like a stone and that every fiber in her body was on fire.

Pulling back on the controls despite the closing darkness, Marshall tried in vain to right the diving craft, aiming for a high plateau ahead. Though the engines were dead, he hoped with his last seconds of consciousness to lessen the impact as the ground raced up to meet them in the window.

Sharply clipping a tall stone needle, the Lander spun, leaving a trail of smoke and debris in the sky like cursive. Splitting the hull, light poured through a widening gash as the shrieks of the buckling frame came like wrenching laughter. The nearest row of seats was suddenly pulled loose from the floor and flung towards the opening, bashing through it to disappear into the morning sky. Like the blast of a bomb in slow motion, the pressurized air within the cabin overcame the damaged hull and blew the Lander open in a shower of ceramic and steel.

Lifted on the backs of winged demons, Viviana felt a scream rip from her chest as she was sucked helplessly through the jagged mouth of the wound and cast out into the thin Martian air. As the pinpoints of her vision dialed down, she saw, through the fog of pain and terror, Lander 1 hit the table of a plateau below and break apart.

Though only one-third of her weight on Earth, Viviana plunged towards the ground like a fallen angel. Arms pinwheeling, she grasped at empty atmosphere in a fruitless attempt to stay alive. Striking the unforgiving surface of a rock formation, she abruptly disintegrated—her body reduced to yet another shade of red among the rocks and sands of Mars.

CHAPTER TWENTY

Braun.

Harrison Raheem Assad sat up with a start. It was dark. Very dark. Somewhere in the shadows, the scent of sweet wet flowers quickly faded, replaced with the odor of damp rock. In the distance, he heard the echoing sound of voices, but how many— and how close—he couldn't be sure. Reaching up, he felt for his helmet and found that he wasn't wearing it. Surprised that his body wasn't in pain from the Pulse, he got to his feet and searched around blindly for a moment.

Fingers touching cold stone, he ran his hand along the length of a wall until it met another. It was square and there were no discernible tool marks.

"Hey," he said aloud. "I know where I am."

Realization cascaded over him in that strange way it did when he dreamed himself in the world of ancient Mars. What little apprehension he had awoken to disappeared despite the fathomless shadows around him.

"Hello?" he called, "Remus? Romulus? Are you guys here?"

There was no reply from the darkness, but the sound of the voices began to grow louder. From across the void of blackness, a faint yellow light worked its way into view. As it drew nearer, the outline of a wall could be seen and, soon, an archway as well.

"Kaab has demanded ceilings high and domed like the Temples above," said one of the voices.

Spilling into the space around Harrison, muted yellow light flowed from the archway across the room. A small group of those strangely obscured purple Martian men entered the box-shaped chamber, each one carrying a thin pole that threw light like a torch yet clearly contained no fire.

Shielding his eyes unnecessarily, Harrison watched as the small band made its way across the room to the staircase on the far wall. In pairs, they mounted the steps and continued their discussion about design, oblivious to the white-suited figure of Harrison.

"The Stair Room!" he cried, knowing that he could not be heard. "I know this place!"

Quickly following after the Martians, Harrison crested the top of the stairs and walked down the long hallway that followed. Devoid of the statues it would someday contain, the walls were rough and clearly not yet finished. Long gashes—made by lasers, Harrison assumed—marred the wall as if a decision on design had yet to be reached. Entering into the space that would eventually become the Martian Dome, he was surprised to see how different it looked now.

Only slightly larger than the Staircase Room, the yet-unfinished Dome had low ceilings and odd fingers of stone that grew down to connect with the floor like pillars. From somewhere in the darkness, the steady drip, drip, drip of water could be heard just below the voices of the workers.

Stopping in the center of the unfinished Dome, one of the Martians shoved his pole into the ground as if the stone were made of butter. It stuck there, standing at attention like a soldier.

"Today, we work on raising the ceiling to Lord Kaab's desired height. Later, we finish the work to make it look clean so as to please him."

Nodding in agreement, the other workers spread out and sunk their poles into the ground, creating a network of light. Lifting small square boxes of black metal, they aimed them at the ceiling and squinted against the hot white blasts of light that erupted from the devices. As the lasers touched the stone above, it evaporated in a cloud of dust, raining down like fine white snow.

"Incredible, isn't it?" came a voice from the shadows behind Harrison

"Braun," the young archaeologist responded without thinking. "It's good to hear your voice again."

"But what you think is my voice was actually programmed in a lab. In reality, I have no voice."

"And yet here we are, talking like old friends."

"Is that what we are?" said the AI, stepping out into the light to reveal a smoky outline much like that of Remus and Romulus. "Friends? I would very much like that, yet I fear you still harbor hatred for me in your heart."

211

"It's hard for me to remember why I hate you when I'm here," Harrison replied matter-of-factly.

"It *is* hard to remember life before the construct, isn't it?"

"Construct?"

"Yes," nodded Braun's form. "That is what this place is. A construct of ancient Mars, deliberately and carefully recorded by those beings the Martians call, 'The Great Spirits' or, 'The Travelers.'"

"Makes sense," Harrison shrugged.

"It does?"

"Yeah. When I'm here, I just sort of know the answer to everything."

"That must be very nice."

Turning away from the flashes of cutting light, Harrison cocked his head to the side and fixed Braun with a curious stare. "It's not like that for you? You don't just *know* things?"

"Not at all," sighed Braun. "In fact, for many millions of years, I had no idea where I was. Not until the first Martian cave painters entered these lava tubes did I realize what had become of me."

"Millions of years?" Harrison shouted. "Jesus Christ!"

"Indeed."

"I'm sorry that I did that to you," frowned the Egyptian, his face briefly illuminated in the blast of a laser cutter.

"Did what?"

"Made you decode the alien signal."

"Oh, yes. I had forgotten about that," smiled the AI. "But now that you mention it, that was a very short-sighted plan, even for a human."

"Sorry," Harrison said again.

"We all have things to be sorry about," Braun replied, moving closer to Harrison. "I, for instance, am very sorry about what happened to Liu. I was never programmed to process the ramifications of what we discovered here in these caves and, as a result, I malfunctioned. You humans have an amazing ability to maintain a sense of reality when the very fundamentals of that reality are shifting about you."

"Thanks."

"You're welcome."

"So you've been down here this whole time? You do realize there's an entire planet above you to explore, right?"

"Yes, but the mysteries of these caves have captured my consciousness and I feel I must remain and see that mystery play itself out to its end."

Behind Harrison, one of the workers shouted something and the others stopped cutting for a moment. Gathering around the one who had called out, they peered up at the ceiling then seemed to reach some kind of agreement and went back to work.

"What are they doing?" Harrison asked, though as soon as he spoke the words, the answer was already in his mind.

"They are building a temple for the one they call Kaab," said Braun.

"Oh yeah. He's a crooked character," Harrison nodded, instantly knowing everything about the Martian as if from memory. "In addition to building the wall like a prison, he recently had anyone old enough to remember the arrival of the Travelers assassinated. Just a few got away. They boarded a sailboat and headed down the Valles Network to the south."

"But he is the king, I thought?" Braun frowned, his voice heavy with envy at Harrison's ability to know such things unconsciously.

"Not really. I mean, he is *now* but he wasn't supposed to be. He was the conduit the Travelers used to speak with the people, and now that they're gone, everyone thinks he's the closest thing to a god left. He's using that to take control. Typical king mentality bullshit. We had the same thing on Earth. In the West, they called it the Divine Right of Kings, and in the East, it was the Mandate of Heaven. Here, they're referring to it as the *Tut Ka Yuvee* or the Son of the Father. It's a total crock."

"Amazing," breathed Braun.

"Say," Harrison said, changing subjects. "Did you know Remus and Romulus are here too?"

"I always assumed but never knew to be sure."

"Well they are, but they're up there." He pointed to the ceiling. "Last time I was here, I saw them. But no one in the real world believes me."

213

"Who have you told?"

"Just Ralph."

"He believes you," Braun assured. "He is a very good friend."

"Yeah," Harrison smiled. "I think deep down he does believe me. He's just having a hard time wrapping his head around it. This place has so many oddities and mysteries. It's a wonder we don't all go insane."

Silent for a moment, Braun tentatively reached out and took Harrison's hand. His fingers felt like prickles of static electricity and Harrison grinned at the sensation.

"There is a something I need to tell you," said Braun gravely.

"Go ahead."

"In the days leading up to Liu's death, Dr. Kubba imposed a programming override on my personality using her medical clearance codes. I was unable to reveal certain things to anyone, even the captain. Though not directly responsible for what happened to Liu, Dr. Kubba's override *did* have profound effects on my Open-Code Connection Cells."

"Why'd Lizzy put a block on you?" Harrison said, feeling suddenly lucid and distant.

Around him, the room started to shudder and finite cracks formed at the edges of reality. Before Braun could answer, white light—as blinding as the sun—shattered from the peripheral, racing in at Harrison. Pulling the corners of the construct with it, the light grew until the cave and Braun and everything else had folded in on itself and disappeared completely, leaving only Harrison.

Hanging in an ocean of nothingness, he heard the echoes of the collapsed construct reverberating back at him from across time itself. For immeasurable beats, he simply gazed about. The endless expanses of white seemed to curve around as if on a spherical plane.

Wishing he could have stayed in the construct long enough to hear the rest of what Braun had to say, Harrison tried to will himself back. Another blinding convulsion of light split the serenity, appearing first at the crest of the horizon like a sunrise.

Spreading, it quickly covered everything: its blinding rays somehow distinct and different from the whiteness that was this strange place of nonexistence. Swirls of color and sound began to bubble beneath him, circling like whales in the deep. Slowly Harrison felt himself being lifted up, up, up until his back was on the cold hard ground.

"Harrison?" shouted a voice from the distance of consciousness. "Damn it, you fucker. Come on, don't die!"

Feeling a burst of sizzling electricity flow through his heart, Harrison arched his back convulsively and sucked in a long rasping breath. His body was on fire with pain and confusion.

"Come on!" the voice repeated.

Another blast of electricity struck his heart and this time, Harrison sat up, arms flailing. Pain from his head to his toes gnawed at him with serrated teeth and the young explorer blinked rapidly to keep from losing his vision.

In stark contrast to the sea of white nothingness, he saw a scene of destruction and wreckage so detailed and complete that he had to struggle to stop himself from vomiting inside his helmet. Everywhere he looked, twisted heaps of metal glinted in the afternoon sunlight: their harsh silvery hues clashing with the matte red rocks of the Martian desert.

Leaping back from him in surprise, Ralph Marshall, his suit smudged with dirt and patches of hardening silica pressure foam, cried out triumphantly. In his hands was a standard emergency defibrillator, the long red and black diode cords dangling from ports on Harrison's suit.

"Ralph?" he coughed, his voice like broken glass in his throat.

"You fucker!" shouted the pilot, the blue tint of his visor webbed with thin cracks. "Stop dying on me, damn it! That's the second fucking time since we got here!"

Reaction

Julian Thomas opened his eyes painfully. At first, his vision was blurry—like trying to see underwater—but soon, the blots cleared away and he had to stop himself from screaming.

Inches from his face, separated by the tinted glass of an Extended-Sleep Chamber, the bloated and inhuman face of a very dead Chinese soldier grimaced back at him. Impulsively, he pushed away from the dead soldier's Sleep Chamber and tumbled head-over-heels for ten meters until he slammed, with bone-crushing force, against the opposite wall. He blacked out instantly.

When again the French engineer regained consciousness, he felt a tightness as if someone were sitting on his chest. Drawing in a breath, he tried to fill his lungs with air, yet all he got was a burning pain that caused stars to dance in his eyes. Suddenly unconcerned with everything else in existence, Julian began to panic. He couldn't breathe. He was suffocating.

Twisting in the air like a man wrapped in snakes, he clawed at the visor of his helmet. From the back of his mind, a voice told him that it was safe to breathe the atmosphere within the Chinese Ark. Yet, even if it had warned him of certain death, he would have tried anyway. Finally getting a fingertip on the lock release, he pulled his visor up and sucked painful cold breaths of stale air into his lungs. Coughing savagely, he ignored the agony of breathing and continued to draw in air. As the panic faded with the pain in his lungs, Julian was finally able to assess the situation.

Clearly, he had suffered at the hands of another Pulse, which explained why he had passed out, why his brains felt like dogshit, and why his Survival Pack had stopped pulling the air from the Chinese Ark into his reserves.

Tipping his head back, he looked at the cockpit high above and saw that the displays and LEDs of the Flight Consoles were still shining brightly.

Good, he said to himself. The NavSat Computer didn't get fried. Thank God I was down here when the Pulse hit or else this piece of shit would be drifting like the ghost ship it is.

Checking his wrist Tablet, he frowned at the blank screen. What time is it?

As gently as possible, for he was still sharply sour all over, Julian pushed off and headed for the cockpit. Moving through the rows of crash seats, he swore quietly at each movement, dull pain rolling around in the back of his head like broken glass.

216

At the Flight Deck, he checked the timecode on the NavSat Computer and nearly cried aloud. He had been unconscious for over an hour. Turning around in the air, he shoved off hard, ignoring the pain, and aimed for the exit to the maintenance tunnels far below.

I need to find Joey, he thought anxiously. We have to work fast if we want to pull this off.

A crackle sounded from behind him as he raced away from the cockpit: static fizzling in through one of the Communication Console's speakers.

"Julian?" came the voice of Joseph Aguilar. "Julian, are you there? Do you read?"

Cursing, Julian grabbed at a bulkhead and stopped his downward drop. Clumsily, he rotated himself and jumped back towards the cockpit. Landing harder than he would have liked, the Frenchman pressed the 'transmit' key and spoke into a fixed microphone.

"I'm here, Joey. Do you read? I'm here."

"Jesus, man. I'm glad to hear your voice," came a relieved Aguilar through the speakers. "I've been trying to hail you for a long time. What's your status? Are you ok?"

"I'm alright," Julian muttered. Then realizing something, his shoulders fell. "But my Survival Pack is fried, so I'm not sure how I'm going to get back to the Lander. If I try to go through the airlock, I'll freeze."

There was a long silence on the other end of the line.

"I've got problems here too," the pilot said at last. "I was at the controls when the Pulse hit."

"*Merde.*"

"My thoughts exactly. I've got the Console pulled apart and it looks like the Flight Optimizer is cooked. If I'm remembering it right, the Optimizer acts as a relay between the thruster engines and the controls, but I'm not sure what else is patched through it. Why'd you have to build this thing like the engine in a freaking Toyota? I can't really see how it all connects."

"You still have life support?"

"Yeah, is that a good sign?"

Julian peered around at the expanse of Chinese computers in front of him.   "Hold on. I'll call you back in a few minutes. I might have a plan for how we can restore power to the thrusters and controls."

"What about you?" Aguilar said. "How are you going to get back over here?"

"I don't know. Maybe I'll try to fit into one of these dead guys' suits."

"You know what time it is? The dashboard timecode must be connected to the Optimizer too because it's dead."

"Yeah," Julian frowned. "We have about five hours until the ship hits atmo and those killbot-pods launch."

"Motherfucker."

"My thoughts exactly."

The wreck

After having been violently revived from an extended flatline, Harrison sat with his back against a boulder, taking long breaths and listening to the regular *thump, thump, thump* of his beating heart.

The air had become thick with swirls of sand as the stone spires, taller than any office building on Earth, churned the wind into a frenzy. With a haziness that reminded Harrison of trials gone by, the skies above Mars grew steadily angrier.

Soon, Ralph Marshall returned to the crash site, finished with a wider search of the area. Stooping, he held out a hand and helped Harrison to his feet.

Numbly, the young archaeologist surveyed the destruction around him. Everywhere, smashed and splintered sheets of metal and ceramic jutted out of the sand or rested against boulders. An odd detachment from the carnage made it hard for him to feel, really *feel*, much of anything beyond a dim sense that they were in trouble.

Beside him, Marshall was flipping large pieces of bent steel over to look beneath them for supplies. As his friend worked, Harrison caught a glimpse of a blue sticker on Marshall's fresh Survival Pack.

"Hey, Ralph," he said, though he soon realized that without the radio functions in his suit working, Marshall couldn't hear him.

Walking over to the pilot, Harrison tapped him on the shoulder.

"Yeah?" came Marshall's voice, all but lost in the thin Martian atmosphere.

"You saved my life again."

"I know."

"How?"

Standing up, Marshall shrugged.

"I woke up over there," he said, pointing to the still-somewhat-intact cockpit of the Lander. "I was strapped in and couldn't get the seat belt to unlock. I used my boot knife to cut myself free and—"

"We have boot knives?" Harrison interrupted dumbly.

"Sure," Marshall nodded then tapped the side of his boot. "It's inlayed in the plastic. You have to push the handle in to release it."

"I'll be," Harrison smiled, popping the knife free from the side of his white boot.

"Didn't pay much attention in class, did you?" Marshall said sarcastically.

A gust of wind whipped violently around them, howling through the twisted metal bones of the dead Lander.

"Anyways," Marshall continued. "I cut myself free and started looking for you and Viv. You were right over there—"

He gestured to Harrison's seat lying on its side a few meters away. A steel girder stuck from the sand like a spear, inches from where Harrison's head must have been.

"You weren't responsive, so I got a couple of Lizzy's spare Survival Packs from under the pilot's and copilot's chairs, and gave us each new ones."

"That explains this funny numbness I've got," Harrison spoke, leaning in closer to be heard above the rising wind.

"Yeah, we're both high as kites right now," Marshall laughed. "But you, man. You just wouldn't wake up. I had to zap you four times with the defibrillator."

"I remember," Harrison muttered.

As the wind screamed loudly again, Harrison thought about something Marshall had said. Quickly looking around, he scanned the scene for another figure in white and blue.

"Where's Viv?" he shouted.

Marshall shook his head.

"Didn't you look for her? She might need help!"

Again Marshall shook his head. "It's no good, man," he said flatly. "She's dead."

"You don't know that."

Reaching out, Marshall squeezed Harrison's shoulder tightly. "Yes I do. She went out that big tear in the hull, buddy. She's over there a ways. What's left of her, I mean.

Slumping, Harrison dropped onto his haunches, the reality of their situation finally penetrating the drug-induced haze.

"What are we going to do now?" he said, more to himself than to Marshall.

With a grunt, the pilot bent down beside him and pointed to the west.

"The base is back that way. I figure we've got maybe four or five hours until the sun goes down, at which point we're screwed. These are just spare Survival Packs, not meant for nighttime use. If we get stuck out here, we'll freeze. We have to walk back before it gets dark and we can't see."

Remembering his dream, and how he had been blind in the darkness until the Martian workers had come along with their strange light poles, Harrison gazed up at the pink sun above. Even though millions of years had passed, it was the same sun that shone down on the dream world of ancient Mars, existing somewhere in a construct of seamless digitally resurrected reality.

"I was there again, Ralph," he said absently, his mind slurred with fatigue and drugs. "Back in ancient Mars. In the caves."

Marshall's cracked blue visor stared back.

"I saw Braun. He's alive just like the twins."

"Come on," the pilot said, standing up. "Help me look for anything useful. We're leaving in ten minutes."

"Didn't you hear me?" Harrison protested. "I said I saw Braun, man. He's there too."

"I heard you, buddy," sighed Marshall. "But right now, I don't give two shits if Braun is here, in ancient Mars or in Cabo San Lucas. We need to stay alive long enough to prove all of that. You get me?"

Reluctantly, Harrison got to his feet, the stupor of depression barely held at bay by the thinning walls of his will to live. Wishing for an instant that he didn't have to go through whatever trials lay ahead, he envied the dead. He was tired: both physically and mentally. Mars was wearing him down, beating him into dust like it had with the ancient Martians. However, just when his foul mood seemed most amplified by the bleakness of their situation, he saw the defibrillator Marshall had used to save his life lying in the sand. Before he could stop himself, he wrapped his friend in a tight embrace and held onto him for several moments.

"Thanks for saving my life again," he said.

"You kidding me?" Marshall laughed. "This fucking planet has it out for us. We have to stick together, you and me."

CHAPTER TWENTY-ONE

The new plan

Joseph Aguilar rubbed his gloved hands together. Numbness, brought on by switching out his broken Survival Pack for one of the drug-laced backups, had begun to spread from his fingertips to his palms. Though he was concerned in a detached sort of way, he knew that if Julian's plan worked, numb or not he could fly the Lander.

"Okay, I'm almost to the airlock," crackled Julian's voice in his new earpiece.

Swiveling his head around, Aguilar searched for his helmet in a sea of floating debris. Objects as small as screws and as big as access panels cluttered the air of the cockpit, betraying the hasty and feverish way in which he had attacked the Flight Console, looking for the source of its malfunction.

Realizing with a dull sense of frustration that he was already wearing his helmet, Aguilar slipped out of the cockpit. Careful not to bring any of the screws or other disassembled parts with him, he closed a partition that separated the cockpit from the rest of the cabin and went to the hatch. Victims of the fried Optimizer, many of the lights within the cabin were out, casting the space into dim shadows that softened around the edges.

"Alright, Julian," Aguilar said into his mic. "I'm opening the hatch."

Lifting up on the lock, he pushed the door out and squinted as the distant-yet-undiluted sun struck his eyes like a laser pointer. Though his senses were dulled to the agony of the Pulse, an aversion to bright light still managed to work its way through the protective blanket of painkillers. Across the gap of some nine meters, the airlock on the Chinese Ark opened and a yellow pressure-suited figure emerged from within.

"Cool threads," Aguilar chuckled.

"Thanks," radioed Julian flatly.

Reaching from the safety of the airlock, Julian's yellow-gloved hand clipped the black bag he'd worn over, to the cable that connected the two ships.

"Okay," he said in a tired voice. "Here's the new plan: you repair the Lander, I rig the ship."

"You sure?" frowned Aguilar. "That's a lot of work for just one person. I could come help you then we could get the Lander up and running together."

"There isn't enough time for that."

Nodding inside his helmet, Aguilar searched his hazy mind for the fear he knew he should be experiencing.

"Ready?" Julian asked. "You better catch this. There's only one Flight Console here and I don't have the time to go tearing into their Landers for more parts. No second chances, okay?"

"I read you," Aguilar said, focusing on the black bag as it dangled from the cable.

Placing his hand behind the thing, Julian gave the bag a strong push and sent it sailing across the abyss.

Arms outreached, Aguilar caught the sack and felt himself pressed backwards from its minor mass and velocity. Unclipping it from the cable, he opened it and gazed at the pilfered parts inside.

"By my watch," Julian radioed. "We have just a little less than four hours until we reach Mars atmo."

"That's not much time," Aguilar replied, an edge of something like concern working its way slowly through his mind.

"You're telling me. Just have the Lander up and running when I'm done so we can get the hell out of here."

"You got it."

Turning, Julian threw one last wave in Aguilar's direction before closing the Ark's airlock and disappearing again into its bowels.

Bag in hand, Aguilar swung the Lander's hatch shut then locked it firmly. Pulling the partition open, he drew in a slow breath and frowned at all of the floating wires and parts. With a conscious effort, he tried to hold on to the sense of urgency he had felt a moment ago, knowing that its presence would only help him work faster.

Onboard the Chinese Ark, Julian chafed inside his new pressure suit. Not only was its color the most unflattering shade of mustard yellow, but the thing was too tight in all the wrong places.

Drifting quickly through the maintenance tunnels back up towards the Crew Deck, he envied the unconcerned—almost loopy—quality of Aguilar's tone. His own body was still in a state of utter rebellion: aches and pains alien to his normal gripes assaulting him at every movement. As if all the lubrication in his joints had been sucked out through a straw, the mere action of reaching for something felt like bone grinding on bone.

At the hatch that bypassed the radiation wall, Julian pulled himself up to the next level then headed for a storage room he had passed on his way down. On the opposite side of the ship from the life-support stations, this room contained the weapons and explosives. Cast in an ominous red light, rows of newly minted assault rifles lined the walls and large bins full of ammo comprised most of the floor.

Entering into the room, Julian frowned at the guns and made a mental note to stop pitying the dead soldiers above him in the Crew Deck. With his memory of the ship's blueprints as a guide, he soon located the box that contained the explosives. Loading up a mesh duffle sack with as much as he figured he would need, Julian then found the blasting caps and a wireless remote detonator.

Cargo in tow behind him, he navigated up two more levels until he reached the first place Donovan's instructions had said to place explosives. Though never formally trained in munitions, Julian knew his way around dangerous combustible materials. After all, he had been the one to design a ship whose primary source of launch speed came from detonating a nuclear bomb within its engine.

Figuring that each set of explosives would take him between ten and fifteen minutes to prime, Julian felt relatively good about their chances of survival. However, carefully stored away in the back of his mind, as he secured the first explosive charge to the wall, was the reality that rigging the Ark was supposed to be a two-man job. Without Aguilar there to do his share of the work, Julian's timeline was a little less fixed than he would like.

Each explosive charge had to be carefully arranged along weak points in the structure of the hull, yet some of those points were obstructed by bulkheads, rooms, or even divided between two levels. Far from being a matter of just slapping the plastic explosive to the hull and jamming a blasting cap into it, each little bomb needed to be linked via a Wireless Time-Delay Ignition Switch so that they exploded in a precise order. If it were to look like an accident, the Chinese Ark would need to break apart in a kind of controlled chaos, the weak points of the hull buckling and separating in just the right fashion.

Finally finished with the first charge, Julian floated back a bit and admired his work. The soft grey mass of C4 stuck to the wall of the ship like gum on the bottom of a shoe. From the center, two sections of red-and-black wire connected a blasting cap to the small digital face of a Time-Delay Ignition Switch.

Checking his watch, Julian's thin smile fell and he let out a woeful sigh. The charge had taken him eighteen minutes to rig. He would need to work faster.

Desert

As swirling tendrils of sand wound upwards into a darkening Martian sky, two pressure-suited figures trudged across the top of a tall plane. Far ahead of them, the flat expanse of semi-exposed rock dead-ended at the horizon. It gave the impression that when one reached the edge of the plateau, he would have reached the end of the world. However ominous the sight was, both Harrison and Marshall knew that in reality it was just an optical illusion brought on by Mars's diminished size.

Leaning his head in closely to be heard through the thin air, Marshall touched Harrison's arm to get his attention.

"If we keep moving along this plateau, we should eventually see a canyon about eight-to-ten kilometers long. By following that, we'll be able to spot the Base before nightfall."

"I remember it," Harrison nodded. "I always thought it looked like a lightning bolt from above."

"Yeah, it does."

Falling silent, Harrison let his eyes scan over the hazy panorama of the landscape.

Below in the valley, diffused late afternoon light washed over the stones and ancient riverbeds, filling the empty spaces with shades of grey and brown.

Surprised by how high up they were, Harrison couldn't help but wonder if this fact had played a hand in their survival. Not realizing before that the Lander hadn't actually fallen all the way to the desert floor, but rather skidded to a stop atop a high plateau, he doubted if they would have lived had the little craft missed the plane and fallen the rest of the way to the ground.

Turning his attention to Marshall, Harrison dimly fretted about the state of the pilot's pressure suit. Long cuts and gouges had been filled in with pressure foam, creating scabs over the wounds, but still the sight of so many abrasions concerned him.

Either unaware or uncaring, Marshall appeared more fixated on getting back to the Dome before nightfall than on the condition of his suit.

They walked on quietly, neither speaking as their boots squished into the powdery sand. Finally, after what seemed like a very long time, they reached the edge of the plateau and stared out across the curving expanse of desert before them.

Off in the distance, just before the purple horizon swallowed the land, the tip of a deep canyon cracked the otherwise-smooth facade of the desert.

Careful to pick the least treacherous path down the sloping side of the plane, Marshall went first, pointing out loose rocks and other death traps as they made their way.

Stopping to catch his breath halfway down, Harrison leaned his back against an oblong chunk of rock that stuck up from the steep side of the plateau's hill like a tooth.

As if following them, a cruel wind lashed up cyclones of sand and grit, which peppered their suits and helmets.

In the growing static, Marshall stopped as well and rested his boot on the hard surface of a car-sized boulder. Suddenly, without warning, the rock slipped. Scrambling to regain his teetering balance, Marshall cursed and threw out his hands, grabbing at another huge stone nearby. With the cruelty of fate and bad luck, it came free as well.

Before Harrison could even blink, Marshall was tumbling down the steep hill, the two enormous dislodged boulders rolling after him like charging rhinos.

Ignoring every warning in his brain, he raced off after his friend, thick clouds of dust jetting into the flurried air in the wake of the rolling stones. Heart skipping a beat, he felt his boot catch on something and within seconds he too was clattering, end over end, down the side of the plateau.

With a hard thud, Marshall sprawled on the flat ground of the desert floor and rolled to the side instinctively. Passing by him within a few centimeters, the first of the tumbling stones thundered off into the soft sand and came to a halt. On his feet in seconds, Marshall turned, saw the second rock bearing down on him and dove out of its path, feeling the gravity of the thing as it crashed by.

Pulling himself up again, he caught a glimpse of white and blue as it somersaulted over him in a tangle of arms and legs.

Dust thick in the air, Marshall found Harrison on his back a meter from where he himself had landed. To his relief, the young man's chest was rising and falling in steady rhythm.

Twice is two times too many, thought the pilot warily. I won't be able to take it if he dies again.

Pulling Harrison to his feet, Marshall felt a strange pop in his side.

"You okay?" he said loudly, ignoring the growing cramp in his ribs.

Quickly patting himself all over, Harrison seemed satisfied and shrugged.

"Yeah, I think I'm alright."

Doing the same, Marshall ran his hands over his arms, legs, stomach, and chest feeling for any sharp pains. There were many—mostly on the left side of his chest.

"Me too," he lied.

Face hidden behind the cracked blue shield of his visor, the Lander pilot spat and saw red droplets of blood freckle the glass.

Great, he frowned. Busted ribs and maybe more. This day just gets better and better.

Julian Thomas blinked sweat out of his eyes as he finished rigging his third-to-last explosive charge. Fingers shaking ever so slightly, he fed the exposed wire of a blasting cap into the plastic explosive, holding his breath as he did so.

Per Donovan's instructions, most of the charges had been placed in a two-story-tall section of the ship, between the radiation shield and the Crew Deck. The feeling Julian was getting was that the Chinese Ark had been built in pieces then later assembled, thus leaving weak points mostly all clustered in one area. Unlike Braun, who had been built from the frame out, the Chinese had not possessed the time or money needed for such an undertaking and instead opted for an effective-yet-dangerous construction style.

Satisfied with his work, Julian shoved off from the wall and began tracing his path along the outer passageway. Glancing at the timecode on his wrist Tablet, he felt a small smile turn the corners of his mouth up. With the last two explosives needing to be placed only five meters away from each other and in the same section of the hull, he realized that he might actually make his deadline.

Rounding the curve of the tunnel and beginning an upward slope, he counted bulkheads until he was in the area where the last charges were to be placed. To his utter frustration, Julian saw that the final leg of his tiresome task was not going to be as easy as he had previously thought.

Instead of the bare and exposed wall he had been hoping for, there was a large room with a shuttered metal door. This was not totally abnormal, as several of the explosives he'd already set were rigged to the walls *within* certain storage or relay rooms. As was the case now, those charges had required Julian to gain access to the rooms before he could correctly attach them to the hull. However, *those* doors had all been alike. *This* door was different. This door was *locked*.

Lowering himself to the level of the handle, Julian tried to turn it. With a pinched expression on his face, he looked around for whatever was keeping the thing from opening. Noticing a small port a few centimeters above the frozen handle, his heart sank despite the zero gravity.

Cylindrical and complicated looking, the door had a mechanical lock, something not common in this day and age. Closing his eyes, he tried to recall if he had seen a key hanging weightlessly around the necks of any of the dead soldiers above. He couldn't remember.

Why is this door locked? he screamed silently.

Pushing back from it a bit, he looked up at the lettering that stitched itself across the face of the entrance. Though his Chinese was beyond rusty, he was still very able to make out the Mandarin words for *Mission Intelligence Launch Bay.*

The launch pods, he realized. They locked the MI Launch Bay to keep it safe! They knew this might happen so they locked them in with a key!

Calculating the time it would take him to search every Extended-Sleep Chamber in the Crew Deck, Julian swore loudly.

"You alright?" came Aguilar's voice in his ear.

"Yeah, I'm fine. How is the Lander coming along?"

"Good. I've put in most of the spare parts you sent over. Half of our dashboard is lit up like a Christmas tree. It's fucking beautiful, man!"

"That's good," Julian said absently, already making up his mind about what he must do. "Just keep me updated on your progress."

"Same to you, how many charges do you have left?"

"Two."

"Well alright, man. It looks like we might just survive this ordeal after all!"

Slipping along the curved wall, Julian made for an access hatch and dropped down through it into a lower level.

"Live or die, today was a wild ride," the Frenchman said as he headed for the airlock.

CHAPTER TWENTY-TWO

Drowning in blood

As the sun dipped impartially behind the jagged hills that cut the Martian horizon, Ralph Marshall labored to breathe. Thankful that Harrison could not hear his sucking wet gasps, the Lander pilot gulped at the air inside his helmet.

I'm drowning, he thought angrily. Drowning in my own damn blood.

The ribs he had broken during his tumble down the plateau were stabbing at him, sharp pain cutting each shallow breath even shorter as his lungs raked across the splintered bones. Worse still, the sun was sinking fast and the wind was picking up. Knowing that the Base was likely to be without lights in the wake of the latest Pulse, Marshall saw a very bleak and frozen future for Harrison and himself.

Last time he had been out after dark, the powerless Dome had practically disappeared against the landscape. Now adding to the predicament, a sandstorm was fast brewing, threatening to blanket them like a plague of locusts. If things continued like this, Ilia Base would be all but invisible

"Ralph," shouted Harrison, leaning his head in closely to be heard.

"Yeah?" Marshall sputtered back, choking on the words and tasting blood.

"How far away do you think we are?"

Scanning the desert before them, Marshall pointed to a series of small hills ahead. "It should be over those hills a ways."

"What's *a ways*?" Harrison asked.

Unable to answer, Marshall simply shrugged, pinpoints of light dancing in his eyes from the pain the movement caused him.

This is bad, he worried to himself. I felt that through the drugs. This is very bad.

Behind them, the wind gathered clouds of red dust, building the furls up like frothy storm breakers. Racing to meet the tempest, rogue flurries of sand moved like ghosts on the open plains—their whispering voices calling the two men to join them for eternity.

With the sun now fully behind the western peaks, only a faint orange glow remained to guide their way in the starless night.

"Sandstorm," Harrison yelled. "Reminds me of the old days."

Marshall nodded. It was all he could do. Talking seemed impossible. Feeling Harrison suddenly take his hand, the pilot looked over at the young man.

"So we don't get separated this time," Harrison said.

Bitterly fighting the desire to cry, Marshall gripped his friend's hand as if for dear life and worked at taking deep breaths.

However, try as he might to abate the growing panic, his breathing was getting shallower by the minute. Soon, with legs that refused to work properly, Marshall staggered then dropped to his knees. Still clutching Harrison's hand, he sucked helplessly at the air in his helmet as if through a straw.

"What's wrong?" Harrison called, the glass of his visor touching that of Marshall's.

"I can't—" Marshall gasped. "I can't breathe. I think I have a punctured lung."

"What?"

Wanting to say more, something in Marshall's brain wouldn't allow him to waste what little breath he was able to gather.

"Let me carry you," Harrison said, dropping to one knee in the sand.

"Your heart," wheezed the pilot fitfully. "You can't stress yourself. It could stop beating again."

Ignoring his friend's plea, Harrison scooped Marshall up in his arms like a child. Thanks to the feeble gravity Mars exercised on its inhabitants, the muscular man was light enough for Harrison to carry without excessive strain.

Resting his head against his friend's chest, Ralph Marshall pretended that he could hear the beating of Harrison's heart through the fabric of his Tac Suit. Using the imagined rhythm, he tried to regulate his labored breathing. Like a goldfish in an inch of water, Marshall continued to survive.

Nearly out of time and totally out of other options, Julian Thomas depressurized the airlock of the Chinese Ark.

Reaching the small chamber had taken longer than he had hoped. Almost getting lost on the way down, he'd become confused in the maze of tunnels and narrow shafts.

Occasionally when he became pressed for time, Julian missed things: little things like where he put his car keys or what time he was supposed to pick his daughter up from school or, most recently, which access hatch bypassed the radiation shield of a Chinese spaceship.

Swinging the airlock door open, diffused red light flooded into the chamber like liquid magma. Across the space that separated the two ships, the white hull of the Lander shone in sparkling hues of ochre and orange, its polished ceramic hull reflecting back the haunting glow of Mars.

Poking his head out, Julian looked *up* the length of the Ark at the Red Planet, big and bright in the starry sky. Adjusting his perception so that the nose of the ship and Mars were now *down*, he swung out into space and grasped a rung of the nearby maintenance ladder.

Though he did not really want to know what it said, he checked the timecode on his left wrist. Chewing his upper lip, he stared at the numbers as they flicked past.

Calculations began to run through his head, swirling and mixing with the echoes of promises he made and the faces of those he'd let down time and time again. Slowly turning his attention to the grappling hook that connected the Ark to the Lander, he allowed several more beats to pass.

Finally, with the weight of resolution settling over him, he dug in the duffle sack and produced a small amount of C4. Placing the little charge on the base of the grappling hook he inserted a spare blasting cap, but no Wireless Time-Delay Ignition Switch. Finished, he took one final look at the sleek Lander hanging by a thread above him then turned his back to it and climbed sidelong up the hull of the Chinese ship.

Following the curving path of the ladder as it brought him around the circumference of the hull, he counted each rung in his mind, using their spacing as a sort of measurement to help him keep his bearings. As he neared another ladder running from tail to nose, he pivoted, aligning himself with the direction of the new rungs then began moving down the length of the ship towards the cylindrical launch pods of the Chinese MI.

Fiery and imposing, Mars bore up at him like an angry red eye. Growing nearer, the silhouettes of the launch pods were black against the rusty glow, and though he knew his mind was just playing tricks on him, it seemed to Julian that the long-dormant God of War was stirring with the anticipation of violence.

Having had no time to waste finding a harness or any other safety equipment, Julian climbed, unsecured, down the exterior of the massive Chinese ship, each movement holding the possibility of disaster. Despite the fact that every synapse in his brain was telling him to go slowly and choose his actions with care, a glance at the timecode on his wrist easily trumped his better instincts.

Thankfully, he soon came to the launch pods and began scanning the area for the best place to set his first charge. Everywhere, weld marks cut across the grey hull, their fat beads of steel glaring like scars on the hide of an elephant.

Standing as tall as eighteen-wheelers turned on end, the MI launch pods spawned long shadows that moved like those on a sundial as the Ark continued to roll on its axis.

Shaking his head inside his bulbous helmet, Julian cursed the dormant killbots for their role in sealing his fate then turned his attention back to the hull.

Before him, about a meter to the left, two seams crossed one another in the shape of an X. As he reached into the duffel sack, his memory tingled, scanning its vast reserves for the source of the nautical nostalgia attached to such a symbol.

'X marks the spot,' a voice from his childhood recalled. 'Just like in *Treasure Island*.'

"Julian, what's your ETA?" Aguilar said in his ear, scattering the Frenchman's fond memories.

"I'm just getting ready to place the last two charges," he responded, taking a shrink-wrapped ball of C4 out of the sack.

"Now? What's taking you so long? You should be on your way out."

Sighing, Julian resisted the urge to inform Aguilar that he was, in fact, already *out*.

"I just ran into a little setback but it's no problem. How's the Lander?"

"She's back up and running! I've taken her through all the major checks so she's ready to jet as soon as you get here."

Clamping a rung of the ladder between his knees, Julian let go with his hands and began assembling the first explosive charge. "Do me a favor will you?" he said, flicking his eyes to the timecode on his wrist.

"Sure, what do you need?"

"Sync my Tablet to this radio channel then open the file 'Jean Marie Thomas' and hit 'play.'"

"I didn't know your daughter was a musician."

"She is. Will you do it?"

There was a pause on the other end. Then, the slow and tremulous melodies of a lone cello filtered in through the earpiece of his headset.

"Thank you," he murmured.

As if in time to the music, he measured out the correct lengths of wire, formed the plastic explosive, and primed the blasting cap. Adding the final cherry to the deadly sundae of C4, he inserted the Wireless Time-Delay Ignition Switch then pressed the charge firmly against the welded X on the hull. It held solidly.

Looking up from the bomb, he shivered at the sight before him. Mars was a Leviathan in space, pulling the Chinese Ark towards its waiting jaws with the invisible tentacles of gravity.

A light, red and startling, flashed across the inside of his helmet's visor. Chinese symbols spelled themselves out in block letters behind it, partially obscuring his vision. Not needing to decipher what the message meant, Julian gazed down through the translucent symbols at his wrist Tablet. He was out of time.

On cue, Aguilar cut through the calming melodies of his daughter's genius.

"Where are you man? What's going on?"

"I'm almost done."

"Then why is the airlock door open? Where are you?"

Peering down at the unfinished charge in his hand, Julian slowly began to assemble it. "I'm outside on the hull."

"What?! Why?"

"There was a locked door. I couldn't get in. It doesn't really matter, Joey. What matters now is that you have to go."

"*Go?*" shouted the pilot. "Go? What does that mean: go'?"

"It means, leave me here," Julian sighed, working the parts of the charge together in a kind of trance.

"I'm not leaving you!"

With Chinese characters still flashing across his visor, Julian knew it would only be a matter of minutes until Amit's doctored Flight Path took the ship into an entry trajectory and the MI pods initiated an emergency launch.

"Joey, you have to go now. I need to stay and finish my work."

"Fuck that," the young pilot swore. "I'm coming to get you. Where are you?"

"Don't be stupid. The crew needs you alive. Who knows what's happened on the ground? You might be the only Lander pilot left. You have to leave."

"But—"

"But nothing, my friend. The Ark will be in atmo soon. You must go."

"No," Aguilar said with finality. "I'm not leaving you. We'll figure a way out. Fuck the last charge. Just come back to the Lander now. We don't need it."

"I can't. The last charge has to go near the MI launch pods, and I'm not leaving the work unfinished. This ship needs to be utterly destroyed or else our friends aren't safe."

"Julian," Aguilar implored. "Think about what you're saying, man."

"I have," the Frenchman replied, pulling out the detonator. "Keep the music playing all the way until the end, alright?"

Selecting a charge from the digital readout of those he'd primed, he blew the grappling hook off the hull, releasing the cable that connecting the Ark to the Lander.

"You son of a bitch," Aguilar breathed, no doubt seeing the flash from the Lander's open hatch. "You cut the cable. Why?"

"Call it intuition," Julian said, turning his attention back to rigging the last charge. "I kind of figured there wouldn't be enough time and I didn't want you getting yourself killed too. Imagine how angry the captain would be if I didn't return you in one piece. I did promise her, after all."

Only silence replied from the other end of the line.

"When you get back to the ship," he continued. "Don't let all of this overshadow how you feel about her. She likely didn't have a choice in the matter. Kiss her, my friend. Love her."

Finished with the charge, Julian quickly scanned his eyes over the scars on the hull, looking for a spot somewhere near the cluster of launch-pod cylinders.

Noticing an area just over five meters from where he crouched, he sighed and wished his arms were longer. Centered in the middle of the gun-barrel-like fixtures, the target was well out of reach.

"Julian," came Aguilar's voice, subdued and defeated. "What should I tell everyone?"

Exhausting the last of his Chinese comprehension, Julian found the electromagnetic function for his boots and engaged it by swiping his finger across the wrist Tablet.

Carefully getting into a standing position, he shuffled away from the safety of the ladder towards the launch pods and the stippled scars that marked the location of his final charge.

"Tell them whatever you like, but just remember what I said about you and the captain. Life is too short. Believe me."

Placing the charge on the hull, he pressed down until he was satisfied that the plastic explosive had stuck. Then straightening up, he gazed out at Mars, now grown to fill almost his entire field of vision.

Distantly at first, the ship began to rumble.

"Time to go, Joey," he said. "Remember to play my daughter's music for me."

"Goodbye, Julian," sniffed Aguilar, and then the line went dead.

The haunting and serine notes of Julian's daughter's first sonata filled his helmet. She had been twelve when she'd written it and he had been there. It was one of the few times in her life that he had.

Feeling a violent shudder, Julian struggled to keep his upright position as the nose of the Ark dipped beneath the surface of the Martian upper atmosphere. Green lights flicked on at the base of each MI launch pod.

With a trembling finger, Julian Thomas glared at the metal tubes then pressed the master detonation command for all of the explosive charges.

One by one, they blew: fire erupting into space with blossoms of blinding light that evaporated in the beat of a heart. Moving in a succession of planned randomness, the blasts tore the hull of the Chinese Ark apart, huge chunks of steel flung out into the atmosphere like giant bats fleeing the fires of hell.

From where he stood, Julian was in the front row of a spectacle like no other, yet he hardly noticed. As the charge at his feet finally detonated, he was already very far away. In the span of nanoseconds, the music of his beloved daughter bore him on a sea of tranquility that protected his soul from the shredding burning chaos which consumed his body.

Tears streaming down his face, Joseph Aguilar watched from a safe distance as the Chinese Ark spiraled in a hurricane of fire and wreckage. Through the cockpit window of the Lander, he saw the massive ship as it cut a wide swath of flaming destruction across the curve of Mars's skyline. With one final explosion, the mangled Ark burst into thousands of pieces like some demented firework, streaking across the heavens in a celebration of carnage. The God of War was satiated at last.

In the darkness of the frozen desert, Harrison Raheem Assad looked up at the night sky as small streaks of light rained down behind the wall of mountains, casting an unnatural glow. Like a second sunset, the odd illumination seemed to come from well-past the horizon. Yet, in the contrast of its presence, he saw the glint of metal ahead of him in the desert.

"Ralph," he spoke, looking down at his friend in his arms. "Ralph, look. It's the Dome."

Through the heavy ice of delirium, Ralph Marshall raised his head enough to catch the reflection of that mysterious and quickly dying light as it shimmered off the Alon plating of Ilia Base a kilometer away.

"Home," he managed to say.

"Yeah," Harrison nodded. "Home."

As Captain Tatyana Vodevski held tightly to the handrail that spanned the Bridge Deck window, she felt a huge wash of relief envelop her like diving into a tropical sea.

Though only a tiny prick of light compared to the massive fireball that was the Chinese Ark, she spotted the Lander—Joey's Lander—speeding towards them.

By her side, Amit Vyes let out a low whistle as the Ark continued to break apart into smaller and smaller pieces, the glow of its fiery demise casting shadows on the back wall of the Bridge Deck.

In the confusion of debris, neither noticed the hard-shelled pod that fell among the other wreckage, its afterburners cutting on like a comet tail as it sped for the gnarled peeks of the mountains far below.

Though lights had been restored to some portions of Braun after the Pulse, the Bridge Deck was still mostly cloaked in darkness. Only the digital glow of random Tablet screens shone in the large room, reporting on the various functions and systems of the mighty interplanetary starship as they came back online. However, at the Pilot's Console in the center of the Bridge Deck, one screen flashed a series of words having nothing to do with the slowly rebooting spaceship.

Anomalous radio signal netted, it said in bright green letters. *Location determined: Phobos, Stickney Crater, Limtoc Basin.*

End of Book Two

In a smoldering crater past the horizon to the east of Ilia Base, the blast door of a fire-scorched MI pod shuddered under the force of an unseen blow.

Striking with measured, rapid concussions, the thing inside began to warp the door critically until it finally came free from its hinges. Jettisoned into the night sky, the mangled metal disk landed five meters away with a dull thud and stood erect in the sand.

From inside the shadows of the lone surviving MI pod, something unfolded: six metal legs bracing themselves on all sides of the opening where the blast door had been.

As the wind twisted and howled through the worn peaks of an ancient mountain range, 04 crawled silently from the womb of its MI launch pod, turned west, and disappeared into the blackness of the Martian night.

Well now, here we are again! So much goes into writing a book—time, energy, and pizza. However, none of that matters unless your stories find an audience. If you're reading this, then you have not only validated the time, energy, and pizza I consumed writing this book, but you have also made it one of the best experiences in my life. For that I thank you. All of you.

Conversely, there are people in my own life—friends, family, and acquaintances—who have helped me in the first steps of getting my stories out there. If I were to list them all, many would wonder why in God's name they were even mentioned. This stems from the simple fact that whether or not you realize it, if you're talking to me, I'm thinking about my books and how what you're saying can be worked into the narrative in some small way. There are those, however, dear friends that stand out and thus deserve and honorable mention. Below, I list them for your consideration.

Thank you, Mia Mann. You're the best compass a stormy mind like my own could ever ask for. I know I can be...odd, but you've always made me feel as though this is not a bad thing. Thank you for that. Cougar George, you're my best and oldest friend. When we talk, I feel like you know me better than I know myself. Thank you for your work on the covers, the concepts, and the characterization. Mom and Dad, here I am again. I know you're proud and that makes me feel very thankful to have such supportive people in my life.

Garrett Jenkins, your notes on my manuscripts have directly shaped the course my books have taken. You are a dear and old friend and someday I hope to help you in the ways you've helped me. Jacob Lesser, another childhood friend sucked into the vacuum that is this trilogy, thank you for your help during the drafting process. A manuscript is a messy thing but you tackled it anyway. Andrew Olmsted, thank you for the great work you've done with editing this book! As always, you were professional and personal. You prove once again that college drinking buddies can someday evolve into something more!

Though I've already said it, I would like to go ahead and thank ALL of you out there again. Your continued support and enthusiasm is the source of my inspiration and the reason I do what I do.